Finding Gracie's Glory

By

Patty Schramm

©2016 by Patty Schramm

Second publication 2018
Flashpoint Publications

ISBN 978-1-949096-15-6

eISBN 978-1-949096-16-3

Cover Design by AcornGraphics

Publisher's Note:

Acknowledgments

First and foremost no book can be completed with any amount of quality without a strong team behind it. Special thanks to our RCE team that, without whom, this book wouldn't have been published for the first time: Verda Foster and Nann Dunne, best editors in the business! Ann McMan—what can I say about my cover except, wow! You always rock it, SB. And thanks to Lori L Lake for her guidance in starting up Flashpoint Publications.

Dedication

To my mom, Mary Jo Schramm. She taught me to get out there and do what I want and gave me the strength and gumption to make it happen. I love and miss you, Mom.

Chapter One

The front door slammed shut, and the walls of the house shook. Grace leaned against the dresser in their bedroom. Her knees grew weak, and she slid to the floor. Blood stained the front of her white T-shirt, but she didn't care. The pain in her arm overrode her other injuries.

Her left arm was bent at an unnatural angle and hung limply at her side. She didn't dare try to lift it. She should call 9-1-1. She needed to get to a hospital, but calling for an ambulance meant that cops would come as well. She wasn't sure she could deal with that. Carly would be pissed.

Grace's chest burned with each breath. Were her ribs broken, too? The blows from the baseball bat hit her everywhere. It hurt to think.

Her cell phone on the nightstand mocked her from the short distance. But who would she call? Matt, her twin brother, would be so angry he'd go after Carly. Maybe her sister-in-law, Sherry, could come get her. No, she had to take care of the kids.

That only left one person. Her mom. She'd help. She'd also tell Grace's father.

Using only her right arm, Grace managed to pull herself the few feet from the door to the nightstand and grasp her cell phone. Her vision blurred, and it took three tries to get her mom's number on the screen and the call through. Marsha Kato answered immediately.

"Hi, sweetie."

Grace tried to speak around the lump in her throat. They'd last spoken a month ago. She choked back a sob. It was the only noise she could make.

"Oh, no," Marsha said, a mix of sympathy and fear in her voice. "Sweetie, are you hurt? Is she still there?"

"Yes...no. Mom..." She just couldn't go on. The tears came in earnest, and she slumped to the floor into a fetal position. It hurt the least.

"We're already in the car. Stay on the phone with me. Okay?"

"Yeah." Grace gritted her teeth in pain. "I'm...sorry...Mom."

"This isn't your fault, Gracie Lee. I love you."

"I...no one else to...I didn't want you involved."

"I'm involved because I'm your mother, sweetie." There was a brief silence. "Are you still there?"

"Yeah."

"Gracie, listen very carefully. You might hear the sirens before we get there. Dad called for an ambulance—"

"No...please..."

"It's already done."

Time slowed, or sped up, Grace couldn't be sure. Her eyes opened and closed as she fought to stay awake. She heard her mom say something but couldn't make out what. After a while she heard, "We're on your street. Where are you?"

"Bedroom."

Grace's eyes closed and it seemed only a few seconds before she heard her father's unmistakable voice. She managed to open her eyes as he fell to his knees at her side. Hariku Kato, Jr.'s, piercing brown eyes met hers. Tears slid along his pale cheeks. He started to touch her but pulled back as if afraid to.

"Gracie..."

"I'll be okay, Dad," she said, though she knew it was a lie. She would never be okay.

Sirens blared in the distance. Marsha appeared beside Hariku and handed him a towel. He gently pressed it against Grace's cheek, blocking some of her view. His usually stern expression was gone, and he looked so vulnerable it broke her heart. How could she have done this to him?

"I love you, Gracie Lee," he whispered.

Grace wanted to reply, but nothing left her mouth as the darkness took her.

****

Disconnected images floated through Grace's brain. A dark-haired man with a kind face; bright lights overhead, shining in her eyes; a woman in pink touching her arm; Carly's face twisted with rage...

Her eyes flew open and disorientation set in. Grace looked wildly around the room, at the pasty white walls, then squinted at the stream of sunlight peeking through the window blinds. The room smelled of antiseptic. It sank in fast that she was in the hospital. Next to the bed was a skinny, green vinyl recliner. Her twin brother, Matt, was curled up on it, asleep.

Every part of her body hurt. Her swollen right eye wasn't open more than a slit. Her left arm was heavy. She tried to lift it, but the pain stopped her. So did the white cast that went from her hand to her elbow. Only the very tips of her fingers were visible, and they looked bigger than normal. She couldn't move them. Breathing hurt, and she knew her ribs were broken. Realization hit her and caused a new pain in her chest.

The woman she loved had beaten her. Again. Tears leaked from her good eye.

A light touch on her shoulder surprised her. She opened her eye and looked into Matt's concerned face. His lightly tanned complexion was pale and his eyes red rimmed. It broke her heart to see the sadness there.

"Hey," she said. Her throat felt like it was lined with sandpaper. "Water?"

"Sure." He held the light-pink hospital cup close to her and put the straw in her mouth. "Just a sip."

"Thanks."

Matt placed the cup on the bedside table and took her uninjured hand in his. "You scared the crap out of me, Gracie Lee."

"Sorry. I don't remember a lot."

"That's probably a good thing." Matt brushed her bangs away from her face. "If you hadn't called Mom, you might have died."

"Died? Carly wouldn't—"

Deep, rich, brown eyes, the one identical trait they shared, narrowed, and she could see his controlled anger. "She hit you with a baseball bat. Repeatedly. The head injury alone could have killed you. If I'd been there—well, the cops wouldn't have needed to arrest her. They'd have arrested me."

"I'm glad you weren't there. Where is she now?"

"Jail. Where she belongs." Matt gently squeezed her hand and swiped at the tear that trailed down his cheek. "Sherry's been to your house. She got most of your stuff out of there and put it into our spare room. We're going to get a bed so you can stay with us. No arguing." He kissed her forehead. "I love you, Gracie Lee. That bitch is never going to touch you again if I have anything to say about it."

Emotion tightened her throat. Tears flowed and she gripped his hand as hard as she could. It was difficult to reconcile that Carly hurt her this badly. They'd had a lot of fights in seven years of marriage, but she'd never hurt Grace like this before. Whatever started the inevitable argument was lost to Grace. She recalled coming in from work—then waking up in the hospital. Flashes of images raced through her brain, but they didn't make much sense to her.

"I'm sorry," she managed to squeak out.

"You have nothing to be sorry for." Matt kissed her again. "I need to tell Mom and Dad you're awake. *Ojiichan* is here, too."

"He is?" *Ojiichan*, their grandfather, lived in the Yukon in Canada. He rarely left his small home except for the occasional holiday or other family gathering. The injuries must be bad to bring him to Seattle. "Matt, how long..."

"Three days. We weren't sure you'd wake up." Tears clouded

his eyes and streamed down his cheeks. "Let me step outside and talk to the nurse, then I'll call the family. I love you. Don't forget that, okay?"

"Love you, too." Grace hated to lose the contact of his hand in hers. He walked quickly out of the room.

Barely a minute went by before the door to her room opened again. Two nurses went through a list of questions for her as they took her vitals and moved around the bed. A doctor soon followed. He did his own examination, told Grace to rest, and left.

When the door opened again, she expected to see her parents. Instead, the slight form of her grandfather appeared. Hariku "Harry" Kato's arms were strong despite the appearance of frailty. His once jet-black hair was completely gray and still cut to military standards, though he'd retired as a colonel over thirty years ago. Grace didn't think she'd ever seen him with his hairline below the ears. She inhaled the familiar scent of Old Spice as he leaned down to kiss her cheek. When he straightened, strong, dark eyes met hers, and Grace nearly broke into tears. She'd expected to see disappointment. Instead, she saw only love.

"*Ojiichan*...you didn't need to come."

"Nonsense." He placed his thin fingers around hers and squeezed gently. "I am here now, and I plan to stay until you are well again."

"I don't see that happening anytime soon."

"You need more faith." He squared his shoulders, and Grace knew the colonel was firmly in place. She and Matt always called him that when he spoke with authority. "I'm here to give that to you."

"Are you staying with Mom and Dad?"

"Yes."

"Are you angry with me?"

"No." Harry released her hand. "Grace, you must first believe that no one is angry with you. Disappointed, perhaps. Never angry. It is done and now you will move forward. We will get you healthy. You will get yourself well."

"*Ojiichan*..."

He held up one hand like a traffic cop to stop her speaking. "Enough said. You will rest." He kissed her on the forehead and left. The colonel had spoken and that was it.

Grace closed her eyes and willed sleep to come. She didn't even want to consider what would happen next. It was all too much. Thankfully, her mind shut down as her eyes closed.

****

Grace had no way of knowing how long she slept. The bright

sunshine was gone, but it wasn't yet full dark outside. She looked up into the concerned face of her mother, who stood beside the bed, holding Grace's hand. Grace knew, deep down, that her mother was disappointed in her, too. How could her child, whom she'd raised to be independent, resourceful, and strong, live with an abusive wife for so long?

Nothing made sense. Not anymore. Grace knew one thing for certain; she was no longer the person her parents had raised her to be.

"I'm sorry, Mom," she said through renewed tears.

Marsha's expression never changed, and her gaze never wavered from Grace's. "You have no reason to be sorry. None of this was your fault."

"It is—"

"Hush," Marsha said. "It doesn't matter what you did or didn't do. I'm thankful you weren't killed."

The door opened and Grace's father, Hariku, walked in. Dressed in a black golf shirt with an air force logo on the breast, and tan slacks, her father made a dashing figure. His jet-black hair was short and trimmed closely above the ears. Despite being retired from the military, he looked every bit the officer he'd always been. He quietly closed the door, placed a hand on Marsha's shoulder, and smiled down at Grace.

"I just spoke to your doctor. Looks like you'll be a guest here for a few more days. Maybe a week."

Grace noted the dark lines beneath her father's eyes. He couldn't have gotten much sleep. She wondered if he was disappointed in her as well.

"Dad—"

He held a finger to his lips to quiet her. "I love you, Grace. We all do. Don't dwell on what brought us here. We're going to move forward." His voice was soft, but it held every bit of the command tone she was used to hearing. Unlike *Ojiichan*, Hariku never learned how to turn that off when dealing with his children.

"I don't know what to do."

"The only thing for you to do is get better. Matt and Sherry will be ready for you, and if at all possible, I'll make it so you never see that woman again."

The tears spilled in earnest now. Grace sobbed, thankful for the love of her family, ashamed by what occurred, and sad at the loss of Carly. Whatever happened between them, Grace still loved her. Loved the woman she married. Loved the comfort they once had; the wonderful times they shared; the idea that somewhere, she didn't know where or when, she'd lost her best friend. And a part of her soul.

Chapter Two

After another week in the hospital, Grace was allowed to go home. Rather, she was sent to Matt and Sherry's house. There was no home for her to go to. Matt took the day off work and, along with Sherry and Marsha, entered Grace's hospital room. Her mother was smiling, but Grace could see there wasn't much happiness behind it. Matt and Sherry looked equally distracted.

"Okay, spill it. What's wrong?" Grace perched on the edge of the bed. She was dressed and ready and now worried that maybe she wasn't going to be leaving. "Did the doctor say something?"

"No, honey." Marsha was by her side immediately and took hold of her uninjured hand. "We got some bad news is all."

"Then you should tell me now. Please."

Marsha hesitated, so Matt finally spoke up. "Carly's out of jail."

"What? I thought you said—"

"I did. She was in jail, but someone paid her bond. She was released yesterday. We only found out an hour ago when the prosecutor's office called me. There's a protection order against her, so she's not allowed within a thousand feet of you."

Grace started to shake. If Carly wasn't in jail, that meant she'd be coming for her. Charges of domestic violence would be a death knell for Carly's career in public office. She worked in grant management for the city but had aspirations of achieving a much higher office. An elected office. Felony charges, whether Carly was found guilty or not, would ruin that. It was the only reason Grace never called the police before. She was protecting Carly.

But that was over now. And Carly would be beyond angry.

"I don't know what to do," Grace said as tears filled her eyes. "I never wanted any of this to happen. She's going to be fired."

"She's already on administrative leave," Marsha said. "Honey, she did this to herself. Let's get you home, and we'll figure all this out. Okay?"

Grace wiped the tears away. "I just hate this."

"We all do," Matt said, placing the wheelchair by the bed. "But that bitch isn't going to come near you. I found a lawyer who is drawing up the divorce papers and will be at the house tomorrow afternoon. You'll be away from her free and clear."

Grace got into the wheelchair. "She can have everything. I don't want a thing from her. Not the house. Not the car. Nothing."

Matt kissed her temple as he started wheeling her out of the room. "I figured as much. I'll take care of you Gracie. I promise."

****

Grace sat on the edge of the twin bed and took in her temporary bedroom. It used to be Matt's business office, but he'd moved his computer, desk, and anything else he could into the master bedroom. He replaced his stuff with a plain, white, chest of drawers and a corner table that held a laptop. Grace's clothes and few possessions now filled the closet.

Sherry'd managed to bring anything of worth from the house Grace and Carly owned for five years. Sadly, not much of it was of any meaning to Grace. Matt retrieved her cell phone and took it to the phone store to get a new SIM card and new number.

The laptop wasn't hers. Matt insisted on getting her one so she could be connected to the world. Or play games. Whatever she preferred. Grace wasn't overly technical, unlike her computer geek brother, but she appreciated the gift nonetheless.

She gazed toward the single window. It looked out over a typical suburban area far enough outside Seattle to avoid the feel of the city. Grace used to love the feel of the city. Not anymore. She needed peace and calm.

A few clouds blocked the late afternoon sun, but Grace considered it a beautiful day. She was alive, away from Carly, and hopefully about to begin her new life. Would it really be that easy? It sounded easy when her family said it to her in the hospital. It didn't sound so easy when she said it in her head.

She got up and leaned her forehead on the cool glass of the window. Traffic was light; a couple neighbors came and went; kids played in and out of the street; and Grace tried very hard to feel settled.

But thoughts of Carly intruded on her peace. She'd so often wait up until the early morning hours wondering if Carly was hurt, in an accident, trouble at work, thinking up all manner of things that could cause her to be late or not come home at all. It didn't occur to Grace until later, after the second affair, that Carly was with another woman.

Every time hurt Grace deeply. Every time she started to leave Carly. Every time Carly would woo her back with promises of fidelity.

By the fourth affair, Carly no longer promised fidelity. She blamed Grace for the need to go to another woman, threatened her with more violence, and eventually Grace stopped asking for fear of losing Carly forever. She still loved her. Crazy, yes, but something she couldn't deny.

Her ribs complained, so Grace decided to leave the window and maybe lie down for a while. Even though nothing would make her ribs comfy. She started toward the bed when she caught movement near the neighbor's green SUV. Not one of the kids; the figure was too big. Then she saw it again. Carly stood there talking to the neighbor. In broad daylight. Despite the restraining order.

Grace backed up so fast she nearly lost her balance.

What now? Yell for Matt? Call 9-1-1? Panic rose in her chest. Would Carly hurt her family? The boys were probably in the backyard playing.

She ignored the pain and rushed out the bedroom door and right into Matt.

"Hey, Gracie. Where's the fire?"

"She's here. Carly's here."

"What?" Matt gripped her right arm when she tried to head for the staircase. "Whoa, wait. What do you mean she's here? No one's here."

"Outside. Talking to your neighbor."

Something changed in his demeanor, and Matt flew down the steps.

"Shit. Sherry! Call the police!" Gracie did what she could to keep up with him, but it just wasn't   possible. She heard the front door slam against the side of the house as he took off. Luckily, he never asked which neighbor and Grace hoped that would stall him until she got out there.

Sherry came running in from the backyard. "What the hell's going on?"

"Carly...she's at your neighbor's house." Grace pointed toward the house in question. "Call the cops. I have to stop Matt."

She didn't wait to hear anything else from Sherry and headed outside. Matt was leaving one neighbor and on his way to the one where Grace saw Carly. She managed to block his path.

"Gracie—"

"Stop. The cops need to handle this, Matt. Not you. Please."

He wouldn't look at her, his eyes wild with anger as he searched the area. "I want to kill her."

"I know you do. But that's not going to happen. Not today." She placed her good hand on his chest, feeling the rapid beat of his heart. "Look at me."

He shook his head but didn't move.

"Matthew, look at me." He eventually did and she saw the anger begin to fade. She held his gaze long enough to be sure he wouldn't go looking for trouble. "We'll tell the cops what happened. Maybe it's enough to get her back in jail. Let's go inside. Sherry's probably freaked out."

"Yeah. Okay." He put his arm protectively around her and led

Grace to the house, where they waited for the police to arrive.

****

By the time the police got there, even though it was barely six minutes after Sherry called for them, Carly was gone. The neighbor gave a statement, and the police left after a brief search of the area.

Once the excitement was over, Grace gave in and took one of her pain pills and did what she could to get comfy in bed. Thanks to Sherry, she had every extra pillow in the house and managed to get into a semi-reclined position. It eased the pressure on her ribs enough she thought she could sleep.

Now if only her brain would shut down.

"Knock, knock. Are you decent?" Matt called from the hallway. Grace left the door slightly ajar to ease her feeling of being closed in.

"I'm decent, you twit."

"I don't want to see you naked." He held his hands over his eyes as he walked in.

"You've seen me naked."

"We were ten. You didn't have anything to see. Now you do."

"You're an idiot."

"And we're twins, so that makes you an idiot, too."

Grace laughed, holding her ribs against the pain. "Fraternal twins. Only you got that DNA. Not me."

"Whatever." Matt pulled the desk chair to the bed and sat down.

"Are the boys okay?" she asked.

"They thought it was cool to see the police car, but they had no clue what it was doing in the neighborhood. Sherry ushered them to their room and got them started on a video game. I'm shocked they even looked out the window to see the police."

"Good."

"Gracie..." Matt started, stopped, tried to start again, and ended up staring at his hands that now held Grace's right hand. While her skin was calloused, his was smooth, like a baby's butt. So obvious he didn't do any real work, as she liked to tease him. She squeezed his hand, hoping to ease his tension.

He cleared his throat and tried again. "Gracie, I think I would have killed that bitch if I'd seen her. I've never wanted to physically hurt anyone before. She came very close to taking you away from us for good. I won't let that ever happen. If I could've done something to stop it—"

"I wouldn't have left her. Mom tried. Sherry tried. Dad yelled. You talked to me, but nothing any of you could have said would have gotten me to leave. I had to do it on my own or—or something like this"—she indicated her broken arm and hand—"had to happen. I'm still here. And you're not going after Carly. Ever. Promise me."

"I don't want to make that promise, but since I already had to make it to Sherry I'll make it to you. I won't. I want to, but I won't."

"Good. She's not worth it."

"But you are. I just want to protect you."

"You can't. Not always."

"I can while you're here."

"Fair enough."

"I'm installing cameras and a security system tomorrow. If that bitch comes within a hundred yards, I want it on video. I want to make damn sure her ass stays in jail."

"Won't that be expensive?"

Matt shook his head. "Nope. I have most of it, and what I don't have, *Ojiichan* has decided to pay for. It's part of what I do for a living, you know?"

"You do the software part of it, not the hardware. Who's going to put everything up for you? You can't be climbing a ladder with your back—"

"I already called my business partner, Jason. He'll be here in the morning."

Grace felt her eyelids grow heavy. The medicine was kicking in. "Did you say *Ojiichan* is paying for it? Did you call him? I thought he was going home."

"He came over to check on you, found out what happened, and delayed his flight home. He's going to sleep on the couch, determined to be our night watchman until I get things set up."

"I love him." Grace smiled and let her head fall back against the pillows. "I need to sleep, Matt."

"I know." He stood up and kissed her on the forehead. "I got your six, Gracie Lee."

"Copy that," she said with a salute. Once the light was turned off, Grace closed her eyes and let sleep claim her.

****

Darkness enveloped her. A heavy weight pressed upon her chest, holding her in place. Pain shot through her ribs.

She couldn't breathe.

She couldn't see.

Her left arm was pinned.

Her heart raced.

She had to get out of there.

She must get up!

Despite the pain, the heaviness of her arm, Grace rolled off the bed. Her legs crumpled, and she fell to the floor with a loud thump.

Dizziness and nausea kept her from moving. The her face lay upon the scratchy carpet. She had to get up. She had to get out of there!

The door flew open as the light came on.

Grace blinked against the brightness, unable to make out who was there. A grayish blur knelt beside her, and she drew back.

Where was she?

Why couldn't she get up?

"Hey, it's okay," the soft, feminine voice said. "Are you hurt?"

"Dunno," she muttered, her addled brain trying to process the name behind the voice. Grace squeezed her eyes shut as nothing seemed to come into focus. The room refused to stop spinning.

Gentle hands touched her head, arm, body, and legs. She didn't pull away, though her instinct told her to.

"I don't think you're hurt. Let's see if you and I can get you back in bed, okay?"

Sherry. It was Sherry. Grace sighed in relief, despite the pain it caused. "I don't know if I can. I'm sitting on my good arm, and everything spins when I open my eyes."

"You're drenched in sweat, too. Matt, get me a wet washcloth and towel."

Grace heard movement and moments later felt relief as Sherry wiped her forehead. "If I can get on my back, maybe I can get up."

"Matthew, please move into the hallway." Harry's command voice was gentle, and it filled Grace with warmth. She'd forgotten he was there. "Sherry, may I?"

"Of course."

More movement and Grace heard Harry's voice very close to her ear. "You are partly under the bed. There isn't enough room to help you. I have called the fire department to assist us in getting you back in bed."

"I can do it, *Ojiichan*. I'm sure of it."

"Shh." He kissed her temple and touched the side of her face. "You will not try. They will help us get you into bed without hurting you. Be patient. I will wait with you."

"I don't understand what happened," Grace said, her heart beat now closer to normal. "I couldn't breathe. I had to get out of here. I didn't even know where I was at first. I was just scared."

"I believe you had a panic attack, Gracie Lee."

"From what? I felt fine when I went to bed."

She heard more movement, like feet shuffling, but didn't dare open her eyes.

Harry said, "I saw it a lot after the war. From my friends. You have suffered a great trauma. Your brain doesn't know how to cope with it." Harry wiped her face again with the washcloth. The motions soothed her.

"What do I do?"

"Right now, you relax. We will get you into bed, and tomorrow we will figure this out."

"*Ojiichan*, they're here," she heard Matt say.

It didn't seem very long to Grace, but perhaps she'd fallen asleep. Her brain was fuzzy, probably still affected by the pain pill she'd taken.

Harry left her side as two people came into the room. Both were men, and with strong, gentle hands, they lifted Grace back into bed. Everything hurt as she rested her head on the pillows.

One of the men ran a battery of questions at her then assessed her to be sure she didn't have fresh injuries before eventually leaving. Grace managed to thank them on their way out.

She was embarrassed. Both by having this panic attack and needing two men to help her into bed like she was ninety years old and feeble. It was ridiculous.

The mattress lowered slightly, and she dared open her eyes enough to see Harry seated there. "Still dizzy?"

"Not so much now. A little nauseous still. Can I have some 7-Up?"

"I'll get it," Matt said. She hadn't realized he was there.

Sherry edged into the room. "Would you like some crackers? Your stomach's got to be empty."

Grace managed a smile. "You're such a mom."

"Guilty as charged," Sherry said. "I'll get Matt to bring some up for you. I'm going to check on the boys, unless you need me?"

"I'm good. Thanks."

"Is that true?" Harry pinned her with an unconvinced gaze. "Are you good?"

"Very sore. Especially my ribs. I just need sleep. Will you stay with me for a while?"

"Of course." Harry met Matt at the door, spoke to him in hushed tones, and returned with the soda and crackers. "You eat a little, drink your soda, and I will do the talking."

"Tell me a story," she said and laughed at the expression on his face. "Like the ones you told me and Matt when we were little."

"Perhaps the story of when I took your *obaachan* to the drive-in movie?"

"Yeah. When you were in the convertible, and it rained, but the top wouldn't come up."

"Eat." Harry began the story as Grace settled her stomach and her mind, listening to the familiar tale and the soothing voice of her beloved grandfather.

Chapter Three

Grace sat on a chaise lounge on the back deck of her brother's house. A cool April breeze brought the scents of spring. The sun shone behind the canopy of trees that surrounded the property, promising a glorious day. She drank her milk. She wasn't hungry enough for breakfast but needed to put something in her stomach to take her pain meds. Last night felt like a distant memory. Harry was currently in the shower, apparently none the worse for wear after sleeping in the desk chair beside Grace's bed.

The fall caused more pain in her tender ribs. As long as she didn't breathe too deeply, she could cope. Rib fractures were common in her line of work as a rock-climbing instructor, even if she was trained on how to fall properly. Truth be told, Carly did more damage to her ribs than climbing and falling ever had.

The porch door, directly behind her, slid open, and a tray of toast, scrambled eggs, and coffee was placed on the wicker table beside Grace. Sherry sat on the chair across from her.

"You have to put more than milk in your stomach."

"I'm not hungry."

"Or course you are. You didn't touch your dinner, which means you haven't eaten a thing since lunch yesterday. Those crackers and soda last night don't count. Don't make me pull out the guilt card and make you eat."

Grace gave her a half-hearted smile. "That's mean."

"I know. But it works. Eat up."

"Fine." Grace took a bite of toast. "Yummy. Satisfied?"

"Not yet. Keep going. Between bites you can talk to me."

"What about?"

"What's going on in your head," Sherry said. Her kind, hazel eyes were on Grace, and Grace knew she'd get her talking whether Grace wanted to or not. Grace sighed.

"Everything is just so messed up. I want to hate Carly, but part of me still loves her."

"Is that why you never left her? It's been going on longer than the last year or so, hasn't it?"

"Yes." Grace ate some eggs to avoid the conversation. Sherry quietly waited. "It happened just after our second anniversary. I don't even remember what the argument was about, only that Carly shoved me against a wall and pinned me there. Her face was nearly touching mine as she screamed. Then she hit me. Not in the face, but in the stomach. I doubled over, trying to catch my breath."

"How could she do that? Physically, I mean. You're bigger and stronger than she is. You were in the army at the time. I know you can handle yourself in a fight."

Grace concentrated her gaze toward the tree line. Anything to avoid the expression on Sherry's face. Even her loving sister-in-law would never understand. "I can't explain it. When she did that—there was something in her eyes. I was scared. I can handle myself in a fight, but that's not what this was. It was Carly being enraged and me being afraid of what she might do. I didn't want to hurt her. So I took it."

"And after she did it, what did you do?"

"I threatened to leave. She said I was welcome to go, but that she'd use some contact she had at the police department and tell them I'd threatened her. She'd get a protection order and make sure my CO knew I was gay. DADT hadn't been repealed yet. And you know how much my military career meant to me..."

"She wouldn't have been able to do that. No one would believe her."

"I believed her, Sherry. Her best friend is a cop, and I couldn't afford to take the chance that she'd do it, get me arrested, or worse, tell my CO. So I let it go."

"And it happened again?"

Grace nodded, feeling her face flush with embarrassment. "Twice more before I had to fly back to Tokyo. When she joined me there for her vacation, she was as sweet as could be. She apologized for hurting and threatening me. I thought that was it. Done deal."

"And then?"

"And then it calmed down. We talked via Skype every day for at least an hour, and I honestly thought we were good. I loved her, Sherry." Grace took a moment to compose her thoughts.

Sherry asked, "Is she the real reason you left the army?"

"Yes. She knew there was a chance I'd get shipped to the Middle East and lost her mind over it. She threatened to out me. And it wouldn't matter if they believed her or not. It'd be enough to get me discharged. I didn't want to take a chance on that. I decided not to re-enlist so I could go out with an honorable discharge instead of a general—or worse, a dishonorable." Grace wiped a few tears from her cheeks. "That's when she got control over me, I guess. After a while, yelling and pushing turned into screaming and hitting. I could hide a lot of the bruises and blame the injuries on my job once I started working as a climbing instructor. Probably why she let me keep that job."

"We should have figured out sooner you were lying," Sherry said. "You're like a monkey when you're climbing. I always wondered why you kept falling. Matt told me you were trying new things; experimenting with new equipment. Was that a lie you told him?"

"It was. And it got easier and easier as time went on. A few times I called Mom, and she took me to the doctor and pretended to believe the story I made up. I know Matt stopped believing my excuses a long time ago. And I'm sure you did, too."

"We were worried about you. I know you and Matt fought about you leaving Carly, but he was convinced this very thing would happen. He was scared you'd end up dead."

"Guess he was right." Grace leaned back in her chair, adjusted the sling, and closed her eyes. "I wish I'd done something sooner."

"It doesn't matter now," Sherry said. "You're here, she's back in jail as of this morning, and we're going to help you get back on your feet. Literally and otherwise. Okay?"

Grace nodded as the words stuck in her throat. At least Carly wouldn't be showing up again. "What do I do in the meantime? I can't just sit here and take up space. I don't have any money, even though my manager said my job would be there if I wanted it back." She lifted her arm slightly. "If I'm able to go back."

"I've got a suggestion." Sherry went into the house and came back with the phone and a business card. "Harry gave this to me. I think he got it from one of the police officers yesterday. Anyway, the woman's name is Abby and she's a counselor who specializes in abuse. All her clients are LGBT." She handed the card and phone to Grace. "You don't have to call right this minute, but I think it'd be a good idea to do it soon. Matt and I will take care of you—so will Harry and your parents. But there are some things we can't help you with. This lady can."

Sherry removed the tray of food and left. Grace could hear her boisterous nephews clamoring for breakfast and took note when Sherry asked them to let Grace be. At least for a while.

She placed the card on her lap and stared at it. It was white with bold, black letters that announced Abby Dumont, Counselor, and her phone number. Grace didn't need to think about it. Sherry was right. No way could she get through this on her own. Her head was so messed up...

She turned the phone on and keyed in the number.

****

Grace's first appointment with Abby Dumont was two days later. Her mom insisted on being the one to drive her. They were quiet during the forty-five-minute trip. It took a bit to find Abby's office amidst a sea of nondescript buildings. Once Marsha found a parking spot, she turned off the engine and looked at Grace. "Want me to go in with you?"

"No. I need to do this alone. But thanks." Grace opened the door and stepped out. Light rain fell on her face. Nerves caused her to sweat on the ride over, and the wetness cooled her.

She entered through a single glass door into a musty hallway. The white walls were dulled with age, and the industrial carpet should have been replaced some time ago. Grace slowed her steps, wondering if this was even a good idea.

The hallway ended at a T-section, and the black-and-white placard indicated office number 10 was to the right. Two doors down and she was there. She adjusted the sling and took a deep breath, which hurt a little. She put her hand on the faded bronze handle and went in.

An atmosphere worlds apart from the entrance into the building met Grace with the calming and pleasing scent of jasmine. Very subtle, but enough to make her smile. To the left was a two-seat Rattan couch with white cushions decorated with purple, blue, and pink flower designs. The room itself measured about seven by fifteen feet, and a second, identical, couch sat angled to the first one. In the   corner where the couches met, stood a rubber tree plant. An old song about an ant ran through her mind and Grace almost laughed. A third wall was taken up by a stereo that softly played an eighties station.

Grace supposed it served to mask the chatter in the next room. She took a seat on the couch, leaned back, and waited.

Less than five minutes later, a short, older woman with pale blonde hair, pink-rimmed glasses, and wearing blue capris and a flowery pullover came out of the office. Her smile lit up her gentle, pudgy face. "You must be Grace."

Grace stood and joined her at the door, drawn to the friendly woman. "Hi."

"I'm Abby." She shook Grace's hand. "Come in, come in."

Abby led the way and pointed to a set of couches similar to the ones in the reception room. The office, which held a desk in one corner, was twice as large, and the couches were adorned with huge, fluffy pillows. Grace hesitated.

"You can sit wherever you like." Abby's soft voice startled her. "I'm going to make some tea. Would you like some?"

"I'm not much of a tea drinker."

"It's Chi tea. Very soothing. I'll make you a cup, and you can decide if you like it. If not, I can offer you a soda or some water."

"Thanks." Grace chose the couch farthest away from the large chair that clearly was where Abby sat. The chair had a back pillow and a footstool strategically placed, as well as a round table with enough room for a drink to sit on. In front of the couch was a similar table, maybe a foot in diameter. It held a wicker basket filled with hard candies.

Grace looked around the room, admiring the portrait-sized photos that depicted various scenes in nature. The areas didn't look familiar to her, but they covered all four seasons. Probably weren't from Washington then. At least not the Seattle area. They didn't get tons of snow, and one photo showed a farm with snow that almost dwarfed the fence that surrounded it.

Abby placed the cups of tea on the tables, picked up a yellow notepad, and sat down. She crossed her legs and put the pad on her lap, apparently not eager to start writing. "Is this your first time seeing a counselor?"

"Am I that obvious?"

Abby smiled. "To the trained observer, I suppose you are. I'll need to get some information from you, but we'll get to all that paperwork stuff later. How about you tell me the reason you made the appointment."

Grace looked at the floor and stared at the lavender carpet. How the hell was she going to begin?

"Maybe I should start with a few questions," Abby said. "Did you get my card from the police?"

"Yes," Grace answered without looking up. "Well, my sister-in-law did."

"Good. How long ago?"

"Couple of days."

"Is that when you broke your arm?"

Grace cradled her arm, even though the gesture hurt. "No. That happened over a week ago. The cops came because she was breaking the restraining order."

"May I ask her name?"

"Carly."

"Your wife or girlfriend?"

"Wife." Grace found the courage to look up and wondered whether Abby knew more about her than she was letting on. "How do you know what to ask me?"

"I specialize in counseling abused people in the LGBT community. I guessed the arm wasn't broken in an accident."

"Oh."

"I want you to know that there's nothing you can't talk about in here. You have my full confidence, and I want you to be comfortable. I don't expect we'll talk about everything in one go. Sound fair?"

"More than fair. It's just that—I don't know what to say. I'm embarrassed that my brother and his wife have to put me up in their house, that my parents are paying my medical bills since I can't work. I have no home, no car, no income—nothing. Sherry packed a few of my things while I was in the hospital, but there wasn't really anything there I wanted or needed. Mostly clothes I guess. I don't even own a CD or DVD. How pathetic is that?"

"Who's Sherry?"

"My sister-in-law." Grace tasted the tea and put the cup back into the saucer.

"Would you rather have a soda? Or water?"

"No, thanks. I'm fine."

"Is your family close?"

"Very. But not for the last few years. Carly didn't like them, and we never went to family functions. I feel like I don't even know my nephews."

"How many nephews?"

"Two. Gregory's seven and Harry Three's five."

"Harry Three?" There was a twinkle of mirth in Abby's eyes. "May I ask about the 'Three' part?"

"He's named after our dad, who's named after his dad. Our dad doesn't much like his own name, which is Hariku, and our grandpa—*Ojiichan*—goes by Harry. So, since he's the third one, my genius brother stuck the poor child with a 'three' behind his name."

Abby's laughter was sweet. "I think it's clever. Now, what did you call your grandpa?"

"*Ojiichan*. It's Japanese for grandfather."

"You speak Japanese?"

"Yes. Matt and I both do. My father insisted we speak Japanese. He's proud of our heritage and wanted to make sure Matt and I were, too."

"And are you? Proud of it?"

"Very. *Ojiichan* was born in Okinawa, Japan. His family immigrated to California two years later. But they never lost their heritage. Up until six or seven years ago, he made an annual trip to Okinawa to visit relatives there. But now that he's in his nineties and has had three heart attacks, he pretty much stays put in the Yukon."

"The Yukon? As in Canada?"

"One and the same. He owns a gold mine there that he says is our inheritance, but really it's his pride and joy. He loves it. The folks that work for him are like family. I used to go there every summer to help out."

"Used to?"

"Yeah. Before Carly forced me to stop going."

Abby didn't comment, but she wrote something on her notepad. Had she been doing that all along? Grace couldn't recall.

"He sounds like an interesting man."

"He is. He's more like my best friend than anything else.

Even though I hadn't seen him for a while, I still got calls from him every week, sometimes twice a week. He was always careful to call when Carly was working or when I was at work."

"You have an amazing relationship. You must feel very blessed."

Grace shrugged. Did she? Was she blessed? Her family was always good to her, regardless of the mistakes she'd made. But how the hell was she going to crawl back from this one? From wasting so many years with Carly? From the stigma of still loving the woman who tried to end her life?

"We've got ten more minutes for today. I'd like you to fill out some forms, if that's okay?"

"Sure. I'm right-handed so it's no problem."

"Great." Abby handed her the paperwork, pulled the table closer so Grace could use it, and patiently waited for Grace to finish up. "I'd like to make another appointment for next week. Would that work for you?"

"So soon? I thought this would be like a once-a-month thing."

Abby gave her that kind smile, her green eyes holding Grace like a hug. "I think it'd be a good idea to see each other more often. I have a feeling there's a lot more for us to talk about."

"Okay." Grace handed her the paperwork and stood. She adjusted the sling for the umpteenth time. "Thanks."

"You're welcome." Abby gave her a business card. "This is my emergency number. If you need to talk—about anything— you give me a call."

"No offense, but why would I call you?"

"None taken. One thing you need to understand is that we've only just barely touched the surface. You'll go through a lot of different emotions, and you could have nightmares or panic attacks. I don't want you to wait until our next appointment to work through those things. I'm here to help you 24/7."

"I'll put the number in my cell phone."

"Good. Did someone bring you?"

"My mom. She's waiting in the car."

Abby held the door for her and followed as Grace entered the waiting room. "Tell her next time to come inside and be comfortable. If you're okay with it, I'd like to meet her."

"Sounds good." Grace turned to go but stopped. Abby was watching her, but her face was a mask. "It will get better, right?"

"That's what we're going to work on."

Grace smiled and headed to the parking lot. Weird that after a very short hour, she felt a little lighter on her feet. As if something positive had just happened. And for the first time in years, Grace felt a little more in control of her own life.

Chapter Four

Two years later...

Grace stood in the middle of Matt's living room, hands on her hips, staring at him. His posture was similar, his face red with frustration. He wasn't yelling, but she knew he wanted to.

"You're not going," he said.

"You don't get to tell me that, Matthew. I am going. I have a plane ticket, my passport, and I'm packed. Mom will be here in half an hour to take me to the airport."

"I can't believe you've been planning this and never told me."

"I didn't tell you because I knew you'd act this way." Grace tapped his chest with her forefinger. "This is my life. Even though you're ten minutes older than me, you don't get to run things for me. I've let you do that for way too long already."

His shoulders slumped a little. "I had to, Gracie. You couldn't—"

"I'm glad you did it. There was no way I could have done anything by myself after Carly put me in the hospital. You and Sherry did more than I ever could have expected or ask for. And I love you both for it."

"I don't understand why you have to go now. We could get you set up in an apartment. I'm sure you'd be able to get a job."

"I know and that might happen when I come back. But right now I'm going to spend my summer at Gracie's Glory with *Ojiichan*. I haven't been to the mine in an embarrassingly long time. Abby thinks it's a great idea."

"Speaking of Abby, what are you going to do about that? You can't just stop seeing your counselor."

"We're going to use Skype. I know it seems weird, but they have technology in the Yukon, too. The connections are spotty, and you have to use satellites sometimes, but it's there. I'll be fine." She wrapped him in a fierce embrace, holding on until he gave in and hugged her back. "*Aishiteimas.*"

Matt kissed the crown of her head and let her go. "*Aishiteimas,* Gracie. Be safe and call me when you get there."

"You're worse than Mom."

"Gracie..."

"Fine. You'll be the second person I call. I already told Mom she'd be the first."

****

Harry met Grace at Whitehorse Airport. He sported an uncharacteristically big smile that virtually split his face. It caused tiny crinkles at the corners of his eyes, and Grace felt a huge weight lift off her shoulders. The deep brown color of his skin was back, and he looked nowhere near his age of ninety-three.

He spread his arms, and Grace walked into his welcoming embrace.

"*Kon'nichiwa, Ojiichan*," she said.

"I'm fine," he said. "Your mother has called five times in the last two hours. You need to call her."

"I will as soon as we get to your cabin. My satellite phone isn't charged up enough. I forgot to plug it in before I left Matt's." Grace put her luggage into the bed of his rickety pickup truck and climbed into the passenger seat.

"You look tired, Gracie."

"I forgot how many times I have to switch planes. The last leg was full of turbulence, so I didn't get a chance to sleep."

"Hmm. Do you want to eat or go to the cabin?"

"Food please. Airport food is beyond horrible. Can we stop at Marge's?" Grace's mouth watered at the prospect of food from the best restaurant in the world. Marge's should be a UNESCO World Heritage site, in Grace's humble opinion.

"Apple pie before or after lunch?"

"Before." She smiled at the grin on his face. "I promise to save room for meatloaf. And mashed potatoes. And brown gravy."

"Now I am hungry." Harry gave her a sideways glance. "It's good to know your appetite is back. You are too skinny."

"I'm hardly skinny, *Ojiichan*."

"Your *obaachan* would disagree."

"*Obaachan* thought everyone in our family was too skinny. She tried to fatten us up like we were destined to be Christmas turkeys." The memory of Grace's grandmother always brought a sad smile to her face. "I miss her and her cooking."

"So do I. This is why I have dinner at Marge's. Better than my own cooking."

"Your cooking consists of using the microwave or reheating a frozen meal in the oven."

Harry shrugged. "And yet I still survive."

"Only because of Marge."

"I'm glad you are back. I missed you."

"I missed you, too. Summer never felt right if I wasn't here mining for gold with you."

"I remember the first time you panned for gold. You found

half an ounce and thought you were the richest person in the world."

"I was four and you gave me fifty bucks. I *was* rich. Do you know how much candy you can get with fifty bucks?"

"Enough to make a four-year-old sick all night." Harry sighed. "*Obaachan* was angry with me for a week."

"I wasn't. Best thing I ever spent money on." Grace leaned back in the seat and gazed out the window as a comfortable silence fell between them.

Harry lived outside of Blue River, to the North of Whitehorse. Situated deep in the Yukon Territory of Canada, the town of Blue River wasn't even the size of a postage stamp. A dozen or so buildings, one of which was the post office, grocery store, and gas station combined, occupied two intersections along Highway Five, and at some point in history, the buildings were given the title of town.

Fewer than 500 people lived there year-round, but when gold-mining season started, thousands occupied the surrounding area and Blue River became a boomtown. As they entered the town limits, a sign announced an Internet Café attached to the four-room motel. They'd entered the twenty-first century. At least in technology, but the place still held the look and feel of its 1840s roots.

The main street barely had room for two cars to pass. Wooden facades adorned each building, and it always made Grace think of the Wild West. Blue River wasn't a major tourist location, but keeping the look of the place didn't hurt business any.

Harry parked in front of Marge's, and they went inside. For Grace it was like stepping into another time. The streets may have been lined with wooden facades, but Marge's was a fifties soda shop, complete with a silvery bar surrounded by metal stools that had red vinyl seats. Grace went to the bar, sat on one of the stools, and spun in a circle.

"I missed this place."

Harry settled beside her. "I can see that."

Grace continued her rotating fun until Harry stopped her with a gentle hand on her back. She was a little dizzy but managed to look across the bar at the waitress, who was on the verge of giggling. Grace broke out a sheepish grin. "I don't get out much."

"Apparently. What can I get you two?"

"Apple pie with cinnamon ice cream," Grace said.

"That it?"

"And two meatloaf dinners," Harry said. "Coffee for me, soda for her. But you can give my granddaughter the pie before dinner."

Grace gave the stool another spin and smiled at the waitress. Kind blue eyes watched her for a moment.

"I don't believe I've ever seen anyone do that and not get dizzy," she said. Her nametag read, "Peggy." She leaned across the bar and in a conspiratorial whisper asked, "What's your secret?"

She was so close Grace could smell her perfume. It reminded her of lilacs. She knew the woman was teasing her, "Who says I'm not?"

Peggy laughed outright and slapped her hand on the counter, causing Grace to jump. With a wink at Grace, she loudly said, "Marge, you owe me ten bucks!"

Someone, Grace assumed it was Marge, grumbled a response from the kitchen area.

Peggy lightly touched Grace's hand. "Be right back with that pie."

Grace stared after her as Peggy sauntered toward a glass fridge full of pies. For the first time in ages, she allowed herself to enjoy the sway of a woman's ample hips. She hadn't looked at another woman in two years.

Harry bumped shoulders with her. "She's taken. Marge is her wife."

"Huh?" It took a moment for Grace to process what he'd said. "I'm not looking for a girlfriend."

"At least you're looking. That's better than nothing. I doubt Marge would mind though." He gave her a sideways glance. "I think it's good you were flirting with her."

"She was the one flirting," Grace said, feeling her defensiveness kick in. "And when did Marge get married? You never told me that."

"Two-and-a-half years ago."

Their conversation stopped when Peggy handed Grace her pie and ice cream and Harry his coffee. Again, she leaned on the counter, this time in front of Harry. "You coming to the game on Friday night?"

Harry sipped his coffee as if considering his answer. "I haven't recovered from last week."

Peggy's laugh was hearty, and her expression full of mirth. "That's my line, you know? I need another three weeks in tips to make up for last week."

"You need to learn how to bluff," he said.

"And you need to not be such a damn card shark, or next time I'll end up naked because my money will be all gone."

Harry looked serious, but his voice was teasing. "If there's a chance you'll be naked, then I suppose I'll be there."

"Harry Kato. Ever the gentleman." Peggy patted his cheek with one hand and wandered off to get their food.

"She's always like that?"

"Always. Not every woman that flirts is cheating on her

spouse." He turned enough to face her. "You can't project your feelings for Carly onto every woman you meet."

"I wasn't—was I?"

"A little."

There hadn't been a woman that Carly didn't flirt with. After the first affair, Grace always wondered if Carly's flirting would or had led to something else. "It's hard. So many things remind me of her. I really thought that coming here I'd be able to get her out of my head."

"That is going to take time, Gracie. But coming here is a good idea. I think you needed to get away from Matt and your parents more than anything else."

"I love them, *Ojiichan*, but I have to take control of my own life. Matt did everything for me after I got out of the hospital. I think the only thing I actually did for myself was sign whatever papers he put in front of me. So much of that time is a blur."

Harry squeezed her hand. "It's better that way. Now, eat your pie before your dinner gets here."

Grace returned his gesture and dug into the lovely piece of pie, doing her best to bury her worries for the moment.

****

Grace took a quick shower and emerged to the smell of cheese and pepperoni pizza. She dressed in sweats and a T-shirt and headed to the kitchen, where Harry was making their late dinner. She wasn't terribly hungry after a big lunch at Marge's, but it was hard to resist the odor that filled her nose with pleasant memories.

"Sit," Harry said. He used the spatula to point toward the kitchen table. "Do you want a soda, too?"

"Sure, thanks." Grace watched the taut muscles of his arms as he removed the pizza to slice it. If not for the gray head of hair and slight stoop when he walked, no one would ever guess his age. She smiled when he presented her with dinner.

He sat across the table from her. "How is my favorite granddaughter now?"

"I'm your only granddaughter."

He waved her off. "Semantics. Tomorrow morning we go to Gracie's Glory. I need to check in with Charlie."

Charlie Townsend, whose name always made Grace giggle, was the foreman for Harry's mine. He'd worked for Harry since the early 2000s. The gold mining season would soon be starting up, and she figured Harry wanted to see that Charlie and crew were ready. They were always ready, but since Harry couldn't participate, he tended to supervise. Though Grace thought it was more like micro-management.

"I can't wait to get out there. I need a good workout. I feel like a walking blob of Jell-O. I'm surprised I could lift my luggage at the airport."

"Me, too. It must have weighed over 100 pounds."

"It did. I need all my makeup or I can't possibly work." It felt nice to be joking with him.

"I think Josie would be upset if you tried to put makeup on her face."

"Heh. Upset? She'd knock me flat on my ass."

Harry grinned. "And you would deserve it." He cleared the table before she could object and pointed to the living room. "Get comfortable. You pick the movie, and I'll make popcorn."

"Is there another soda in that dinky fridge of yours?"

Harry didn't respond, only pointed to the green recliners.

"Why are you letting me pick the movie? You never let me pick the movie."

"You're my guest."

"No, I'm your granddaughter. There's a difference."

Harry gave her a fresh drink and shrugged. "Enjoy while you can. Next time, I pick."

"Okay, but I'm putting *Rent* in."

She heard his not-so-subtle groan, popped the DVD in and got comfy. He pretended to hate musicals, especially this one. Not because of the storyline, but because he'd made the mistake of letting her watch it over and over again when it first came out. He knew it as well as she did, and it was pretty much expected they would watch it at the beginning of every mining season. It wasn't until that moment that Grace realized how much she'd missed coming to the Yukon.

"*Aishiteimas, Ojiichan.*"

Harry settled into his chair as the movie started. "I love you, too. Why do you look sad?"

"I missed this. Missed coming to see you. It's been five years, but it feels more like a couple of decades."

"You're here now." He took the controller from her and turned the volume up. "Now hush. I like this first song."

****

Gracie's Glory wasn't a large operation as far as gold mines went, but Harry owned 105 acres of precious land around it. Land that hundreds of other mine owners tried to buy from him over the years. Money wasn't the reason for Harry's investment in mining, and he'd turned down each one. He considered himself an amateur miner, but Harry was a shrewd business man. Each year his venture turned a profit and made the surrounding ground valuable.

The following Monday, Grace turned Harry's old GMC truck down the familiar trail to the mine, passed through the open gate, and soon parked alongside a log cabin. Built the year Harry started mining, the one-story building had three rooms—two of which held a single bed. The big room, a combination kitchen and living room, served as a resting place for the workers. A Port-A-Potty stood like a lone sentry behind the building.

An old construction trailer converted into an office sat next to the cabin. A generator kept it moderately warm inside so that Harry or Josie wouldn't freeze while doing paperwork.

Four RVs were lined along the opposite side of the cabin. One of them belonged to Charlie Townsend and his wife, Josie, but Grace didn't recognize the others.

It occurred to her then that, if not for the Townsends, Harry would have been forced to close his operation years ago.

She parked in front of the cabin, got out, and stretched after the hour-long drive. Harry stepped out and headed right for the office. Grace took a moment to look around and re-familiarize herself.

Not much about the camp had changed in the years since her last visit. A red canopy covered the clean-out tent where the recovered gold was cleaned and separated from other rocks and debris. She loved working in there as a kid. Seeing the tiny gold flakes trail into the collection pan was exciting. Sometimes Harry would let her cook the gold, the last step in making it as pure as possible before sending it to an assayer for payment.

Beside the tent was something new. A very large, red, container box. It reminded Grace of containers she'd seen on the barges in harbors along the Atlantic coast. She enjoyed watching the giant cranes load and unload the units like they were playing an enormous 3D version of Tetris.

She loved that someone used black paint and wrote, "Gracie's Glory" on the bright red sides of the unit. She suspected Charlie was the culprit.

Speak of the devil...Charlie came roaring toward her on the four-seat Gator. He jumped out, picked her up, and swung her around like she was a ten-year-old kid.

"It's about time you came back here, young lady!" Charlie put Grace down and pulled back enough to take a long look at her.

"It's good to see you, too, Charlie."

"Josie was excited to find out you were coming for the summer," he said then whispered, "You doing okay?"

"I'm fine, thanks. Where's Josie?"

"She had to get to town." He looked worried and his gaze moved to Harry, who joined them. "She's gone to get a surveyor."

"What for?" Grace noticed Harry's expression change to

serious with an edge of controlled anger hanging in the air.

Charlie said, "David, from TNT, has his crew blocking me from working on the north cut."

"Why would he do that?"

"He says it's TNT's claim that I'm on."

Harry climbed into the Gator. "Take me up there."

"Now, Harry," Charlie said, "we need to wait on the surveyor. He'll come up and—"

"Take me up there." The colonel was in charge, and Charlie got behind the wheel.

Grace jumped into the backseat. "What's up with TNT? I thought you guys got the claim borders straightened out last season."

Harry looked directly ahead and kept quiet.

Charlie said, "So did we. But David says his GPS shows we're two meters onto their claim."

Grace held on as the Gator rocked and bobbed them toward the northernmost edge of the claim. "Isn't that the area where you found good gold last season?"

"Yep." Charlie's voice was tight, and she could tell he was pissed off. "I kept going as long as possible, and we got a little over a hundred ounces on that one section. I was up there this morning moving pay dirt when the little—when Jonas Templeton's son showed up."

"How long ago did Josie head to town?" Grace asked.

"'Bout an hour. I expect she'll be back soon—if Tony's in his office."

Tony Black was the government surveyor and, at the start of each mining season, was rarely in his office. New miners came in, claims exchanged hands, and all of them needed to be sure they weren't on someone else's land.

Ten minutes later, they arrived at the disputed section. On their side, the yellow D10 dozer sat idle where it had been scooping mounds of dirt into a well-used dump truck. Opposite the dozer, a group of five people gathered around what looked to Grace like a boundary marker. A stick in the ground had an orange ribbon tied to the top of it and a number plaque nailed to the side.

Charlie jumped out of the Gator and made a beeline for the group. Grace jogged to keep up with him. He stopped in front of a tall, muscular man that Grace found slightly familiar. His light blue eyes narrowed at Charlie.

"I'm not arguing with you anymore, Townsend. Get off our claim."

"It's not your land, you little bastard. And we got Tony coming up here to prove it."

"I don't give a shit what Tony says." The man waved a handful of papers in Charlie's face. "These plans and our GPS prove we're in the right spot. Now get out of the way so I can get my guys started."

Charlie slapped at the papers, and they went flying everywhere. Tall Guy quickly stooped to catch them, while Charlie continued his rant. "Your daddy needs to get his ass up here and settle this right now. We been mining here for years. Everyone knows that Harry owns all the way up to Oak Creek. Now get!"

"Listen, you old—"

"David, stop." Harry moved between them, his gaze locked with Tall Guy. "Let's not speak words we may regret. Tell Olivia I'll meet with her and your father on Wednesday. I'll have Tony survey the area, and we'll settle this then."

David opened and closed his mouth twice before speaking. "Yes, sir." He clearly respected Harry, but he didn't miss the chance to glare at Charlie before gathering his crew and leaving the area.

"That was Jonas's son? I thought he was still in college," Grace said.

"Timothy's in college. That was David. He started working the mines a few years ago, but last season Jonas put him in charge of the Clear Creek operation, which borders our claim. Jonas's daughter, Olivia, runs the company."

Grace scanned the area in dispute. Most of the trees had already been cleared, and she could see Oak Creek in the distance. The ground between where they stood and the trees along the creek was flat and ready to be cleared by the dozers that would move the dirt until bedrock was hit. That section was where they hoped to find gold.

"So now what?" Charlie asked.

"We talk to Tony." Harry headed to the Gator. "While we wait, I want to see the last survey for that area."

"Sure thing." Charlie settled in the driver's seat. He glanced over his shoulder as Grace joined them. "Welcome back."

"Thanks."

****

Once back at camp, Harry and Charlie headed to the office to work out the boundary issue. Grace remembered Jonas Templeton, a bear of a man with a gentle manner and open smile. She was probably ten when she first met him and thought he was a giant. It gave her a laugh now, but she suspected he'd still seem pretty damn big to her. She couldn't remember meeting any of his children. She only knew of them from stories Harry told her.

She wandered around the claim, finding her way through old

and new. Along with the new D10, Harry had purchased a new wash plant. Not new in the sense that it was fresh off the factory floor, but new to Gracie's Glory. She hopped into the Gator and drove to their current mining location.

Where they mined changed with each season, sometimes moving to a different claim. Harry owned a total of ten claims on 243 acres of gold-rich land. As technology for retrieving gold improved, Harry would have the tailings from previous claims put through the wash plant again. The last time he'd done that, they found enough gold for the deposit on the D10, which amounted to just over six thousand dollars.

The new wash plant, situated about three miles from camp, shone like a blue beacon in the late morning sun. She'd never seen one so big before. Harry could probably run several hundred tons of dirt every day. The last wash plant she'd worked with could do a few dozen tons. She wondered whether Harry was planning to increase production, or had the older plant just worn out.

If Grace hadn't grown up around gold mines, she'd never have known what the contraption was used for. This one stood at least twenty-feet tall and was three times as long. The hopper, where the gold-rich dirt went in, was the highest point. Grace parked the Gator to get a closer look. From the hopper, the dirt was fed into a round tube called a trommel. The tube spun as jets of water sprayed forth into it from the hopper.

Gold comes in nuggets or flakes. Rocks larger than two inches in diameter moved to twin conveyors. From there they were washed into piles, called tailings, off to one side of the machine. The rest would be sent to the final collection point known as a sluice box. This is where they hoped to find the gold. Water moved everything along riffles that would catch the heavier gold nuggets and flakes. Beneath the riffles were tightly woven mats called Miner's Moss, designed to entrap the gold.

Grace loved every piece of the process and simply couldn't wait to see this new, shiny machine up and running. Accomplishing something few others could do meant more to her than the thrill of getting rich. Finding yellow flakes buried beneath tons and tons of dirt fascinated her. Perhaps Harry was right. She'd gotten hooked with that first nugget all those years ago.

"You do know you're supposed to wear a hard hat around the wash plant. Right?"

The voice sounded harsh, but Grace heard the gentle teasing in its tone. She turned to her left and opened her arms to embrace Josie, Charlie's wife. A faded pink hard hat adorned her head. Deep auburn curls peeked out around the edges. She and Josie were the same height and when Grace pulled back, she looked into light-gray eyes that shone with the kindness she remembered.

"We cannot go this long again without seeing each other," Grace said. "I missed you." She embraced Josie again, sniffing back sudden tears.

"We missed you, too, Gracie. But you're here now, and I heard Harry say you're planning to work with us." Josie touched her cheek with her warm, calloused fingers. "You sure you're ready for that?"

"I need it. I need to be outside doing something I enjoy and feeling like I'm necessary. I could have gotten my old job back, but I needed a change."

"I know," Josie said. Her hand gripped the arm Carly had nearly destroyed. "I only want to know that you're strong enough."

"The doctor said I'm good enough to climb a mountain, so I'm good enough to work the mine." Grace laughed lightly. "Besides, *Ojiichan* is making me nuts already and I've only been here a day."

"Bullshit." Josie also laughed and hooked their arms together as they started back toward camp. "I have it on good authority you've been staying up late watching musicals and eating pizza."

"Well, your authority has a big mouth. And we had sandwiches yesterday, not pizza."

Josie gave Grace's arm a tug. "Oh, felt like something nutritious did you?"

"Yep. Tomatoes, ham, and onions."

"Ick! You and I will go shopping for real food tomorrow. You, young lady, need to cook for that old fart or you'll both get ulcers."

"It's not that bad. Some of the pizzas had veggies on them."

Chapter Five

Liv Templeton stretched languidly and enjoyed the peacefulness of the morning. Sunlight streamed in between the slats of the blinds on her bedroom window. The blinds made straight lines across her and the naked woman lying next to her. She ran her hand along the soft, tan ass, along the curve of her back and down again.

A quiet moan muffled into the pillow. The woman turned sleepy, green eyes on Liv. "Morning."

"Hey, Sara. Want breakfast?"

"Will it be the same as dinner?" Sara was obviously sleepy, but Liv knew she'd be up for more sex if that's what Liv wanted. Friends with benefits always sounded so stupid to Liv. But with Sara...they'd managed to make it work. At least for now.

"Nah. I think I actually need food. I'm going to get a shower. Why don't you put some coffee on?"

"Coffee. Mmm. Good idea."

Liv crawled out of bed and laughed when Sara didn't make a move. "You actually have to go into the kitchen. It won't make itself."

"What good is technology if we can't have coffee made for us?"

"We had the technology. If you recall, you broke the technology last month. So, it's your fault I don't have a decent coffee maker. Until I get time to find one I like, you get to be the coffee maker instead."

Sara gave her a squinty glare. "How do you survive when I'm not around?"

"I don't. I'm just a shadow of myself without you." Liv threw a pillow at her and headed to the bathroom. She called over her shoulder, "Coffee!"

Sara's choice of words would mke a sailor blush.

Half an hour later, Liv and Sara were seated at the breakfast bar. The coffee was a bit strong for Liv's taste, but it helped wake her up. They both munched on Pop Tarts—Sara's daily choice for breakfast. Today's flavor was S'mores. Liv would have to brush her teeth twice to keep them from rotting from all the sugar.

"How is it you stay so damn skinny and eat all this junk food?" Liv asked, gazing at her long-time friend. Sara maybe weighed a hundred-twenty-five pounds wet, even though she was almost as tall as Liv's five-ten.

"Great genes—and fast metabolism. It's a curse."

"Curse? If I let you fix me breakfast every day, I'd weight three hundred pounds inside a month."

"Nah. You work your ass off. You'd lose the calories fast." Sara made a point of ogling Liv's rear and gave it a slap. "I like your ass, though. I wish you wouldn't work it off."

"You want my job then?"

"Hell, no. I like my leisure time." Sara finished her coffee and headed into the kitchen for more. "Trust me when I say that working at a bank is much preferred to getting dirty and slimy at a mine."

"You don't know what you're missing. Gold mining is the most amazing thing in the world. And it's the best job ever."

"It's the best job because you're the boss," Sara said.

"I don't like being the boss. I'd rather be out there on a dozer or running the wash plant. The paperwork sucks. The surveyors suck. The safety guys suck."

"Your brother sucks."

"He does." Liv wasn't looking forward to the talk she'd have with David later in the day. He'd caused a lot of unnecessary trouble with Harry Kato, and it was Liv's job as the operating officer of the company to fix it. "I love him, but he's such a douche bag. One of these days I'm going to let him get his ass kicked. I think it's overdue."

"Me, too." Sara leaned her hip against the counter as her friendly gaze found Liv. There was   something behind that gaze, and Liv was intrigued. Sara never looked at her like that. Like there was more between them than casual sex. Sara said, "Tell me again why we broke up?"

"Because we're better off as friends. We sucked as girlfriends." Liv stood so she could kiss Sara on the forehead. "Two years in the same space, and I don't think we went an entire day without a fight. I work too much, you're home alone too much, I want to go hiking, you want to go dancing, blah, blah, blah."

"Yeah. I get the most amazing lover in the entire Yukon, someone completely and perfectly compatible in every way but the one that really counts. Karma's a bitch."

Liv laughed. "Maybe. But if you'd just be open to the idea of dating, you might find that perfect match. She's out there, Sara. I'm sure of it."

"And in the meantime?"

"You've got your very best friend." Liv wrapped her in a big hug. "Promise."

"Thanks." Sara snuggled into Liv. "Okay, sappy moment over. You available for lunch today?"

"No. David really fucked up, and I have to fix it. Plus, Dad wants to go to Gracie's Glory after I talk to dumbass. I have to apologize on behalf of TNT."

Sara rolled her eyes. "Of all the people in the world, David had to upset Harry Kato. He must have done something huge. Harry's the sweetest guy ever." She held up her hand when Liv started to explain. "I don't want to know. I'm just sorry you have to keep cleaning up after him. Anyway, drop me off at the bank, since that's where my car is. I need to get home and change. Mom and I are going shopping this afternoon."

"Oh? Imelda Marcos needs more shoes?"

"Ha-ha." Sara shoved her playfully and started cleaning up their dishes. "*Donna* needs a new dress. Dad is taking her for a night on the town for their fortieth anniversary."

"Cool. They deserve it."

"Liv, do you seriously think I'll ever find someone that I can spend that much of my life with?   Someone to be with forever?"

Liv wrapped one arm around Sara as they headed out of the house. "I'm sure of it. I'm the only woman in the territory dumb enough to break up with you. That being said, we're going to the Pot O'Gold on Saturday."

"As long as you're not thinking of setting me up with someone, fine."

"Would I do that?"

Sara narrowed her gaze at Liv. "You would."

"Yeah. I would."

****

The office of TNT Mines was in the center of Whitehorse, in what was once a Victorian home. Liv's parents lived in the house, but when Jonas turned the running of the business over to Liv, with some responsibility going to David as well, he and her mother, Ellen, moved out of the city. Their comfortable, one-story home was modest in size and pointedly did not have an extra bedroom. It was their way of telling the kids the nest was empty and they liked it that way.

The downstairs of the family home now held offices. On the second floor, David set up an apartment for himself with an extra bedroom for their younger brother, Timothy, on the occasions he came home from university.

Liv's office was near the back of the building where the old dining room once looked out over their spacious backyard. She'd made it her mission to keep up with all the amazing flowers and plants put there by her mom, and in the spring, as it was now, she loved to open the windows to the wonderful mixture of scents.

Beyond the yard, on a clear day, she could see the magnificence of Grey Mountain.

She stepped in ten minutes before nine. David was seated on the leather sofa in her office, waiting for her.

Liv parked her butt on the edge of her desk and waited for him to speak.

"I already got my ass chewed by Dad. I really don't need it from you, too."

"I think you do." Liv stared at him, but David wouldn't meet her gaze. "Harry's a friend of the   family, David. You can't just go pushing him off his own claim without—"

"The GPS said we were in the right area."

"The GPS isn't 100 percent reliable, and you know it. That's why there's boundary markers all over the place. Besides, you know damn well where Harry's claim ends. What were you thinking?"

David shrugged, but Liv knew he did nothing by accident.

"Dad put you in charge of Clear Creek. He told you what sections he wants you working on this   season, and those sections don't come close to Gracie's Glory. If I hear about you getting into it with Charlie or Harry or anyone over there again, I'll have to move you back to the shop."

"You can't move me anywhere!" David shot to his feet, as did Liv, and they stood toe-to-toe. David was a head taller than Liv, but that never stopped her from standing up to him. He shoved his finger into her chest. "I don't give a shit what you say, Liv."

"You better because Dad left me in charge of this entire company. That includes the mines and the shop. So I'm going to leave you with a choice. You do things the way I say, or you go find somewhere else to work. Period. I'm done taking shit from you, David."

"This is bullshit, Liv. I do a damn good job."

"Yeah, most of the time you do. But when you fuck up, it's big and I'm left having to fix it for you. I'm tired of doing that. Straighten up or find another job." She turned away from him and sat behind her desk. "I got another meeting in an hour I need to get ready for. Get up to Clear Creek. The wash plant conveyor belt broke, and Sam's supposed to be there with a new one. He's going to need help."

David hesitated. Liv made it a point not to look up until she heard him close the door. She leaned back in her chair and breathed a sigh of relief. She and David used to be close. Growing up they played at the mines, learned everything they could from their dad and the other workers, and were inseparable. Timothy, being ten years younger, always stayed with their mom during the gold mining season.

Most people thought David and Liv were twins. Seventeen months separated their births, but as kids few people could see that. Both had wavy, brown hair, athletic builds, and identical sky-blue eyes. When Liv saw the hurt and anger on David's face, she nearly caved. Which is exactly what she'd done every other time before. Her resolve to make him sit up and listen left an ache in her chest, one that wasn't caused by his finger jab.

She missed her brother. Plain and simple.

"Good morning, Liv."

The deep voice came from the vicinity of her doorway, and a smile spread across her face. Her father had a way of doing that just by his presence. Jonas Templeton strode into the office and plopped his large frame onto her couch. His once blond hair was nearly white now, belying his fifty-eight years. She wondered if she and David caused the early loss of color.

"Hey, Dad. You just missed David."

"I saw him in the driveway. He didn't look all that happy."

"What'd he say?"

"Not a damn word." Jonas grinned at her, and she saw a hint of pride in his eyes. "He tucked his tail and left. I think you got through that thick skull of his."

"I hope so. I hate doing that to him. But dammit, he shouldn't act like such a dick."

"No, he shouldn't. So, you ready to go see Harry?"

"Yeah, I'm ready. It's not like I need to do anything but apologize. Charlie was right and David was wrong. But I'd like to see Harry. And I don't mind getting out of the damn office for a while, even if I'm two days behind on paperwork."

Jonas stood and opened the office door for her. "Now you understand why I retired."

"Semi-retired, and yes. I get it. Paperwork sucks."

"Hell, yes."

The ride to Gracie's Glory started out in comfortable silence. Liv was rehearsing the apology in her head, while wondering if she'd said enough to keep David in line or if she'd be firing him before the   season was over.

"Hey, you okay over there?" Jonas asked. He sneaked a glance at her, and Liv saw he was frowning.

"Fine. Why?"

"Because that's the third time I asked you. What's going on?"

"Just thinking about David and if he's going to keep screwing up. I have to think he's pushing me to fire him on purpose. But I don't know why he'd do that."

"To see if he can push you that far or not. Don't give in to him, Liv. That's what he wants."

"I know." She turned her gaze to the wooded landscape as they sped down the remote, two-lane highway.

"Let's change the subject. Harry and I talked about a few other things when he called me this   morning."

"Good or bad?"

"Depends on your take. His granddaughter, Grace, is staying with him this season."

Liv recalled some old photos in Harry's cabin but didn't remember meeting his family, other than his late wife. "Didn't she used to come up here all the time but stopped a few years back?"

"Yep. Harry didn't go into detail, but he said something about a bad relationship."

"Wow. Not cool."

"Nope. And worse yet, she doesn't really have any friends, other than her brother who lives in Seattle."

Liv gazed at Jonas, already knowing where he was heading. "And she needs some friends here, right?"

"There's more to it than that. Now, don't get the wrong idea here, but the reason he came to me about it is because Grace is gay. He thought maybe you could introduce her around, get her to go out and have some fun."

She let loose with a laugh. "Seriously? Why? Am I a lezzie guide to the Yukon? Dad, please."

"It won't hurt to be nice to her, Liv. Besides, you might actually like her. She's been working Harry's mine since she was three."

"So she's a lesbian and a gold miner. We should be instant buddies."

"Enough with the sarcasm."

"Sorry, but I don't have time, Dad. I can barely take a breath as it is. You know David is zero help to me, and while Kurt is doing a great job running the repair shop, I still have to check in there every week. Plus, you want us to start on the East River claim, and if I don't go up there and start shoving the guys around, they'll never get started."

Jonas was uncharacteristically quiet, and Liv worried she'd made him angry. She was totally a daddy's girl, and making him upset hurt her more than it would ever hurt him. She sighed heavily and twisted in her seat so she could see his profile. His prominent jawline was tight, showing how tense he was.

"Dad—I'll see what I can do. Maybe Sara can help me out. She could stand to go out more often."

"Are you really that busy? Have I put too much work on you?" He didn't move his eyes from the road. He gripped the wheel so tight his knuckles turned white.

"Sometimes, but I like being busy." What she didn't tell him was how being busy kept her mind off how lonely she felt. Her occasional tryst with Sara did nothing to alleviate the despair that often clenched her heart. That feeling that she was not just alone, but that she'd always be alone.

"That's not what I meant for you to be doing, Liv. I want you to enjoy the work, like I did."

"I do. I promise. Especially when we get out of the office together. That's the best part." She reached over and touched his shoulder. "It's fine. I promise. Once I've been doing this for a few years, I'll be as good as you were. Or close to it anyway."

"You'll be better than me. I'm sure of that." He pulled onto the path that led to Harry's claim. "So you'll introduce Grace around?"

"Sure. No problem."

"Thanks."

"Thank me later, after I make nice with Harry."

Jonas finally grinned at her. "You already have."

****

Grace looked up from the paperwork in her hands when the car stopped at the mine's office. The beat-up, black-and-red jeep looked familiar. So did the bear of a man that climbed out the driver's side. His hair was whiter than she remembered, but the broad smile and unmistakable dimples could only belong to one person. Jonas Templeton. She couldn't help grinning as she went outside to greet him.

"Hey, Jonas," Grace said as she descended the steps.

"Whoa," Jonas said. He gathered Grace into a smothering hug. "Gracie Kato—when did you grow up?"

"Too many years ago to count." She backed away from him but held onto his strong arms. "When did your hair get white?"

"Too many years ago to count."

"Touché." Grace turned from him as a woman got out of the jeep. Nearly as tall as Jonas and with identical dimples when she smiled, the woman was nothing short of stunning. Her unruly, wavy, brown hair fell to the top of her shoulders and framed her round face perfectly. Sky-blue eyes looked toward Grace, and she felt the breath leave her body. Their gazes held for an incredibly long time before the woman strode toward Grace and offered her hand.

"Hi. Olivia Templeton."

Grace, still working up the ability to speak again, took the hand in hers. It was warm, gentle, yet strong, and she knew she held it far too long. Her hand felt cool when she released Liv's. "Hey."

"How come I never met you before?" Liv asked, her eyes still on Grace's.

"I haven't been up here in a while."

"Six years," Harry said, startling Grace as he joined them. "I think Liv was still in university the last time Grace worked the mine."

Liv finally looked away from Grace, whose breathing had become faster than normal.

Liv said, "Six years ago? Yeah. I was working on my masters then. But we've met now." She tossed a sweet smile to Grace and gave her full attention to Harry. "And I want to apologize for David. He knows better. Please let me know if he or any of the guys on his crew give you any trouble. I promise I'll take care of it."

"I accept your apology." Harry half-bowed to her. "Now, Jonas, you and I have business to discuss. Grace, why don't you and Liv head up to the creek and see if Charlie needs any help."

"I still have some paperwork to finish for you, *Ojiichan*."

He waved his hand dismissively. "Paperwork can wait. Charlie cannot. Go."

Grace hesitated, but the look on Harry's face gave her the motivation to move forward. To Liv she said, "I usually walk to the creek, unless you'd rather take the Gator?"

"I always choose walking. I spend most of my time behind a desk. I need all the exercise I can get."

Grace had to laugh at that. One look at Liv's well-muscled body, and she doubted any fat existed there. "You don't look it."

"Guess I got you fooled. I sometimes wish I'd never agreed to take over the business from my dad."

"You run TNT?"

"Yup. Four mines, equipment repair shop, and this year we opened a Caterpillar dealership. We sell and rent. We just sold Harry a used D10. So I'm almost as busy in the off-season as I am now. In fact, it's busier as new miners come in for equipment or come here to find they didn't prep their stuff for winter properly and now need repairs or new stuff."

"Wow. I had no idea TNT was so big. Last time I was here I think your dad just had the one mine on North Ridge. Right?"

"That's where he started. He saved money until he could buy up the land around it and then branched out to Clear Creek where my idiot brother was supposed to be yesterday instead of causing you guys trouble."

"I've never seen Charlie so pissed off. I got the impression they'd been fighting about it for a while."

"Wouldn't surprise me," Liv said. "But enough about me. Tell me about you. Where do you work?"

"I don't. Not anymore." Grace kept her gaze away from Liv. She'd never gone more than a week without working since she turned sixteen. It'd now been two-and-a-half years.

"Why not?"

Grace shrugged, not sure she wanted to get into this conversation. Liv was easy to talk to, and she didn't want to push her away, but she wasn't certain her past was a good topic. How do you tell a stranger—especially a nice stranger—that your ex-wife beat you so severely you spent two years in rehab?

"Hey, I didn't mean to pry. Well, I meant to pry, but not upset you." Liv stopped in front of Grace and waited for Grace to look at her. Kind eyes stared into hers, and Grace felt like she could melt right into them. "You okay?"

"I was a professional climber." The words tumbled out so fast they surprised Grace.

Liv raised one corner of her mouth in a crooked smile. "What'd you climb? Corporate ladders?"

"Ha-ha. I'm not homicidal enough for a permanent desk job." She enjoyed seeing the amusement in Liv's eyes. It warmed her entire body in a way she wasn't familiar with. Her stomach fluttered with sudden nerves. "I used to climb rocks, mountains, ice. That sort of stuff."

"Cool. I love rock climbing. Never been a fan of the ice, but I'm not a big fan of snow either."

"You live in the Yukon, and you don't like snow?"

"Not really. My dad swears I'm adopted." Liv stepped aside and they walked in tandem again.

"Yeah. You can't possibly be from here. I used to love to be here for the first snowfall. It's amazingly beautiful. Peaceful."

"Peaceful? It makes everyone stupid. Like they've never seen the stuff before. Tourists come and drive like morons, pissing off the locals so they end up driving like morons, then you get a bunch of accidents. When it snows more than a meter, everything shuts down and if you don't have enough supplies—sucks to be you. The only good thing is that the ice roads form, and we end up with a lot of business coming in."

"You drive the ice road?"

"Hell, no!" Liv laughed, a deep and hearty sound that sent pleasant shivers down Grace's spine. "We've been doing summer repairs on equipment for the diamond mines and sending the equipment back via the ice road from Yellow Knife. That's why Dad opened the dealership. There's a huge demand for new equipment, especially up north. Everything from generators to dozers. I expect this winter to be kick-ass busy."

"Your dad's a good businessman."

"He's really an idea guy. It's the running of the business that tends to go over his head. I think that's why he sent me to university. It was all part of his evil plot to sucker me into running things for him.”

“Hey, Gracie!” Charlie called to her as he jumped down from the loader he’d been operating. He jogged toward them. “What are you doing up here?”

“*Ojiichan* said we should see if you needed help.”

“And I think he wanted me to apologize to you, Charlie,” Liv said. “David’s an idiot. I’ll do my best to keep his ass at Clear Creek and away from here. Okay?”

Charlie said, “No worries, Liv. You can’t always control him. It’s not your fault.”

“It is because I didn’t keep track of him.”

“It’s over and done. So, you girls serious about helping me?”

“If it keeps me out of that damn office, then yes. I want to help out.”

Charlie clapped Liv on the shoulder. “Think you can handle an older D9?”

“Who the hell do you think fixed it over the winter?”

Grace said, “So you run the company, and you do repair jobs. Anything you don’t do?”

Liv seemed to consider how to reply. “Lots of things I’d like to do, but we’ll discuss that later. Okay, Charlie. What do you need from us?”

****

The day was far too short. At least in Liv’s opinion. She had a great time with Charlie and Grace. Especially Grace. Quiet, hard-working, and absolutely adorable in the few moments Liv could get her to smile. She had a feeling that Grace could be a lot of fun to hang out with. She certainly wasn’t hard on the eyes. Lean, strong, with well-muscled arms all told Liv she worked out. Her straight, black hair, tied into a ponytail, shone in the bright sunlight. Liv really wanted to give it a playful tug. When Grace looked at her with those deep, brown eyes, her expression was bashful. Liv found it adorable. Only a thin, white line marred her otherwise perfect face. The scar created a jagged line from the edge of Grace’s left eye down the side of her cheek. Liv wondered what or who had caused it.

She glanced at her watch. It was past five. Jonas went back to Whitehorse hours ago, leaving Liv to fend for herself. She suspected he’d done it so she’d have to get a ride from Grace. Which was fine with Liv. After a long day, she was famished and planned to ask Grace to dinner. She glanced at her hands and realized she’d need a shower first. “Shit.”

“Shit?” Grace stood a few feet from Liv. “Something wrong?”

A very familiar tingle hit Liv when Grace’s chocolate-brown

eyes met hers. "I need a shower."

"Me, too. I'm sure I stink."

Liv sniffed the air. "Nah. Even if you did, I wouldn't be able to tell past my own stink. Now that we got that cleared up, how about we go get a bite to eat?"

"Because I'm dirty and stinky?" Grace laughed softly.

"None of that will matter at the place I have in mind."

"And where would that be?"

"The Pot O'Gold."

"Best lesbian bar in the territory."

It was Liv's turn to laugh. "Best wings, too."

"Okay. Let me at least wash my hands. I guess I'll need to drive, huh?"

Liv shrugged. "We could walk. We'd get there in time for lunch tomorrow. Or you could drive."

"Yeah, smart-ass. Let me make sure *Ojiichan* is good with eating alone tonight. I don't want the poor man to starve."

"I would never starve. I'm quite capable of cooking." Harry stood a few feet from them, his arms akimbo, his dark eyes filled with laughter. "I need to go over some things with Charlie. I'll get him to take me home." He tossed his keys to Grace. "Don't wreck my truck."

"How would you ever know it was wrecked?" Grace asked through her laughter.

"I know every scratch, dent, and location of duct tape on that vehicle, young lady." Harry narrowed his gaze, but it only brought more laughter from Grace.

Liv was enjoying their exchange. It reminded her of the way her dad was always teasing her.

Harry said, "Go before I change my mind."

Liv took the cue. She hooked arms with Grace, pointed her toward the truck, and called over her shoulder, "Thanks, Harry!"

****

The Pot O'Gold was exactly as Grace remembered it. Placed in the midst of a variety of similar bars in the heart of Whitehorse, it looked like a fish out of water. While the other bars looked like bars, the Pot O'Gold was fashioned after a British pub. Forest green highlighted the multi-framed front window and the wooden door. An oval sign, displaying a very drunk leprechaun chugging a mug of beer, hung above the window. It must have been touched up because Grace remembered the sign being more faded.

They walked in, and it took her a moment to adjust to the dim lighting. Booths lined the right side of the room, with round tables and mismatched chairs in the center. The bar took up most of the left side. Toward the back, near the tiny dance floor, were tables you needed to stand to use. Grace never liked those. She wanted to sit and relax, preferably in a booth. It was more fun to watch the other people than be one of those being watched.

Music piped overhead, but it was low and Grace couldn't make out the song. It didn't really matter. She was only there for food. She hoped it was still as good as the last time she'd been there.

Liv steered her to a booth and signaled the young woman at the bar. Her purple, spiky hair caught Grace's attention as she came toward them.

"Hey, Izzy," Liv said. "How about we start with a couple beers. That sound good to you, Grace?"

"A Coke would be better, thanks."

Izzy gave them a toothy grin. "Got it. Want some chips and dip?"

"Works for me."

"Spicy sauce," Grace added.

"Oh, a woman after my own heart." Liv rubbed her hands together. "Love me some hot sauce."

"The spicier the better. They still have cayenne pepper sauce for the wings?"

"Hell, yes. My favorite." Liv leaned forward and winked at Grace. "I knew I liked you for a reason."

Grace felt the blush creep up her cheeks and was glad for the dimmed lights. Izzy came back with their drinks, took their food order, and sauntered away. Grace couldn't help staring at the tight fit of her jeans over her ass.

"She's sexy and she knows it," Liv said, taking a swig of her beer. "That kid could have any woman that walks in here."

"I bet."

"And she's taken." Liv sighed dramatically. "And way too young."

"Were you interested?"

"Nah. But she's fun to flirt with. Besides, her moms own the place. No way would I ever piss them off by chasing their kid."

"Smart woman."

"So, what's that name you keep calling Harry?"

"*Ojiichan.* It's Japanese for Grandpa."

"Cool. You speak Japanese?"

Grace said, "*Watashi ga yarimasu.*"

"Heh. Teach me to ask a dumb question."

"We grew up speaking it and English. Sometimes drove my mom nuts. She's not fluent, so Matt and I would chatter to ourselves in Japanese and most of the time she couldn't figure out what we were saying. It's hard enough to understand a four-year-old, but if they're both baby-talking in Japanese..."

"That would have made me crazy. I barely speak English."

"Your English is just fine."

"You should hear my French."

"Oh?"

Liv raised one eyebrow, and Grace saw mischief in her eyes. "Yeah. Comes out every time my idiot brother pisses me off."

Grace nearly spewed her drink. "Funny."

"I can be, when I'm with the right people."

There was a twinkle in those amazingly blue eyes, and Grace realized Liv was flirting with her. The last time that happened— Carly happened. She averted the searching gaze before her and cleared her throat. She was saved from any reply when Izzy brought their food.

"Liv, how come you're here without Sara?" Izzy asked.

Liv shrugged. "Just am."

"Huh." Izzy put a plate in front of Grace, her stare not exactly subtle. "Been awhile since I've seen you without Sara."

"Been awhile since I've been here." Liv narrowed her gaze and Izzy took the hint, leaving the table. "She can be a pain in the ass."

"Is Sara your girlfriend?"

"Ex. We're still friends and we go out sometimes. But I have to warn you, Izzy is the world's biggest gossip. Everyone that comes in here in the next few days will know we were together. They'll assume we're dating, blah, blah, blah. Just don't be surprised if you hear stuff."

"Won't bother me. I probably won't be around here much. When I'm not at the mine, I'll be with *Ojiichan*. I'm not a big social butterfly."

"Now that surprises me," Liv said. "You're easy to be around, fun, nice. I'd have thought you were the life of the party."

"Maybe. A long time ago..." Grace remembered those times like they belonged to someone else. She had friends, parties to go to, nights to dance through, music to enjoy...

"Hey," Liv's soft voice brought Grace out of her reverie. Liv's fingers caressed her hand where it lay on the table. Her touch was electric. "Are you okay?"

"Sometimes yes, sometimes no." Grace gave her what she hoped was a reassuring smile and pulled her hand away. "I probably should be getting back, though."

"You've hardly touched your dinner."

Grace looked at Liv's very empty dishes. "And you've practically licked your plate clean."

"I was hungry. It's been awhile since I did any real work." She patted her belly. "Got to replenish my resources."

"Well, my resources don't need as much replenishing as yours do."

"Are you saying I'm a pig?" Liv arched an eyebrow at her, and it made Grace laugh. "I'll have you know I have a very fast metabolism. I might even eat after I get home."

"You do that." She reached for the bill, but Liv beat her to it. "Hey!"

"Nope. My treat. Think of it as my final payment for the idiocy of my brother."

"Fine, but you can stop apologizing. It's over as far as I'm concerned."

"Deal." Liv tossed some money onto the table and stood, waiting for Grace to join her. They walked out together. Liv placed a hand on the small of her back and guided her outside and toward Grace's vehicle. "I can walk home from here."

"I don't mind giving you a lift."

"Thanks, but it's a nice night and I like walking, remember?"

"I do." Grace stared at her feet, not sure why she suddenly felt shy around a woman she hardly knew.

"Dinner was nice," Liv said in the sexiest voice Grace had ever heard. "I'd like to do it again sometime."

"Sure." Grace couldn't find anything else to say. Like her voice was stuck. Nothing else came out.

They were standing beside the driver's door to Harry's truck. Grace fiddled with the keys in her hand, not aware of how close Liv was until she felt a gentle hand on her chin. She allowed Liv to tilt her face upward, surprised by the tenderness of her lips as they touched Grace's.

Grace closed her eyes and let herself enjoy the fleeting moment. When she opened her eyes again, she found Liv smiling at her, dimples adorning her face.

"Does this mean you'd like to do this again sometime?" Liv asked.

"I think it does." Grace watched Liv step away from her. "When?"

"Saturday? We can go to Rock World, do some climbing, get lunch. Maybe dinner and a movie. Whatever."

"Sure."

"Cool."

They stood a few feet apart for what felt to Grace like forever. Eventually, Liv took a few more steps backward. "I'll see you in a few days then. I'll come get you from Harry's cabin. Okay?"

"Sure." It seemed like the only word Grace knew at the moment.

"Cool."

Both of them giggled at the weird awkwardness. Liv waved

and turned away, strolling down the sidewalk in the direction Grace assumed was her home.

Grace got into the truck, sat behind the wheel, and wondered what the hell she'd just done.

Chapter Six

Wow. Just...wow. Liv touched her lips, pleased by the still present feel of Grace's mouth against hers. The kiss, while short and sweet, sent tingles down her spine. She'd wanted so much more, but her gut instincts stopped her.

Grace Kato was like a deer caught in headlights. Each time their eyes made contact, Grace looked away. If they touched, Grace pulled back. If the conversation bordered on intimate, Grace changed the subject. Liv's dad said she'd had a bad relationship, and Liv certainly understood how that could make a girl gun shy.

But that kiss...Grace never made a move to stop it. She leaned into Liv, and the slight movement affected Liv in ways no other woman's kiss had. What was it about this woman? She simply couldn't get her out of her head.

Liv could count the number of serious relationships she'd had on the fingers of one hand. Sara was the last, and while that didn't end badly, it still ended. Probably because Sara was right about one thing: while she and Sara fit well together, Liv never truly made herself available. Liv still cared for her and considered Sara her best friend. She grinned stupidly. It was kinda cool that they kept their "benefits," but she knew that had to stop soon. Especially if Liv was seriously interested in Grace.

Was she?

That was a good question. Liv was serious about Sara, yet not enough so that she tried hard to make it work. Why was that?

"Because you're a great big chickenshit," she muttered aloud. The streets weren't exactly deserted, and her comment garnered a few stray glances. Liv increased her pace, intentionally taking a longer route to her house.

The idea of going to an empty home was depressing. Not that it wasn't her own fault.

Jane thought differently, of course. Their relationship lasted four years, and for Liv those years were amazing. In the end, Jane broke her heart. No, she'd ripped it out and stomped all over it. Sara once commented that Jane ruined Liv for any other woman. Maybe Sara understood more than Liv gave her credit for.

Liv shook her head as if that would rid her of all thoughts of Jane.

Grace.

Now that was an image she didn't mind conjuring.

Chocolate-brown eyes she could fall into; silky, jet-black hair that begged to be played with; and that body...wow. Athletic, well-defined muscles, tight ass, and very, very feminine curves that screamed to be touched—and loved. Oh how Liv longed to spend hours worshipping that lithe body. Lavishing careful attention to every curve until neither of them could move and exhaustion claimed them.

A dampness between her legs warned Liv to slow down, both in her steps and her thoughts. A smile spread across her face, and Liv wondered whether she looked ridiculous. She didn't care. The notion of making love to Grace was so vivid in her mind that she knew her only real option now was a long shower with a very useful, pulsating, showerhead.

"Damn," she muttered.

Her house came into view, and Liv was glad. Her cheeks were warm, and she really needed to get inside for some relief.

She unlocked the door and reached for the light switch by habit, but it was already on. That could only mean one thing—Sara has there. She was the only other person with a key to Liv's house.

"Sara?"

A sniffle from the vicinity of the living room was the only answer she got. She hurried into the room and found Sara curled on the couch, her arms wrapped around her knees. Tears streaked down her reddened face.

"Hey," Liv spoke gently as she knelt on the floor in front of Sara, covering Sara's hands with hers. "What happened?"

Sara hiccupped twice. Liv handed her a box of tissues and waited.

"I...had a date tonight."

"I'd say it's about time, but I get the feeling it wasn't a good night."

"She asked me after lunch. Came by the office. She was so sweet..."

"Who?"

Sara shook her head. "No. I'm not telling you her name."

When Sara raised her head, anger stirred in the pit of Liv's stomach. A red welt marred her beautiful face, just above her cheek and to the side of her right eye. "What—what happened?" Liv spoke through clenched teeth. Containing her temper was never something she was good at.

Sara wouldn't meet her eyes. For a moment, Liv wasn't certain Sara would answer her. "It was my fault."

"Bullshit. If you tell me you fell..."

"I didn't. She hit me."

"Sonofabitch."

"Liv—"

"I want her name, Sara."

"No."

"Do I know her?"

"Yes." Sara started crying again, and Liv climbed onto the couch and pulled her into a comforting embrace.

"I'm sorry if—I'm pissed that someone hurt you, Sara. Please tell me what happened."

Sara clenched her fists into Liv's shirt and leaned her head against Liv's shoulder. "We went to dinner, had a wonderful evening, but there was no spark. Ya know?"

Liv nodded, not trusting herself to speak.

"So after dinner we went to our cars. I gave her a kiss goodnight and thanked her for a nice evening. I started to get into my car when I felt her hand on my arm. I turned around, and she started kissing me again—it was pretty obvious what she wanted." Sara paused to blow her nose. "I tried to stop her and push her away, but she was strong and kept hold of me. I had to bite her lip to make her stop. That's when she hit me."

"She deserved it."

"Maybe."

"What happened after that?"

Liv felt Sara stiffen, and a knot formed in her stomach. Sara said, "She grabbed my arms and pinned me against the car. I guess she thought something was going to happen after dinner. Actually expected it apparently. I told her to let me go, or I'd start screaming my head off. For a second...I wasn't so sure she'd let me go. The look in her eyes—she scared me, Liv. She was so damn strong."

Liv massaged Sara's upper arms and fought back her own tears. She wanted to grab the bitch that hurt her friend and strangle her. After she beat the shit out of her.

Sara must have sensed Liv's mood change and finally met her gaze. "She didn't do anything, Liv. She shoved me against the car, cussed me out, and stomped off. I didn't leave until I was sure she was gone. She knows where I live, so I decided to come here."

"Why didn't you call me?"

"I don't know. I guess I needed to figure out how to tell you without telling you her name."

"She threatened you. You need to call the cops."

"No way."

"Yes way."

Sara pushed back and moved away from Liv. "No. I'm not calling the cops. Liv, you don't understand."

"Of course I don't. You won't tell me who she is, and you won't call the cops. There's a lot I don't understand."

"I work with her."

Liv stood and began pacing. The bank wasn't all that big, maybe midsized for a city like Whitehorse. Probably twenty or thirty people worked there. She knew most of them. Which ones were lesbians?

"She's not a bank employee," Sara said and got up to stop Liv's pacing. "I work with her as an assistant loan officer. She's a client."

"That doesn't narrow it down."

"I know and I won't tell you anything else." Sara placed one hand on Liv's chest, her sweet, greenish-blue eyes pleading with Liv. "Please. Let me handle this."

Liv brushed her fingers along the growing bruise on Sara's face. "I can't let someone hurt you, Sara."

"I'm not your responsibility."

"You're my best friend."

"I am. And as my best friend I'm asking you to back off. I need you to make me feel better, not fight my battles for me."

Liv sighed heavily. "You are one stubborn broad."

The smile on Sara's face warmed Liv's heart. "And this is why you love me."

"No," Liv said and kissed her on the forehead. "This is why we broke up. I love you because you're the best woman I've ever met."

"Flattery will get you whatever you want."

"This I know." Liv opened her arms and gathered them around Sara, holding her close. "My protective streak is a mile long. I won't guarantee how I'll react when I eventually find out who she is."

"By that time, she'll be the one with the bruises." Sara pulled back. "Now, if you really love me, you'll get that tub of double-chocolate-fudge ice cream out of your freezer, gather two spoons, and help me eat the whole thing."

"The whole thing?"

"Well, I'll let you have some, but I need comfort food."

That made Liv laugh as she headed to the kitchen. "How about I get a beer and let you eat out of the tub. I don't really feel up to ice cream tonight."

"Works for me." Sara climbed onto one of the stools at the kitchen bar. "So, why'd you get home so late? I thought you'd be here when I came in."

"I also had a date—sort of."

"What?" Sara nearly fell off her stool. "I'm glad you said that now, or I'd have spewed ice cream everywhere. Who was she? Did you have a good time? Where'd you go?"

"Whoa! One thing at a time." Liv gave a slight laugh. Sara was so good at easing away tension. "Grace Kato, yes, and the Pot O'Gold."

"I don't know any Grace Kato. She related to Harry? And couldn't you think of anywhere nicer than a bar?"

"It's a pub, and you clearly haven't noticed how dirty I am. So was she. We did a lot of work out at Gracie's Glory so the bar sounded like a good option. And she's Harry's granddaughter."

Liv put the tub of ice cream in front of Sara, and it took only seconds before Sara dug in and shoveled a spoonful into her mouth. Liv took a sip from her beer and watched, always amazed at the amount of food Sara could put away.

"Why don't you enjoy your comfort food while I get a shower and put my jammies on?"

"Only if you give details when you're done."

"Details?" Liv asked.

Sara gave her the "duh" look and spoke around the impossibly large amount of ice cream she was about to eat. "I need to know everything about this woman."

"You need to know?"

"Hell, yes. I have to vet her. Make sure she's good enough for my best friend."

"It was a date. Not a marriage proposal. There's no U-Haul coming over tomorrow."

"Pity. But you do have a second date, right?"

Liv's only reply was a not-so-subtle grin as she walked away.

****

Liv woke the following morning with Sara plastered to her side as they lay together on the bed. The bruise on Sara's face had turned dark along the edges. Liz determined to figure out who that bitch was and make sure it didn't happen again. Sara might not want a protector, but she damn sure had one.

Liv gently untangled herself and padded to the bathroom. When she was done, she noted that Sara had yet to move. That would likely change once breakfast was cooking. Nothing woke Sara Hyatt faster than the smell of food.

True to form, half an hour later Sara trudged out of the bedroom, her eyes still laden with sleep. She plopped onto a stool at the breakfast bar. "Do I detect maple bacon frying in that pan?"

"You do. I've got eggs, cheese, bell peppers, and onions for the omelets. If you think you can handle it, I'll let you butter the toast."

"I dunno, Liv. You know I haven't a single gene in my body that allows me to cook. I'll burn the toast."

"Ha-ha. I'll put them in the toaster. You just butter them." Liv put a tub of butter on the counter in front of Sara and handed her a knife. "What kind of lesbian can't even use a toaster?"

"The kind that doesn't own one. This is why God put restaurants on the earth. So someone else can cook. Besides, I'm a whiz when it comes to using the microwave."

"Seriously, Sara, you're going to end up with diabetes. The crap you put in the microwave will kill you. And don't get me started on why Pop Tarts and diet Coke are not a meal."

"And this is why we're not a couple. Healthy eaters and junk food eaters aren't a good fit."

"Heh. That's for damn sure." Liv handed Sara a plate of toasted bread. "But we make good friends."

"We do." Sara carefully got to work on buttering the toast and said, "So, about Grace Kato. I'm sure you thought you got away with not giving me details but think again. How did you meet her?"

Liv kept her back to Sara as she finished up the bacon. The warmth she felt was a sure sign she was blushing. When the hell was the last time she'd done that? "Harry asked Dad to ask me to meet her. It's been a few years since she's been to the area, and she just got out of a bad relationship. I guess he figured since I'm a lesbian and she's a lesbian we'd be instant friends."

"And was he right?"

"I think so." Liv closed her eyes for a moment and pictured Grace. "She's beautiful. Hair as black as night and pulled into a tight ponytail that shows off her face. Her eyes are like black pearls, and when she looks at me, it's like she can see the real me. Like I could never hide anything from her. In the instant she looked at me, it was like we knew each other."

Liv faced Sara, who was still putting butter on the toast. "The only other person I found so easy to talk to was you. I've just never connected with someone so damn fast."

"That's amazing," Sara said, her voice softer than normal.

"Are you okay?"

"Yes, of course." She kept buttering an already buttered piece of toast. "Why do you ask?"

"Because that bread has enough butter on it to give a pig a heart attack." She gently took Sara's hand and stopped her motions. "Talk to me."

"The bacon is going to burn."

"It's already cooked and on the plate. Talk."

"I just feel a little jealous. That's all."

"Jealous of what?"

"Grace."

Liv was clearly missing something. "Why are you jealous of her? I've only known her a day."

"And you feel a connection with her." She looked up at Liv with sad eyes. "I've dated a lot of women, and you and I spent two years together. I never felt a connection with you, and I don't think you've ever told me you felt that strongly about any woman you were with. Not even Jane."

Liv stiffened at the mention of her ex. "Jane was completely different from Grace."

"I know. That's my point. You've never talked about anyone like you're talking about Grace. And after one day—that's amazing. I don't know if I should be happy for you or worried about you."

"Why would you worry?"

"Because you, my friend, have a tendency to jump into relationships. Should I list the ones that came after Jane left? None of which, may I remind you, lasted longer than a few weeks."

Liv shook her head as if to deny what her friend was saying. But she knew Sara was right. She'd ruined a lot of relationships by diving in without ever taking a moment to breathe. Her relationship with Sara was the only one she managed to salvage after the inevitable breakup.

Liv said, "I like her. A lot. We shared one kiss, and with a little luck, we might share another one. I can't explain it, Sara. She's special. Different from all the others."

Sara got up and pulled Liv into a tight embrace. "Be careful. Promise me."

"I promise. Now, can we eat? I'm starved."

"Sure. But we need fresh toast. I told you not to let me touch the food."

Liv picked up the offending bread and tossed it into the trash. "It's okay. I'll take care of the food. You get a shower. I promise a hot meal when you're done."

Sara kissed her on the cheek. "Thanks."

"Sure." Liv watched her walk away, hoping she wasn't making a mistake by telling Sara how she felt about Grace. She didn't understand her own feelings, and she'd blurted them out without thinking first. Now Sara was upset about Liv's possible new girlfriend and still hurting over the treatment of her date from hell the previous night.

Liv went back to cooking and hoped she'd manage to salvage the rest of the day without doing any more damage.

Chapter Seven

Grace set up her iPad and signed in to Skype. Normally, she would be going to see her counselor, Abby, the first Wednesday of the month. As that wasn't practical from the Yukon, they arranged to meet via Skype instead. She waited patiently for Abby's smiling face to appear on the screen. She didn't need to wait long.

"Hi, there," Abby said with her usual cheer.

"Hi, Abby. This is kinda weird. I miss your hugs."

Abby's smile widened. She always greeted Grace with a hug and never let her leave without another one. Her touch was loving and kind, and Grace hadn't realized she'd miss it. "It's one of the few things they can't do with technology. When some scientist perfects a transporter, you'll get plenty of hugs from me. Unless I can convince my husband to go on vacation to the Yukon."

"Well, there's plenty to do here. Skiing, hiking, rock climbing—I'd even give you private lessons."

Abby made a sweeping motion across her full figure. "This is not a body made to climb anything more difficult than stairs." They shared a laugh. "So tell me what's new. Have you made any new friends yet? Things going well with your granddad?"

"*Ojiichan* is wonderful as always. It's nice to spend some quality time with him without doing so from a hospital bed." Grace recalled those long hours when she wasn't able to do much more than go from her bed to the toilet and back and even then needed help. Harry spent hours with her, keeping her company, holding her when she cried, and entertaining her when she was bored. Her family was a constant presence during that time, but Harry was the one who could always reach her best.

Grace gave herself a mental shake and said, "My first night here, Harry put *Rent* into the DVD player. I think he missed me as much as I missed him."

"I'm glad you're catching up. What else is going on?"

"He's letting me work the mine. I was pretty damn tired after the first couple of days, but I got into the rhythm again. I love the hard work. Keeps my body fit and helps me think."

"And what are you thinking about?"

"Hmm, you would ask that." Grace scrunched her face into a fake frown. "I've been thinking a lot about Carly."

"What specifically are you thinking about?"

"How it was when she would be kind and loving. And how,

even during those moments, I never felt a real connection with her. Now all I feel is anger."

"And that's acceptable. Though I sense there's something else you're not telling me."

Grace sighed. "Am I that easy to read?"

"You are."

"It's hard, Abby. The anger is hanging on even though I know I should be past it by now. So is the hurt. And at the same time...I met someone."

Abby's face split into a wide grin. "I want to hear all about her. But first, let's address the Carly issue. Anger isn't easy to turn off. You've got plenty of reason to be angry with Carly. She hurt you in unimaginable ways. I think you need to consider why it is that you still care about her."

"I don't care about her," Grace said, though she heard the doubt in her own voice.

"You do and you likely always will in some ways. She was a huge part of your life. I'm not suggesting that you're still in love with her, or that you even like her, but you do have to deal with the emotions and not chastise yourself for having them. You're human, Gracie. We have emotions whether we want them or not. They're ours to own and no one, not even ourselves, should say we can't have them. I know you hate it when I say this, but you're normal. You're having human reactions to an incredibly difficult situation."

"I do hear you. Honestly. But how can I go on with anyone else when I can't seem to get rid of all these old feelings?"

"That's not the right question. You should ask yourself, where can I put these emotions so they're tucked safely away. You can't get rid of them. You have to find that safe place for them to reside in your mind."

"And that would be where?"

"That's up to you. I can't create that place for you. But I can see you're getting there. It's the first time you haven't argued with me about being normal."

"I'm tired," Grace said but didn't hide her grin. Abby was right. She was starting to feel as though she'd made progress with her emotions regarding Carly.

"Of course. Now, why don't you tell me about the woman you met?"

"We sort of have a date on Saturday."

"Sort of?" Abby lifted a manicured eyebrow in question. "Define sort of."

Grace laughed softly. "Her name's Olivia, and she took me to dinner at a gay pub."

"And from the look in your eyes I can see you enjoyed yourself."

Grace recalled their all-too-brief kiss and licked her lips. "You could say that."

"Spill."

Grace laughed again and "spilled" the details to a very amused Abby.

"That's wonderful," Abby said when she'd finished. "I hate this part, but our time is up now. Before I go, did you get my email about the group I found for you?"

"I did, but do you really think I need to go to group therapy? I don't know that I'm ready to start telling strangers about what happened."

"You're ready. Trust me. They all feel or felt the same way you do. It'll help to talk to people with shared experiences. You don't have to call ahead or schedule a time to be there. Just show up. You don't even have to talk to anyone at first."

"I'll think about it."

"Fair enough. Same time next month?"

"Yes please."

"I'm sending you love and hugs, Gracie. Remember, you can call me if you need to."

"I will. Thanks." Grace disconnected Skype and turned off the iPad. She got off the bed, grabbed her coat, left a note for Harry, and went for a walk. She had a lot to think about.

****

Grace returned to the cabin in time for lunch. She could smell another store-bought pizza the moment she opened the door. Harry lived on them. A smile adorned her face as she walked into the kitchen. "Please tell me that pizza has pineapple on it."

Harry set two plates on the table and scowled at Grace. "Pineapple on a pizza is unnatural. You get pepperoni."

"You are so very boring."

"I happen to like boring." He nudged her with his hip. "Did you have a nice walk?"

"I did." She sat down and leaned back in her chair with a sigh. "Abby and I talked about my feelings for Carly."

"And?"

"It feels wrong that I still care about her. I guess I'm worried about what people will think of me."

"No one is going to think badly of you, Gracie. You're an adult and allowed to feel the way you do."

"You sound like Abby."

"I'll accept the compliment."

"It's just that I get these doubts sometimes. I'm never completely sure what other people are going to say or do. I don't want to disappoint anyone."

"Nonsense. Remove those thoughts from your mind. No one is disappointed in you."

"I didn't say it made sense. It's just how I feel. Abby's been working with me to stop the doubts, but they creep up every now and again. She really wants me to go to group therapy."

"If Abby thinks it's a good idea, perhaps you should go."

"Maybe. I don't feel ready."

Harry was quiet, and Grace got the impression he was backing off so as not to push the issue with her. He said, "When you're ready, I believe group therapy will help you. I did something similar after I came home from the war." When he turned to her, his eyes were filled with sadness. "The other men there experienced some of the same things I did. It was good to talk to someone who understood. Your *obaachan* loved me and tried very hard to get me to open up, but I never could. She could never know what I'd been through. She was empathetic and did everything possible to make things easier for me, but again, she didn't know.

"I don't believe I can explain it to you very well, Gracie. The first session wasn't very helpful. It was new and the psychologists weren't trained to do such things. But eventually, once we all started talking, it became healing. The setting was safe, and all of us were comfortable enough to talk about the things we saw and did. If it hadn't been for the group therapy, I would never have stayed in the military and I might not have stayed married. To say it saved my life is an extreme understatement."

Grace had no idea what to say. Harry never spoke of the war. It was the most he'd ever said about it in her entire life. Her chest tightened to think of the trauma he must have gone through. Worse yet, it had never occurred to her that he could have been so affected by the war. Harry was the center of the family—the keystone that kept them all together. Always strong. Always calm. Always very much in control. She was seeing a part of him that she didn't know how to understand.

"How did you know it would even help?"

"I didn't. But I had to do something. We all did. No person can carry that kind of weight with them. No one."

"So you're telling me I should go?"

Harry sat beside her and took her hand in his. Thin, wrinkled fingers gripped hers gently. "I'm telling you to consider it. I want what's best for you. I know that you've been getting help from Abby for two years now, but sometimes that's not enough. She knows you. I know you, and I know that group therapy works."

"I'll look into going, *Ojiichan*. I promise."

"Good enough." He kissed her forehead and got up. "Now, I've worked all morning on heating up this pizza." Harry removed the food from his oven and set it on the counter. "Come get a few slices and pretend to enjoy my boring meal."

"I would take your boring meal over any five-star restaurant. Even Marge's."

"Your taste buds must be broken. I would never take my cooking over Marge's."

"Does that mean we can go there for dinner tonight?" Grace asked with a hopeful grin on her face.

"We can. I need to go into the city anyway. No point in waiting until we get home to eat."

"What do you need in the city?"

"It's not for me. It's for you." Harry got his pizza and headed into the living room.

Grace was close behind him. "I don't need anything. What are you talking about?"

He nodded his head toward the front door. "I have only one vehicle. If you're going to work the mine, you need transportation. I called a friend and offered to buy his old Jeep Wrangler. Not a fancy vehicle, but it runs well and will get you where you need to go."

"You shouldn't be spending so much money on me, *Ojiichan*."

Harry looked at her sideways, and the grin he had showed nothing but mischief. "He owes me. I beat him at our poker game three weeks ago. He didn't lose a lot of money, but his wife didn't know he was there."

"So you covered for him?"

"In a manner of speaking. I didn't confirm he was there, and she took that to mean he wasn't. Had she known, it would have caused a lot of problems for him. In his words, I saved his ass. Now he owes me a favor. The Jeep is not going to cost me much money. Besides, what do I need extra money for? I can't take it with me when I die. I would rather spend it on the people I love. Make them happy first. So we get the Jeep, and you can do what you want and not rely on an old man and his old truck."

"I love you."

"I know. Now eat your pizza before it gets cold."

****

First thing Wednesday morning, Liv stopped by Sara's office to see how she was doing. Sara was too busy on Monday and Tuesday with meetings, so Liv hoped she'd be free today. Sara still hadn't told Liv the woman's name and insisted she'd handle things in due course. Liv wanted to deck the woman and see how she liked being hit.

Liv waved at the two clerks behind the customer counter as

she entered the old bank. The sparse décor and antique furnishings provided a certain amount of comfort. The wooden counter curved outward like a horseshoe. Directly behind it, the two hundred-year-old vault was still in use. The monstrosity of gun-metal-gray steel took up an area roughly ten by seven feet. Liv had only seen it opened once and was impressed by how well it still worked. The door was more than two feet thick, and the lock was on a timer. Not a lot of fancy technology, but there was no way anyone was getting in it.

Technology was served by the hidden cameras and silent alarms that were all over the main area of the bank, a little secret Sara let her in on years ago. It made Liv feel better about Sara working in a potentially dangerous place.

Opposite the counter sat four tall-backed oak chairs, separated by a potted fern. Straight ahead were three offices. That's all the small operation needed. Sara's was the first on the left. Liv rapped lightly on the solid, cherry-red door. A moment later, Sara's smiling face met her.

"Hey, come on in. I'm not busy."

Liv followed her and got comfortable in one of the two leather-back easy chairs in front of Sara's desk. She glanced at the tidy space and was a bit jealous. Her desk was twice as big, but she rarely ever saw the thick, oak surface. Unlike her office, Sara's was little more than a ten by ten room with a hutch behind her that held all manner of financial forms and her printer/fax machine.

Sara clicked her mouse a few times then gave Liv her full attention. "So, what brings you here?"

"You make it sound like I never come for just a visit."

"Because you never come for just a visit," Sara replied with a smirk.

"Busted. I wanted to check up on you."

"I'm fine, Liv. Promise." She absently touched the side of her face. "At least the bruise is faded enough I can cover it with makeup."

"Has she called you?"

Sara shook her head and shifted her gaze to her computer screen. "I don't expect that she will. It's okay. I'd rather not talk to her again."

"But you will since she's a client."

"Yes, and I'll keep it all business. It's not like I have an assistant I can pawn her off on. I am the assistant."

"If you'd tell me who she is, I'll talk to her. Make sure she keeps it only business."

"No way. You'll lose your temper, and things could go bad. Very bad. And not just for you, either. What if she closes her accounts with us? The bank would lose a ton, and I can't afford to let that happen. Besides, I really think it was the alcohol that got her riled up."

Liv leaned forward in her chair and waited until Sara met her gaze. "I don't care what her reasons were. There's no excuse. Period."

"Can we talk about this later? I've got an appointment in five minutes."

"I'm not done with this."

"I know," Sara said. Clearly, she was resigned to Liv's relentlessness and knew she wouldn't let go of the matter easily.

"Stop by if you need to talk," Liv said. "I'll be at the office late tonight so I can get done everything I need to before Saturday."

Sara's expression showed surprise. "You're not working over the weekend? Are you ill?"

"Ha-ha. I'm going to Rock World with Grace Kato."

"A second date? Awesome."

"Hardly a date. Just an afternoon out. Maybe dinner and a movie." Liv realized what she'd said and ended up laughing along with Sara. "Okay, fine. It's a date. But just as friends."

"For now."

"Call me."

"I will."

Liv stepped out of Sara's office and nearly ran into a woman who was coming in. She recognized Angel Harrison instantly. Nearly as tall as Liv and always stunning in her business attire, Angel had smoldering blue eyes. God the woman was sexy. Her brown hair, highlighted with blonde streaks, was pulled back into a French braid. But Liv hardly ever noticed her hair. It was usually the low-cut blouses that caught her attention. She swallowed and forced herself to keep eye contact.

"Hey, Angel."

"Hey, Liv," Angel said in that low, husky voice of hers. "Heading out?"

"Yep. Just stopped by to say hi to Sara. You?"

"Got a meeting with my loan officer," she said and pointed to Sara.

Liv followed the slender finger, and when her eyes met Sara's, she knew. The color drained from her friend's face. Angel was the woman that hit Sara. Liv clenched and unclenched her fists to keep her cool. This was not the place to confront Angel about it. She'd do that later.

"Well, hope all goes well. Hey, it's been awhile. Why don't you stop by my office when you're done. Love to catch up."

Angel placed a hand on Liv's shoulder in a gesture meant to be intimate, but in reality, her touch was a complete turn-off for Liv.

"See you in an hour?"

"You bet."

Liv briskly walked out of the bank and straight to her office. She had an hour to figure out what the hell she was going to say to Angel—and to calm herself down so she didn't beat the shit out of the woman.

It felt like a lifetime ago when Liv had briefly dated Angel. Somewhere between the heartbreak of Jane and the endearing friendship of Sara, Liv was no stranger to the ladies. She couldn't remember the names of most of them, since very few merited a second date, but Angel was one of those.

Tall, curvy, and feminine in all the right places, Angel was incredibly beautiful. She could spark Liv's hormones with a single glance...and that's what she'd done today. Sex was never the issue between them. Money was. Or rather Angel's insatiable need for more of it.

The woman was one of the richest people in the territory, and not a single penny was made from gold. With the sharpest business mind Liv had ever known, Angel spent the nominal amount of money she'd gotten when her grandfather died, on investments. At first it was houses that she'd buy cheap, fix up, and flip for astounding prices. That moved her into the realty market, and since then, she'd been comfortably seated at the head of one of the largest realty firms in the Yukon Territory. She sold everything from empty parking lots to gold-mining plots. If it was sellable, Angel found a way to become the broker.

Sara's recent appointment to assistant loan officer meant that she dealt a lot with Angel, who used The First National Bank of Whitehorse to secure loans for her clients. She sent thousands of dollars to the bank, and of course, Sara wouldn't want to lose her business.

Now, how to avoid Angel getting so pissed off she stopped using First National? Liv sat behind her desk, rested her elbows on a pile of folders, and sank her chin into her hands. This sucked.

****

Exactly one hour later, Angel glided through the door to Liv's office and settled into a chair in front of Liv's desk. She crossed her legs, allowed her skirt to ride up enough to show off her shapely legs, and gave Liv her most seductive smile.

"It's been too long, Liv. I've missed you."

"I doubt that." Liv leaned back in her desk chair. "You're too busy to miss anyone."

"True. So, to what do I owe the pleasure? Please tell me you want to ask me out. That would simply make my day."

"Nope." She kept her eyes on Angel. "I want to talk to you about Sara."

"Oh?" If Angel was surprised, she didn't show it. "Something happened between you two? I know you broke up."

"Yeah, we broke up, but that's not what I want to discuss. It's about your date with her the other night."

"Date? Well, I guess it was a date. We went to dinner."

"And you hit her." Liv decided to get straight to the point. "You came on strong, she didn't want to, and you hit her."

"What are you talking about?" Angel's facial expression didn't change, but Liv saw the look in her eyes. She'd hit the target head on.

"Don't lie to me, Angel. You've always sucked at it." Liv stood up so she could look down at Angel. "So here's the deal— first, you'll apologize to Sara. After that, you will never go any closer to her than the width of her desk. Don't ask her out, don't ask how she's doing, nothing. You go in for business, you talk business, and you leave."

"And if I don't?"

"That's not an option."

Angel looked down at her skirt and picked off invisible lint. Her voice was calm and cool, but Liv understood her nervous ticks. "I'm not going to do that."

Liv was around the desk in a flash, grabbed the arms of the chair, leaned down, and stared into Angel's face. She was inches from her nose as she spoke. "Not. An. Option. Apologize. Leave her alone. Period."

"Or what?" Angel shoved against Liv's chest, but Liv didn't budge. "You can't force me to do anything."

"If you don't, I'll make sure that everyone in a hundred-mile radius knows that you tried to force yourself on Sara, and when she fought back, you struck her. I bet that won't be very good for business."

"It'd be bad for Sara, too. If I lose business, so does the bank." Angel had to crane her neck to move away from Liv. Her eyes flashed with anger, but Liv knew it wouldn't last.

Liv said, "The bank will be fine. With our new business starting up, they'll get plenty of loans from us. And honestly, who do you think people will believe? A respected person like Sara, or a pariah, bottom feeder like you? Everyone knows you will fuck over anyone you need to in order to get more money. And if you actually think that's not true, then you're delusional."

"You wouldn't," she said, but the look on her face told Liv she knew damn well that Liv would do exactly what she'd said.

After a moment, Liv stepped back so Angel could get up. "You'll do this, and you'll do it immediately."

Angel shuffled so that the chair was situated between them. "She had it coming."

"No, you've got it coming. And if you don't get the hell out of my office right now, I'll let you know what it's like when someone bigger and stronger than you smacks you around." Liv pointed to the door. "Leave. Now."

Angel looked like she was about to respond, but she stormed out instead.

Liv paced the office, circling her desk until she was certain she'd wear the floor down so much she'd fall into the basement. Eventually, she folded her arms across her chest and stared out the window to the backyard.

She had no clue how long she stood there, but she jumped when she heard someone come in. She expected it to be Sara and couldn't turn around and face her pissed-off best friend. "I'm sorry."

"For what?" It was David.

Damn. Liv faced her older brother and sighed. He was covered in dirt, which he'd tracked all through the room. Liv's desk was never in order, but she liked to keep the office tidy. "Never mind. Thought you were someone else. What's up?"

"I need two more dump trucks for Clear Creek."

"Why? What's wrong with the ones you have?"

"One of them blew a piston through the engine block, and the other one isn't fast enough to keep up with the wash plant."

Liv never got headaches, except when she talked to David. The one she felt coming on was sure to last for days. "Both those trucks are only two years old. What the hell happened to them?"

"I'm running 24/7 in order to hit 2000 ounces this season. I need three trucks. We can make the slower one work for now, but that other one is going to need a new engine. I already told Hank to take a look, and it's at the shop right now. We're sitting still with several tons of pay dirt waiting to be run."

"David, you have to take it easy on the equipment. I don't care if you hit 2000 ounces if it means we have to replace half your equipment in the process. A new engine is going to run us into the thousands."

"You should have given me the new trucks I asked for."

"I gave you trucks that were hardly ever used. Two trucks are enough to run dirt to the plant from your cut. Now you want three? On top of having to replace one of them?"

David hesitated. "If I get 2000 ounces, then Dad will let me expand Clear Creek. You know there's good gold over there, and if I can get more land, I can make us a couple million each season."

"It's not about the amount of gold you get, David. Dad wants to see that you can handle things before he lets you expand.

Breaking shit isn't what he's wanting to see."

"Hank thinks the slower truck needs a new fuel pump, and he's going to work on that this weekend."

"Wait. Who broke the truck?" Liv knew the answer by the way David hung his head. "Fuck. Hank. He was drinking again."

"I think so, but none of the guys in the shop would say for sure. He said he replaced the fuel pump last week."

"But?"

David hesitated. "But I checked it over, and I'm pretty sure he never replaced it. I'm not even sure he worked on the damn thing."

"Then he's fired."

"Let me talk to him first, okay? I heard he's having issues with his wife."

"He's drinking again, David. The last time he nearly killed someone when he drove his truck home and ran that kid off the road. If he'd done that during the season, I'd have fired him then. Only thing that saved him was the kid wasn't hurt and it was during the winter."

"And he spent eight weeks in jail, sobered up, and hasn't had a problem since. That was two years ago."

"I know. But this time it affects us. What if next time he fucks up and causes an accident? What if someone gets seriously hurt? Then what? We can't risk it."

David said, "Instead of firing him, let me talk to him. I want to be sure I'm right about the fuel pump, and I don't want to fire our best mechanic. Not if we don't have to. Liv, he's never done wrong by us, and if he is having trouble at home...you know that can affect work. I'm not trying to make excuses. I just don't think firing him is the right move."

Liv saw the compassion in his eyes and relented. It was true that Hank never gave them problems, and while her instincts screamed he should be fired, she decided to let David handle things. She wanted so badly to trust him and decided this one time she would. "Fine. But this is the last time. He breaks anything else, he's gone. And if he's ever drunk at work, he's gone. Deal?"

"Thanks, Livvy." He used her nickname, and it almost made her smile. He always used it when he wanted something. "So can I have two more trucks?"

"Only if you promise me they'll survive the season. We can't afford to keep breaking them."

"I'll do my best." He started out of the office and paused in the doorway. "Livvy, I was a total dick about the stuff with Townsend over at Gracie's Glory. And with you. I'm sorry."

"It's fine." She met his eyes and smiled. "Now get back to work before I dock your pay."

He laughed on his way out.

****

Saturday could not come soon enough to suit Liv. Rock World would be the first stop, of course, but if this was going to be a date, Liv planned to make it as fun as possible. Would Grace see it as a date? A very big part of her hoped so.

She pulled her Dodge Ram into Harry's driveway just as Grace stepped out with a duffle bag slung over her shoulder. Liv jumped out and took it from her and grimaced at the weight. "Damn, woman. What do you have in this thing? The kitchen sink?"

"I told you I used to rock climb. I always bring my own gear. Never trust anyone else's equipment."

"A real pro, huh?" Liv put it behind the driver's seat, where her own bag was stowed. "I'm a rank amateur so be kind. Okay?"

"You need lessons? I'm not cheap."

Liv gave a hearty laugh. "I have so many comments in my head right now."

"Keep them there."

Liv gave her a playful shove. "You ready?"

"Yes. Let's go before *Ojiichan* comes out to tell me to be careful. Again."

They climbed into the truck, and Liv waved at Harry as they drove away. "Wow. You're good. I think he was planning to chat with us."

"Of course he was. He worries like an old mother hen."

"And he gets this twinkle in his eyes whenever he talks about you and your brother," Liv said, with just a touch of jealousy. "I never knew my grandparents. Mom's parents died before she married my dad, and Dad's died not long after David was born."

"I'm sorry."

"Thanks. I was at university when your grandma died. I hated missing her funeral."

"I thought her death was going to break *Ojiichan*. But he's the strongest person I know. He kept going. I don't know how he did it."

"Because he is strong. I suspect you're a lot like him."

Grace grew quiet, and Liv was afraid she'd said the wrong thing. The silence was nearly uncomfortable before Grace spoke again. "I saw you the other day in town. I was going to say hello, but you didn't look all that happy."

"Was it Wednesday by chance?"

"Yep. You were coming out of First National."

"Ah. I was pretty pissed, so it's probably better you didn't come near me."

Grace twisted in her seat to look at Liv. "Why? You get

violent or something?"

"Nah, but I can be a real bitch."

"Noted. Leave Olivia alone when she's pissed. Got it."

Ordinarily, Liv would correct someone who called her by her full name. She'd never liked it, probably because it sounded too girly to her ears. But when it came from Grace, it sent pleasant chills through her. "I like a smart woman."

"I'm very smart. But I'm even better at climbing. You sure you're up for a workout?"

Liv could tell she was teasing and gave her a crooked grin. "Um, again, I've got lots of comments going through my head."

"Your head is a scary place."

"You have no idea."

****

Rock World was on the edge of Whitehorse, and the one thing Liv left out of her tales of spending hours there was that it had been months since she'd stepped through the doors. The moment they were inside, Liv and Grace were met by a fluorescent splash of color. Oranges, greens, vibrant blues all dotted the multi-angled walls, some ceiling high.

Liv paid the entrance fee and followed Grace to the locker room. Once there, Grace set her bag on a bench and slipped off her baggy jogging pants. Liv's jaw dropped. Black Lycra shorts clung to Grace's muscular thighs and accented her sexy ass. Which Liv had difficulty taking her eyes off when Grace bent over to retrieve bright-green climbing shoes from her bag. Liv forced her mouth closed and restrained a wandering hand from touching the smooth contours so dangerously within reach.

She moved her gaze to Grace's slender, well-muscled legs. A white scar crisscrossed the back of her left leg, from the ankle to just below the knee. Liv wanted to ask about it, but Grace straightened and Liv was caught by intense, dark eyes.

"Ready?"

"Uh, sure." Only then did Liv notice Grace had put her shoes on and removed her sweatshirt. The green of her short-sleeved, Lycra shirt matched her shoes perfectly.

Grace raised a dark eyebrow, her expression doubtful. "You're climbing in that?"

Liv frowned. "I didn't know there was a dress code. I thought jeans and T-shirts went with everything."

"No dress code, but are you going to be comfy and able to move around? Those jeans are sort of tight."

"Thanks for noticing," Liv said and smiled at the slight blush on Grace's cheeks. "I like tight clothes, and besides, your clothes are way tighter."

"I like tight clothes, too, but these are designed so I can move easily in them. Yours aren't. You don't climb a lot, do you?"

"That obvious?"

"To an experienced climber, yes."

"I started last year, but it's been a few months since I've had the time to come here."

"All work and no play?" Grace bumped hips with Liv.

"Something like that."

"Well, today we play. Let's start by getting you properly outfitted. I'll even give you free lessons."

Liv wisely kept her thoughts to herself. Instead she allowed Grace to walk ahead of her. "Lead the way."

****

Half an hour later, Liv stood next to Grace at one of the colorful walls. Handholds of various shapes and sizes loomed before her in intricate patterns that reached to the top of the wall. The height was easily four meters, a little more than twelve feet. Not overly intimidating, but this was a lot different than Liv remembered.

Grace's light touch on her arm startled Liv. "Ready for your refresher?" she asked.

"I don't think I climbed one this high last time. But I could be wrong."

"It's okay. I'm going to get you started on the one with a safety harness."

"Cool. So, you train people to climb these things?"

"I teach people to climb lots of things. I much prefer to be outdoors. There's no adrenaline rush quite like the one you get standing hundreds of feet above everyone else, knowing you got there on your own. It's exhilarating."

The spark in Grace's eyes pulled Liv in. She so wanted to kiss her right then. "Think we could do that sometime?"

"Depends on how you do here. It's best to start out small and work your way up."

Liv's libido was in overdrive, and she gave herself a mental slap when she considered working her way up Grace's naked body. "If you can teach me how not to kill myself, I'd love to try climbing outdoors with you."

"Deal," Grace said. She ushered Liv to a gray wall adorned with less colorful handholds. A ladder of silvery bars started at eyelevel and went well over Liv's head.

"What's all this stuff?"

"Warm-ups. It's best to begin here. Plus I can teach you the proper way to use the handholds."

It'd been long enough since her last visit, that Liv couldn't remember much of the stuff she'd learned. She was eager for more instruction. Plus the sultry sound of Grace's voice was something she could listen to all day long. "So where do we start?"

"I'm going to explain things like you've never done this before. That way I know you've got the basics, okay?"

"Yep."

"Good. Now, this pouch is full of chalk. You need it to keep your hands dry, but don't use too much. Always slap the excess off." She reached into the round, floppy pouch that hung from her belt, at her back. She rubbed the chalk on her hands then slapped them together, creating a poof of white.

Liv said, "Chalk for hands. Check."

Grace laughed and the sound was sweet to Liv's ears. "Next you're going to warm up by climbing up and down this campus board. Remember, this will use muscles in your fingers and tendons you're not accustomed to using, so expect to be sore tomorrow."

Liv almost asked if she'd get a massage if she did well, but she bit her tongue. How was it that this woman, whom she barely knew, was bringing out the playful side of her? "Gotcha."

"Now, watch and learn." Grace gave Liv a coy look and was off.

Liv's gaze widened as Grace easily lifted her lithe body with only her fingers curled around the lowest of the silvery practice bars. She pulled herself along the ladder, which was about twice her body length, to the top. Liv watched the muscles of Grace's arms flex as she practically glided back down.

A slight sheen of sweat formed on Grace's brow. Her eyes shone with exhilaration. "So, if you're not a regular climber, why'd you suggest we come here?"

"You told me you're a climber, and I figured it was something we had in common. Sort of. It's a start anyway. I wanted to get to know you."

"You wanted to get to know me?"

"Of course. You're a good-looking woman, so I was interested right away. Besides, the old biddies known fondly as Jonas and Harry asked me to get to know you. They think all lesbians automatically bond and become best friends." She held her hand up when Grace started to speak. "I'm sure they meant well, but Harry's worried you won't get out and have fun. My dad volunteered me, and honestly, he didn't have to. I like you, Grace. I don't think I needed an excuse to ask you out."

The expression on Grace's face was somewhere between embarrassed and bemused. "I'm flattered. I think. *Ojiichan* is totally capable of matchmaking, and I wouldn't be surprised if that's his end goal. I'm only surprised by how fast he got started."

A wide grin spread along Liv's face. "When motivated, most guys work fast. Except my brother. But that's another story."

"You've never met my brother, Matt. We might be twins, but the only thing we have in common is that we both like girls. I don't think he could do anything fast if his life depended on it."

"You're a twin? I don't remember Harry telling me that. That's cool."

"Sometimes. It sucks at birthdays, especially when we were little." She leaned closer and in a stage whisper said, "I was not good at sharing."

"Ah. That would suck. David and I were thick as thieves until I left for university. We were good at sharing—we shared a mutual disdain for our baby brother, Timothy, who's eight years younger than me. We got very good at ignoring him."

"Poor kid."

"No. Timothy's the baby. Nothing 'poor' about him. He's momma's boy and the biggest queen you'll ever meet."

"Wow. Timothy's gay? Is David gay, too?"

Liv barked a laugh. "No way. David's straight as an arrow and as bad at relationships as I am. So the only disappointment so far for our parents is that none of us have produced grandchildren."

"Your parents are okay with two gay kids?"

"We live in Whitehorse. Gay capital of the Yukon. Yeah. They're fine with it." Liv watched something flicker in Grace's expressive eyes before she turned away. "Were your folks okay with it?"

Grace didn't respond immediately, and Liv figured she'd gone too far. She was about to apologize when Grace said, "My dad wasn't happy. He's air force, and I guess he thought that's where I was   heading—as a kid I wanted to be a pilot like him."

"I guess he didn't take it well?"

"At the same time I told him I wasn't going to join the air force, so that was a double whammy. We already knew Matt had no intention of going in—he broke his back when we were fourteen, and while he's okay now, it disqualified him for service."

"And what did your dad do?"

"Got very quiet, and for us that's worse than yelling. Took him a few days, a fight with my mom, and me crying before he came around." Grace rubbed her left arm absently.

"At least he came around."

"Because of a call from *Ojiichan*. He's the reason I joined the army. I'm sure you know that *Ojiichan* retired with the rank of colonel after over thirty years in."

"I do. I've seen the pictures in his cabin. He's an awesome role model, so I can see why you'd choose to follow him. Guess it really bruised your dad's ego."

"It did. But I went in after ROTC, and when I got out, I'd made the rank of lieutenant. He was proud of me."

"And if you're a daddy's girl like me, that's the best feeling in the world."

"It is."

"Why don't you use the Japanese words for mom and dad? I'm just curious."

"My dad didn't want us to get teased in school. He insisted we learn Japanese, but only speak it at home, not at school or around our friends. He got bullied a lot as a kid because he has an accent. Something he did his best to make sure we didn't have."

Liv fell silent as even this topic was heading into a downturn. She wanted their outing to be fun, not full of heavy talk. But it felt so easy and natural to talk to Grace. It was hard to switch gears. "So, let's begin my lessons. I want to get to climbing."

Grace flashed a most adorable grin at Liv. "Okay. Just make sure you let me know when you're tired, okay?"

"Seriously? I told you I'm in great shape. How hard can this be?" She showed off her bicep. "See?"

"Muscles don't mean you've got stamina." Grace gave the muscle a squeeze. "Not bad, though."

Liv was mortified to feel a blush creeping along her cheeks. "Thanks. So, shall we?"

****

An hour later, Liv lay on her back for the umpteenth time in a row. The safety mat cushioned the fall, but it didn't cushion the growing ache in her limbs. So far she'd managed to get a whole meter up the wall before losing her grip and falling. Served her right for wanting to climb without the safety gear. It meant she couldn't climb as high, but it was more freeing. At least it was the few times she'd gotten past that first meter.

She was mortified each time she made a not-so-graceful dismount from the wall. It wasn't as if there weren't plenty of handholds and spots to dig her toes into. And Grace made it look so damn easy. She'd grasp one of those tiny holds with the tips of her fingers, lift her body up, swing it to the side, and go from point to point with such ease and grace—Liv doubted she'd ever be that good.

Grace knelt beside her, and again Liv noticed Grace wasn't sweating nearly as much as she was. Liv felt as if she'd need two showers to feel clean again. Grace asked, "You okay?"

"Yes," Liv grumbled and accepted her offered hand up.

"You did great."

"What? You're nuts. I fell, in case you didn't notice. I'm pretty sure the mat is now dented with the outline of my ass."

"I noticed, but this time you got halfway up. That's the farthest yet."

"I did? A whole meter?"

"Meter and a half, but yes. You hit the halfway spot. And don't be so damn grumpy. It's supposed to be fun. For a beginner, you're doing an awesome job."

Liv eyed her suspiciously. "The damn wall hates me. There's plenty of those big holds to use, and I still lose my grip."

"You're using muscles you haven't really used before, remember? You might be strong from lifting things, but your fingers aren't used to zigzagging and being the point of contact that keeps you going upward. It takes a long time to build up that strength." Grace absently rubbed her left arm again. She walked away from the mat, and Liv got a good look at the underside of her arm. A scar started above her elbow and disappeared into her palm.

"You made it look so easy, though. It took you like a minute to reach the top of that really big wall."

"Fifty-three seconds," Grace said. "But that's not my best time. Should be more like forty."

"Seriously?"

"I'm a little out of practice, but yes. It shouldn't take more than forty seconds to go a few meters."

"Have you ever gotten hurt doing this?"

"Lots of times."

Liv reached out and traced the light scar that ran the length of Grace's left cheek. "That how you got all these scars?"

Grace pulled back as if Liv's touch burned her. "Yes. Some of them. Anyway, how about I show you again how it's done?"

"Sorry if I—I didn't mean to make you uncomfortable."

Grace shrugged. "It's not something I like to talk about."

"Okay." Liv moved a step closer, willing Grace to stay put. She placed a soft kiss on the scarred cheek. "So, you said you were going to show me how to get up?"

"I believe I did."

"Good. I'm going to sit down and nurse my wounded pride."

"You do that." Grace patted her on the head and returned to the wall. She spoke to one of the   employees, who was clearly her spotter now, and began her ascent.

Liv envied the young man who stood below her. He had a perfect view of a lovely ass. Despite her aches and pains, Liv felt a burning deep in her belly. Grace smoothly moved along different routes, each move reminding Liv of a carefully choreographed dance. Sinewy legs swung back and forth, finding placement as if

Grace knew every centimeter of the wall. She took no time to actually look where her hands and feet went; she simply moved upward faster than Liv thought possible.

At the top, Grace waved to Liv, a goofy grin on her face. Liv figured she'd at least matched her record time for the climb. She descended with the same amazing movements as she used to ascend, but near the middle of the wall, her hand slipped and she fell to the mat.

Liv was on her feet in seconds and rushed to Grace's side. The spotter was already pulling her to her feet. "Hey! You okay?"

Pain was evident on her face, and she held her left arm close to her body, rubbing near the scar. "I got an adrenaline rush and went too fast. No big deal."

"Your arm—is it hurt?"

"It's sore. An old injury."

Liv suspected there was more to that story but didn't push. She walked alongside Grace and away from the wall area. "You're okay though. Right?"

"Yup. My spotter gave me a ten for my landing skills."

"Shouldn't he have done something? You looked like a turtle on its back when you hit the mat."

"Which is why I got a ten. Liv, I'm an instructor—I perfected the landing you tried so hard to get right."

"I did pretty damn good. You said so yourself." Liv put her hands on her hips to feign indignity.

"I give you a six at best."

"I had a lousy teacher."

Grace playfully punched her in the arm. "Maybe you're a lousy student."

Liv pouted. "A student who now requires first aid and nourishment. In that order."

"Nourishment I can do. First aid? You're on your own." Grace headed for the locker room.

"Wow. You suck."

"You wish."

I sure do, Liv thought, forgetting her pain as she hurried to catch up. She was going to have fun getting to know this woman. A lot of fun.

****

Grace didn't want the day to end. Even if her body was complaining from using muscles that hadn't been properly worked out in months. Even if her brain told her to keep some distance. Grace preferred to follow her heart. Once parked in Harry's driveway, Grace waited for Liv to open her door. She'd picked up fast that Liv enjoyed doing small things like that for her. It was a sweet gesture and something she could get used to.

They were quiet as they walked to the porch. Liv kept her hand on the small of Grace's back. When she removed it, Grace immediately missed the warmth of her touch. She stopped on the first step so that when she turned, she'd be eye to eye with Liv. Laughing eyes stared back at her.

"What?" Grace asked.

"Just had to make yourself a little taller didn't you?"

"Maybe I did it so I could reach you easier." Grace took hold of Liv's shirt with both hands and pulled her close enough their noses nearly touched.

"Is that all?"

"No." Grace's voice dropped to a whisper. "I thought I'd do this, too." She pressed her lips to Liv's in what started as a soft, goodbye kiss, but became so much more. Liv's arms snaked around her body, one hand on her back, the other rested at the nape of her neck. Grace felt a groan escape her throat as she pulled back slightly. "Wow."

"Yeah, I know, right?" Liv's eyes were still closed, but a huge grin adorned her face. "Can we do it again?"

"You have to ask?"

Liv's fingers traced Grace's jawline. "Just being polite."

Their lips met again in a deeper kiss that sent tingles through Grace's body. Liv's hands held her securely, and Grace was certain that she'd swoon otherwise. No one, not even Carly, had ever kissed her so thoroughly. Right here, right now, Liv ignited a passion Grace never thought possible.

But reality crashed in on her as she realized where they stood. Her face warmed with a blush as she placed her hands on Liv's chest and gently moved her away. "I think," she said breathlessly, "we should stop right there. Otherwise, *Ojiichan* might see things he doesn't want to see on his front porch."

Liv averted her gaze from Grace, but not before she saw a hint of embarrassment in her eyes. It was endearing.

"You're probably right." Liv took a step back. "So, uh, want to do this again?"

"What? Kissing, or rock climbing?"

Liv gave her that crooked smile. "Whichever you want."

"Ah, such a democratic answer." Grace reached out to touch Liv's cheek. "I like both, but I'm not sure my body can take more climbing just yet." She flexed her sore arm. "I need a bit of rest."

"No problem. I found muscles I didn't know I had. I think I'd rather forget about them again."

"So, kissing it is." Grace laughed at the goofy expression on Liv's face. "Unless you have other plans?"

"Well, how about we go hiking next weekend? Then we can, um, maybe do more kissing."

"It's a date." Grace stepped off the porch and stood on tiptoes to kiss Liv once more. "I like the kissing. A lot. Come over for breakfast next Saturday. *Ojiichan* makes amazing omelets."

"You got it." Liv turned and got into her truck. She rolled the window down to wave as she backed out of the driveway.

Grace watched until she was out of sight before going inside. She opened the door and saw Harry seated in his recliner, grinning like the Cheshire Cat.

"What?"

"Nothing."

Grace narrowed her eyes at him, knowing full well he'd spied on them. "How much did you hear?"

Harry leaned back but kept quiet. To Grace, the silence spoke volumes, and she felt another blush creep along her cheeks.

Grace dropped into the opposite recliner. "I like her a lot, *Ojiichan*. Maybe more than I should."

"How so?"

"It's like there's this instant attraction between us, but we barely know each other. It's exciting and scary at the same time. I've never felt this way before. Not even with..."

"Carly." He finished the sentence for her. Harry was quiet for a few moments. "Olivia is a good woman. Try not to compare her or any other woman to Carly. It's not fair to her, and it's not fair to you." He leaned forward and rested his elbows on his knees. "You deserve better than that. If you feel something for Olivia, then you should explore it, but be careful. Don't rush anything."

"I think the rushing part has already happened. If we'd been alone tonight..."

"You were alone."

Grace smiled warmly at him. "I mean somewhere no one could see or hear us. Like her house, for example. We'd have slept together."

"Don't you think it's a bit soon for that?"

"That's the problem. I don't."

"Be careful, Gracie. I don't want to see you get hurt."

"Me either. I'm not looking for a girlfriend, just someone I can have a good time with. Would it be so bad if that included sex?"

"For some people, no." Harry's eyes caught hers, and she saw the concern in them. "For you, I think so. You once told me you could never have sex with someone you weren't in love with. Has that changed?"

"Yeah. I was sixteen when I had that idiotic idea in my head. I don't think love exists the way I fantasized about it. Not for me, anyway. I want to enjoy my life. I want to have the kind of fun I've been missing out on for years. I can't even remember the last time I went to a bar to go dancing. I used to do that every weekend until Carly broke my ribs when she thought I was flirting with some woman on the dance floor."

Grace sighed heavily. "*Ojiichan*, I feel as though I've missed a chunk of my life. Maybe it's selfish or even immature, but I want some of that back. I want to be carefree and do whatever feels right in the moment. Does that make sense?"

"It does, but you must be careful. You're not a child so I won't lecture you. I only want you to make good choices, just as your parents do. I ask that you think before you make those choices. It must be right for you—not right for you in the eyes of others—whether that be me, your parents, or Olivia Templeton."

"That's what I'm trying to do—concentrate on what's good for me. I spent too many years doing for one other person. Abby has been trying to get me to put myself first."

"She's right. The person you need to please most in this world is you. Just don't be careless. Okay?"

"I'll do my best."

"I know. So, did you and Olivia enjoy yourselves today?"

"We had a great time." Grace rubbed her left arm. "I think I overdid it a bit. I haven't climbed much since my last surgery, and I guess I got overzealous trying to impress Olivia."

Harry smiled again. "And did you?"

"Did I what?"

"Impress her."

"If that kiss was any indication...I think I did."

"Good. Why don't you make us some tea, and you can tell me all about your day."

"Don't expect a lot of details. I don't want to give you a heart attack."

Harry scoffed. "It would take more than your exploits to surprise me, Gracie. After ninety-three years, do you really think there's something I haven't heard?"

Grace headed for the kitchen, not sure she wanted to answer that question. "How about we agree not to look for things you haven't heard? I think that would be scary."

"Agreed. For now."

Chapter Eight

Hiking had to be postponed due to rain. Torrential rain that would only add more work for Liv at the mine. Too much rain could flood their mining operations. She called David and did her best to trust him to make sure things were taken care of.

Rather than waste the day, she called Grace to change their date to a movie. It didn't even matter to Liv what they saw. She was only concerned with spending time with Grace.

They strolled out of the theater two hours later, still laughing. "I love Sandra Bullock. She never fails to crack me up," Liv said.

"Her comedies have always been my favorites, though *The Lake House* is her best romance I think."

"I've never been a big fan of Keanu Reeves, but I've got to admit those two have chemistry."

Liv delighted in the twinkle in Grace's eyes. Every time she looked at Grace she felt a certain *chemistry* low in her belly. "Same here," was all she could manage to say. Her cell phone rang and saved Liv from an awkward moment. The ring tone was Katy Perry's "Roar," announcing the caller was Sara. "Hey woman—"

"I am so pissed at you right now." Sara's voice was uncharacteristically harsh, and Liv stopped dead in her tracks. "How could you?"

"How could I?" She knew it sounded dumb to repeat Sara's words, but Liv was scrambling to come up with a better response. She also knew damn well what Sara was talking about. "Because I care about you, that's how. That bitch had no right—"

"No. You had no right. Dammit, Liv, I told you not to fight my battles for me. You're not my girlfriend anymore. I can deal with people like Angel. What I can't deal with is you feeling the need to threaten her. What were you thinking?"

Liv sighed heavily. Grace had walked a few feet away to give her privacy, and she was glad for it. "I didn't threaten her. I made a promise. I told her that if she ever touches you again I'll beat the shit out of her. And I also told her to keep quiet about it. So how did you find out?"

"She told me. She came into the bank this afternoon, sat down in my office, and told me what you'd said."

"And?"

Sara hesitated. "And she apologized."

"Good."

"Not good. I was serious when I asked you to stay out of this."

"I know you were. I'm sorry if I upset you, but you're my best friend and I love you. I couldn't sit by and not do something. I know we're not together anymore, and it might not be my place...but I won't let someone hurt you like that. Not ever."

A pregnant silence followed. Liv heard Sara's breathing hitch. She was crying.

"It's okay, Liv. I probably shouldn't be so pissed off. Sometimes...sometimes I wish we were still together. It'd make things so much easier."

"I know." Liv blinked back her own tears. "We okay?"

"Of course we are. Sorry if I ruined your date."

"It's not a date, and you're fine. You couldn't possibly ruin anything."

"Call me tomorrow and give me details."

"I'll call tomorrow and *might* give you details."

"Spoil sport."

Liv released a nervous laugh and ended the call. She rejoined Grace near the truck.

Grace asked, "Everything okay?"

"It is now." Liv sighed again and leaned against the truck bed. "Sara's pissed because I had a talk with a woman she went out with a couple weeks ago."

"Dare I ask why that's a problem?"

"I have this protective streak. Especially where Sara's concerned. She's not a pushover or anything, but she gets hurt easily." Liv folded her arms across her chest. "She went out with this woman named Angel. We've both known her for years, but it's the first time they went on a date. I guess they got to kissing, and before Sara knew what was going on, Angel was getting more aggressive. Sara told her to stop, they argued, and in the end, Angel hit her."

"Hit her? Did she call the police?"

"No. She got in her car and drove to my house."

Something changed in Grace's eyes—something Liv couldn't quite define. She watched Grace start walking back and forth beside the truck like a caged animal. Anger clearly flowed through her body, and when she looked at Liv again, the anger she saw made her flinch. "Her ass needs to be in jail."

"She's not going to do it again. I'm sure of that."

"There's no way in hell you can be sure!" Her fists clenched and unclenched as Grace started pacing again. "People like her— you think they're okay and that maybe it's a one-off, but you're wrong. She hit her once, she'll do it again. Maybe not Sara, but someone else."

"I think you're maybe blowing this out of proportion. I made damn sure Angel won't ever touch Sara again. I think she learned her lesson—"

"It's not that easy. It's not a lesson she can learn. She lashed out with her fist when things didn't go her way. How do you know she hasn't done this before?"

"I guess I don't." Liv pushed off the truck and blocked Grace's movement. "She was probably drinking too much anyway."

"Oh, so that's the excuse? She got a little drunk?"

"Grace, what's wrong? Why are you acting like this?"

"Like what?"

"Like it's your problem to solve."

Grace didn't speak, but her body was shaking. She was clearly somewhere between angry and hurt. All Liv wanted to do was embrace her and tell her everything was okay, but she knew immediately that was a bad idea.

"Maybe we should go home?"

"Yeah." Grace didn't say another word as she climbed into the passenger seat.

Liv slowly got behind the wheel and wondered what exactly she'd done wrong.

****

The drive back took just short of an hour. During that time, Grace leaned her forehead on the window of the passenger door and stared until her sight blurred. How was it that Liv could be so cavalier about the abuse of her friend? Didn't she realize that women like Angel went on to abuse others—maybe with more physical force than a slap?

Grace absently rubbed the scar on her left arm, her constant reminder of what Carly had done to her. Of how the woman she loved—thought loved her back—had nearly killed her. Grace was lucky to have survived, but every day was a challenge. Now, two years, three months, and five days later, every minute was precious to Grace. She was grateful to still be alive, away from Carly, and finally getting on with her life.

But her body held a lot of scars given her by Carly. Her wife. Her lover.

Tears pooled in her eyes, and she hastily wiped them away. She hated that Carly still had the power to make her cry. Hated that she still held such a powerful place in her life. Grace needed to call Abby.

Liv pulled the truck into the driveway, and Grace was out the door before she'd come to a complete stop.

She hadn't quite reached the porch when Liv stopped her. The hand on her arm was a shock, and Grace reacted instantly. With her free hand she grabbed the front of Liv's shirt, wrapped her leg around one of Liv's knees, and tossed her to the ground. Adrenaline still pulsed through her, so she stepped back to keep from doing any further damage.

Liv stared up at her, eyes wide in shock. "What the fuck was that?"

"You grabbed me," Grace said in way of an explanation. "Don't do that."

"Could have warned me," Liv grumbled, getting to her feet. "I was trying to get your attention. You didn't have to toss me on my ass for it."

"Don't touch me," Grace repeated with more force than necessary.

"Don't worry. I won't." Liv dusted herself off and kept distance between them.

"Fine."

"Fine."

Grace turned away from Liv and climbed onto the porch. Unexpected tears rolled down her cheeks. She couldn't suppress the sob that tore from her throat. She'd taken out her frustrations—her hurt and anger against Carly—on a woman who didn't deserve it. It made her no better than Carly. She wouldn't blame Liv if she never wanted to speak to her again.

When was she ever going to learn that she didn't deserve a woman like Olivia Templeton? Normal. Stable. Kind. Amazing. Carly made sure to beat it into Grace that she wasn't worthy of anyone decent. That she was only worthy of Carly. Of a woman who would rather beat her to death than see her happy.

Grace leaned against the porch rail, covered her face with her hands, and cried. She couldn't even manage a friendship. How pathetic was that?

Her knees weakened, and she crumpled to the wooden floor.

Gentle hands pulled her into a loving embrace. Grace rested her cheek against a soft shoulder until she felt the sobs subside. Tissues were handed to her so she could blow her nose. The strength in the arms around her comforted her, and it took Grace a few moments to realize it wasn't Harry that held her. It was Liv.

She looked up through puffy eyes and saw Liv's compassionate gaze staring back at her. Liv brushed her fingers along Grace's forehead to push back errant strands of hair. She didn't talk, though her actions spoke volumes.

"You didn't leave," Grace rasped.

"Of course not. What kind of bitch would I be if I left you crying on your doorstep?" Liv leaned back a bit and cupped Grace's cheek with her palm. "I'm sorry for whatever I did wrong. I didn't mean to hurt you."

Grace placed her hand over Liv's. "You didn't hurt me. That was done by someone else and—I shouldn't have attacked you like that. I know you weren't trying to hurt me. It's just that..." Grace shook her head as if that would help her find the right words. "I don't know how to explain."

"Try me. Let me know what's going on in here." Liv kissed her temple. "I like you, Gracie. I'd love to get to know you better."

"I'm not a very good person. You don't really want to know me."

"Clearly, you don't know me too well either. Yet." Liv situated herself so she was sitting beside Grace, both of them leaning against the railing. "Talk to me. I promise not to judge."

"I don't know that I can." Grace stared at her hands, folded in her lap.

Liv took one of those hands into hers and squeezed a little. "I can wait. I'm not asking for details. Just give me an idea of what's going on. Why did you flip out on me? And literally flip me?"

"I flipped you because I'm trained in self-defense. I spent a few years in the army."

"So that's *how* you flipped me, but not why. Did you think I was going to hurt you?"

Grace shrugged, afraid of how Liv would react. "I'm not sure. I know I overreacted, but I have to. I can't let myself get hurt again."

"I'd never hurt you, Gracie. Not physically and never on purpose."

"You don't know that. Just like you don't know if Angel will never hurt another woman. Abusers don't wear signs, and there's no way to tell them from anyone else."

"Abusers?" Liv squeezed Grace's hand a bit harder, as if to reassure her. "You were abused?"

"Yes. By my wife—ex-wife."

"Bitch. I hope she's rotting away in jail."

Grace was surprised by Liv's vehemence. "She is. But she's set to be released in a about six months. Some sort of early release program for first-time offenders."

"That's bullshit. People like her should get life."

"Tell that to the Washington State Justice Department. They only gave her four years to serve and she'll be getting out without having to do that fourth year."

"Well, at least she'll be in the states." Liv leaned closer to Grace and said, "But if she steps one foot into my country, all bets are off."

"Don't." Grace wasn't sure whether Liv was joking or not, and it scared her to think that confrontation could actually happen. "She'll have to stay in Seattle for a while. I'm sure my brother Matt will give me the details. That's why I'm staying here as long as I can."

"Well, you've got a six-month visa. I could help you out with that if you want me to."

"How?"

"I can hire you. Get you a work visa. You can stay as long as you're employed. I've done it several times for one of the guys in our machine shop. He's working on getting a legal residency, but until then, I just keep renewing the work visa. It's easy, once you know what you're doing."

"You'd do that for me? You don't even know me."

Liv laughed softly. "I know you're Harry's granddaughter, and that's good enough for me. So no worries. We'll keep you in Canada as long as possible."

"I'll, um, I'll keep that in mind. Thanks."

"Of course."

Grace got to her feet with Liv's help. They stood barely a foot apart for what felt to Grace like a terribly long time. "I had fun today, despite the drama," she said.

Liv gave her a lopsided grin. "Me, too. I'd like it to end on a nice note. If that's okay with you."

"What did you have in mind?"

"I want to kiss you." Liv moved a bit closer, her head slightly bent forward, her eyes searching Grace's.

"I'd like that," Grace said.

The kiss was tentative at first. Liv was letting Grace have control, something Grace wasn't used to. She put her hand behind Liv's neck and pulled her closer and their kiss grew deeper. Tongues moved in tandem as Liv's hands found their way to Grace's hips.

Grace felt the heat of their bodies and knew she wanted more. So much more. But she couldn't. Not then. She placed a hand on Liv's chest, feeling the rise and fall beneath her touch. They parted, Liv's pupils round with desire. Her kiss-swollen lips formed an adorable pout. Grace ran her finger along those lips and smiled. "It's not the right time, Olivia. I'm sorry."

"Don't be sorry," Liv said and kissed her finger. "I was just as into it as you were, but you're right." She nodded toward the window behind them. "I love Harry, but I'm not ready to know him as a voyeur."

Grace laughed outright and it felt freeing. "I'll let him know you said that."

"Don't you dare." Liv feigned embarrassment. "I won't be able to hold my head up in public again."

"Pity. You look prettier when your eyes are visible."

"You think I'm pretty?" Liv asked, one eyebrow cocked

in surprise.

"Gorgeous, even." Grace brushed her lips across Liv's. "What do you think about getting together tomorrow?"

"I think it's a great idea. I'll take you hiking, if you think you're up for it. There's an amazing trail pretty much only us locals use. The view is well worth the effort."

"I'm up for anything about now, but won't it be muddy?"

"Not too bad. There's a lot of gravel. It's a beginner's trail with an amazing view."

"Cool. I love *Ojiichan*, but I'm bored. Come pick me up?"

"I'll be here at nine in the morning. We'll make a day of it."

Grace felt the heat from her sudden blush. Spending a day alone with Liv, along a trail that few knew about, was an enticing offer, and one she wouldn't soon stop thinking about. "Cool."

Liv started toward the porch steps, turned back around, and kissed Grace fully, leaving nothing to her imagination as to what Liv really wanted to do. "See you tomorrow." She jogged to her truck, climbed behind the wheel, and was gone before Grace could form any words.

****

Two weeks later, Grace maneuvered the D10 along the edge of the new cut. The dozer's blade scraped along the ground, removing the layer of earth known as the overburden. It covered the area all miners strive to reach—bedrock. Here the ancient gold lay waiting to be removed. Grace loved the entire process, even if she could never be completely sure that her work would prove fruitful.

She hoped this new cut would produce enough gold to cover the season's expenses and leave Harry with a healthy amount of profit in his bank account. Money was unimportant to Harry, but she felt more comfortable knowing he'd have more than enough. She was there to work, and taking care of Harry gave her purpose.

Aside from Harry's well-being, Grace honestly thought she could make Gracie's Glory a more profitable business. She'd gone over all the accounting for the company, and while the finances were in a good place, with tighter management they'd be able to afford another dozer and a much-needed new backup generator. Perhaps next season they could hire a few more workers as well. Charlie and Josie wouldn't be able to work the mine forever, even if neither of them would admit it.

As if reading her mind, Charlie's voice came over the radio and disrupted her thoughts. "What's up?" Grace said into her hand mic. That was another thing she wanted to buy. Hands-free radios.

"Josie's got dinner ready, so come on back. I'm starved."

Grace laughed. "You're always starved. I need to check the

wash plant, then I'll be there." She laughed harder at his grumbling. After she finished the area she was working on, Grace drove the dozer onto the one-lane road back to the truck-staging area. Last year, Harry's crew created the one-lane road to circle between the cut and the wash plant. It towered over the areas they had, and those they were mining, by about twenty meters.

Since the trucks were too big to run side-by-side, and building a two-lane road took up too much   precious acreage—acreage that could contain gold—the road was one way.

While their operation was small, the road was still efficient and time-saving. And that reminded Grace to look at her watch. In half an hour she'd be calling Liv for their evening chat. That brought a huge smile to her face. Two weeks passed since their date. Liv tried hard to make time to see Grace, but it hadn't happened. She'd canceled their hiking date, and Grace missed Liv a lot. If not for their nightly calls, Grace would be worried that Liv didn't want to see her.

Their chats always lasted more than two hours, the most recent one ended only because Grace's sat phone's battery died. Today she'd remembered to bring her power cord. She hoped the backup generator, which powered the cabin, wouldn't break down again.

Thoughts of hearing Liv's melodic voice sent chills down Grace's spine. The entire day they were together, Grace found each touch brought forth visceral reactions. And when they kissed...Grace never felt that way before. It was nearly indescribable. Amazing, though terribly overused, might work. Incredible was too lame. Exciting? Enticing? Regardless, she couldn't get Liv's touch out of her mind.

Grace parked the dozer beside Little Blue and climbed down. Mike, Charlie's nephew, was teetering at the top of the wash plant, where the dirt was put in. He was half in, half out of the chute, where the pay dirt was loaded into the plant.

"Mike! What are you doing?"

He popped up and said, "Trying to get the damn gate cleared. There's a boulder stuck between the grates, and I can't get it loose."

"Hang on," Grace said and climbed the ladder to join him. Mike was at least a foot taller than Grace and maybe weighed a bit over 170 pounds. While his wiry arms showed good muscle definition, Mike didn't have the power behind him to lever the rock free. Grace elbowed him when she was close enough. "Seriously? You think you can do this by yourself?"

Mike ran a grubby hand through his dark hair and squinted at her. "Would I be up here if I didn't?"

"As Charlie would say, 'you ain't got enough ass behind ya to get it done.'"

"Charlie's an ass."

"But he'd be right."

Mike rolled his eyes and pointed to the crowbar. "If we both give it a good push, we should be able to get it freed up." He looked at her butt and grinned. "I think you've got a nice enough ass to get it done."

"Thanks, I think." She elbowed him again. They both grabbed hold of the crowbar and tried their best to free the rock. "This isn't working," Grace said. "Maybe we should lever it from two sides. I don't think we're getting enough force behind it with just the one crowbar."

"It's the only one up here. But," Mike squeezed behind her on the plank that surrounded the chute, "I've got a shovel. Let's see if that works."

Grace waited patiently while he got the shovel. Once back, they took up positions side-by-side. Mike said, "I meant to tell you this morning that I found an awesome crag to do some climbing. It's not in a tourist area, and it's already got a route with bolts. I hear the view is amazing from the top. Whatcha think? You game?"

Grace couldn't stop the grin that spread across her face. Was she game? To finally get out and do some real climbing? "Hell, yes. When?"

"Saturday. Got a couple of buddies that've done the climb before so it should be fun. Bring your   girlfriend."

"My what?" She let go of the crowbar to face him. "Where'd you hear I have a girlfriend?"

Mike shrugged. "Charlie. Guess Harry told him. Anyway, bring her. We'll have a campfire   afterward."

"Damn gossipy men," she mumbled. Though secretly she was excited that Harry considered Liv her girlfriend. It was nice to feel a bit of normalcy. "Okay, enough chatting. On three. Ready?" Mike nodded and Grace counted, "One...two...three!"

Grace leaned all her weight on the crowbar and felt the rock start to give. Creaking noises came from between the rock and the bars as they continued to work. Her strength was flagging seconds before the rock came free. And so did Mike's shovel. The last thing Grace remembered was a terrifying moment of weightlessness before she blacked out.

****

Liv rarely drove over the speed limit. It always frustrated Dave to no end. But this time was different. She heard the call go out for the fire department and ambulance to Gracie's Glory. She called Grace and got no answer. She got through to Josie and ran to her truck as soon as she heard Grace was injured. She knew no details as Josie didn't stay on the line to tell her much. Liv raced toward the mine. A tightness formed in her chest, and she wished her truck were faster.

She barely knew Grace, yet there was this intense connection between them. One she'd never felt with Jane. Hell, she'd never felt it with anyone. It terrified and excited her at the same time. Right then, it scared her. Grace was hurt enough to need an ambulance.

Her cell phone rang, and Liv nearly ran off the road to fish it out of her jacket pocket. "Yeah?"

"Slow down," Sara's controlled voice filled her ear. "She's fine. She might have a concussion and broken ribs, but she's otherwise fine. Now slow the hell down before you crash and I kick your ass for being reckless."

Liv eased off the gas but was still well over the speed limit. "How the hell do you know?"

"I won't tell you until I know you've slowed down."

"Fuck." Liv let up on the gas. "I'm going 120 kilometers now. Happy?"

"Not really, but that'll do. I called my friend Betty at dispatch when I heard on the scanner that the ambulance was being sent to Gracie's Glory. Betty told me that Grace was conscious and talking. You can't be conscious and talking if you're not okay."

Liv released the breath she'd been holding. "Thanks. God, Sara. I've never been so scared."

"You'd have been less scared if you'd called to find out what was going on before taking off like a bat out of hell. Listen, you and me are going to have to have a talk. You're going too fast with this one, Liv. I don't want you to get hurt."

"I know and I love you for it, Sara. I'll call you later. I promise."

"You better." Sara disconnected and Liv put the phone back into her jacket pocket.

Sara might be right. She probably was going too fast with Grace. But it was hard not to follow her heart. And one thing Liv learned long ago was to always follow her heart. If she had, things with Jane might have gone a lot differently.

Liv finally reached the entrance to the mine and came to a stop in front of the old cabin, next to the ambulance. She was out of the truck fast and had to slow to a jog, fighting the urge to run in there. Charlie met her at the door.

"Hey, Liv, what're you doing here?"

"I heard the call go out for the ambulance. I called Josie, and she told me Gracie got hurt." She anxiously looked behind Charlie, wishing she could see through the closed cabin door. "She okay?"

"The medics are in there with her now, trying to talk her into going to the hospital."

"Stubborn woman," Liv muttered. She thought she saw a smile spread across Charlie's face before she moved past him and into the tiny cabin.

Grace was seated with her arms resting on the rickety, square table. She shook her head at whatever the medic asked her. "I'm fine. Just a little tired."

"Grace," the man said with a lot more patience in his voice than Liv felt, "you need an x-ray. We can't be sure you don't have broken ribs, but I'm sure you have a mild concussion."

"I don't—"

"Have x-ray vision so you don't know if anything's broken," Liv said. She squatted next to Grace and gently placed a hand on her knee. She was trembling. "Besides, concussions can be serious. Please, Gracie. You need to be checked over."

"I've had them before—broken ribs and a concussion," Grace said, her voice barely audible.

Liv swallowed the lump in her throat. The way Grace spoke, she suspected her ex-wife had been responsible for the injuries. "So have I. But do this for me, please? Otherwise I'll worry about you and probably won't sleep for weeks." She put on her best, teasing smile and waited for Grace to look at her. When she did, Grace weakly smiled back.

"Fine. But only if you take me. I don't need to go in an ambulance."

Liv glanced at the medic on the other side of Grace, her eyebrows raised in silent question.

"If you won't let us take you in the ambulance, at least let me tape your ribs so you've got some stability."

"Sure." Grace raised her hands to unbutton her shirt, but couldn't get her right arm high enough. Pain was written across her face.

"Let me," Liv said and gently reached around from behind and undid the buttons. She slid the long-sleeved shirt over Grace's head and then let it rest on her arms. Liv sucked in a breath. Bruises marred the perfect, light-brown skin of Grace's right side. "Oh geez, Gracie. How..."

"I don't know what I hit. I don't remember anything except falling."

"It was my fault," someone behind them said.

Liv moved aside to let the medic work on Grace. Mike was standing there, his pale face smudged with dirt and tears. He was shaking.

"What happened?"

Mike went into a fast-paced description of trying to get the rock free. He ended it with, "...the handle on my shovel broke, and the piece in my hand hit Grace in the stomach. She went over the side of the chute. I almost went with her, but I did try to grab hold of her. It all happened too damn fast."

Liv knew Mike and didn't think he had a mean bone in his lean body. She reached out to pat his trembling hand. "That's why they're called accidents and not intentionals. Chill out. She'll be fine."

"I'm fine, Mike," Grace said, even though her voice was laced with pain.

The medic turned to Liv as he started taping Grace's ribs. "This isn't going to help much with the pain. I can't be sure whether the ribs are broken or not."

"Are you sure it's okay for me to drive her?"

The medic shook his head. "No. I don't recommend it, but I can't force her to go."

"Gracie—"

"I'm fine, Liv. If you're not good with driving me, I'll get Charlie or Josie."

"No, that's not it." Liv knelt beside her after helping Grace put her shirt back on. "It's not about what I can or can't do." She touched the side of Grace's face with her palm and gently turned her head so they were face-to-face. "It's about what's best for you. It's my opinion that you should let these guys take you to the hospital. They can make your more comfortable and be sure they get you there safely. I don't want something to happen to you on the way. I can't drive and take care of you at the same time."

Tears pooled at the edges of Grace's eyes. "Okay. I'll go in the ambulance."

"Good." Liv softly kissed her on the mouth and stood. "I'll be right behind you. Charlie, would you and Josie call Harry—"

"No." Grace spoke loud enough that she startled Josie. "Please. I asked them not to call him when I got hurt so he wouldn't rush out here. I don't want him rushing to the hospital, either. I promise to tell him everything when I get back. I don't want to scare him. Besides, he's seen enough of me in the hospital." Tears shimmered in her eyes as she stared at Josie. "Please."

Josie hesitated. "He's going to kick my ass so you better call me the second you know anything."

"Thanks."

"Want me to come, too?" Mike asked.

Josie guided him toward the cabin. "You need to stay here. Liv'll take good care of her."

****

Several hours later, they pulled into Harry's driveway. The porch light was on and Grace saw Harry's outline in the doorway. She regretted not calling him sooner than a half hour ago, but she didn't think she could handle being in the hospital with Harry at her side. Again. The trip to the emergency room already brought back too many memories.

She reached for the handle to open the door of the truck and winced at the pain. Bruised ribs were just as bad as broken ones. She tried again, but this time the door was opened by Liv. She held her hand out to Grace.

Grace said, "I'm not that broken."

"But you're a little broken." Liv held her arm as Grace climbed out.

"Thanks."

"You're welcome." Liv kept hold of Grace's arm as they went up the porch steps. Harry greeted them at the front door.

"Do you want to go to bed or sit in a recliner?" he asked.

"Recliner please. I don't think I can lie down."

Liv guided her in and helped her get as comfy as possible. "Can I get you something to drink or eat?" Liv glanced over at Harry. "She wouldn't let me get her anything at the hospital."

"I'm fine."

Harry placed a glass of water on the side table next to Grace. He spoke to Liv. "She's stubborn. Gets it from her father."

"I'm not stubborn," Grace protested, even though she knew he was right. "I just don't need anyone's help."

Liv knelt in front of her and rested a hand on her knee. "You're very cute when you're being stubborn."

Grace hated how easily she blushed in front of Liv. She tried to give her an evil eye, but it only made Liv giggle. "You're mean."

"Maybe." Liv moved forward and gave her a gentle kiss on the lips. "You really scared me, Gracie. Please don't do that again."

"I'll do my best."

"Good," Harry spoke from behind them, a grilled cheese sandwich on a paper plate in his hand. "Eat." He gave the food to Grace. "What did the doctor say about your head?"

Grace fingered the tender area near her left temple. "I'm fine. Mild concussion. He told me to get some rest and, if I have any symptoms, to get to the hospital right away."

Harry grunted his discontent. "Did you tell him your history?"

"I did." Grace hoped he'd stop the interrogation. At least until Liv was gone. She didn't want to go into her entire medical history just then.

Liv held Grace's hand and brought it to her lips for a soft kiss.

"I should go so you can sleep. I'll come by tomorrow afternoon."

"You don't need to."

Liv cupped her cheek in her palm, and Grace leaned into the touch. "Yes, I do. Call if you need   anything."

"I will."

Liv got up and handed Harry the pill bottle from the hospital. "The ER doc gave her a few pain meds, but she can't have them until tomorrow. He wants her to follow up with someone by Wednesday."

"I'll see to it. Thank you, Olivia." Harry walked with her to the door. They spoke in hushed tones before Harry closed the door and sat in his recliner.

"Are you angry with me?" Grace asked.

Harry was quiet for a moment, and she worried that he was indeed mad at her.

"I'm not angry. Upset. Disappointed, perhaps, but not angry. Did you expect I would be? It was an accident, Gracie Lee. There was nothing you could have done to prevent it."

"That's not why I didn't call you."

"Why then?"

"I didn't want you to have to see me in the hospital again. We had enough of that already. Besides, I wasn't hurt badly. Scared more than anything else."

"And you should have called." Harry met her gaze, and she saw the concern in his dark eyes. "I wanted to be there with you."

"I'm sure you did, but it was as much about me as it was about you. If you'd been there—the ER brought back enough memories. Besides, Olivia took good care of me."

"She cares for you. But I must ask you never to do this again. Don't forbid Charlie and Josie from telling me what's going on. Neither of them can keep a secret from me."

"Did they call you?"

"No. Jeffrey from the fire department did. That's when I called Charlie, and eventually he told me you'd been hurt. And that you didn't want me to go to the hospital."

"I'm sorry, *Ojiichan*. I meant no disrespect—"

He waved her comment away. "That is not the point. Promise me you will tell me if something happens...if you get hurt. I want to know right away. Promise me."

"I promise," Grace said, feeling appropriately chastised.

"Good. Then it's done. Now, you must be hungry. Please eat."

"I'm more tired than hungry. Maybe I could take a nap and eat a bit later?"

"Of course." Harry got up and left the room. A few moments later he returned with a blanket and pillows. "First we get you comfortable. I think you might be sleeping out here for a few days."

"You're probably right." Grace let Harry get her settled again then reached for his hand. His aged fingers tightened around hers. "*Aishiteimas, Ojiichan.*"

"*Aishiteimas*, Gracie Lee. Now go to sleep."

Grace closed her eyes and did as she was told.

****

Liv pulled into her driveway and parked beside Sara's car. Sara was seated on the porch swing. She got up when Liv climbed the porch steps, strode purposefully toward her, and punched her in the arm. Hard.

"Ow!" Liv rubbed the sore spot. "What the hell was that for?

"For driving like a maniac. What were you thinking?" Sara's face was red with anger. "No, don't answer that. You weren't thinking. You were being suicidal."

"You're overreacting. I was driving fast, not crazy."

"Exactly what did you expect to do? Provided you didn't kill yourself on the way there?"

Liv stared at Sara, both shocked and angry at her reaction. She was right about one thing. Liv wasn't thinking. She simply reacted the second Josie told her Grace was hurt. Only one thing was on her mind. Getting to Grace.

"I care about her, Sara. We've only known each other a short time, but it feels like a helluva lot longer."

Sara's shoulders sagged a bit. "Maybe that's my point. You're going way too fast. It's only going to end up with you getting hurt."

Liv reached toward Sara, but she backed up a step. "I don't think so. It's so much different with   Gracie. It's like we've been friends our whole lives. And when she kisses me—Sara, I swear I've never felt this with any other woman. I know it's crazy, but I think I'm falling in love with her."

"That's not crazy. It's scary."

"Why?"

Sara stepped close enough that Liv could see the tears in her eyes. "Because I don't want you to get hurt. Not again."

"You can't stop that. But if I don't at least try to build something with Grace, I'll regret it for the rest of my life." Liv placed a hand on Sara's shoulder. "I get the feeling this is more than whether or not I'll get hurt."

"I'm worried about you. That's all."

"Yes, but it's not all. Sara, I'm sorry. This means that we— that you and me—" Liv put a little distance between them. Her heart sank as she realized that she and Sara would no longer be enjoying the "with benefits" part of their relationship. It never once occurred to her what that would do to Sara.

"Don't you dare apologize, Olivia Templeton. We both knew that if either of us found someone else it would be completely over between us. It was more a fantasy for me anyway." She swiped at the tears on her face and cleared her throat. "I really am worried about you. Just remember that I'm still your best friend, and you can come to me if you need to talk. Okay?"

"Of course. As long as you remember the same." Liv wrapped Sara into a warm hug. "Don't worry about me. I'm a big girl, okay?"

"A big girl with a big heart." Sara patted Liv's chest. "If she breaks that big heart, I might be forced to break her in half."

That comment made Liv bark a laugh. "I would pay money to see that."

"I'm just as protective of you as you are of me."

Liv sighed. "You're still mad at me about Angel, aren't you?"

"Not so much mad as frustrated. Maybe more so at myself than you."

"Why?"

"Because, deep down, I love that you want to protect me. I love having you there to save me—even if I don't need saving."

"Sara—"

"Don't." Sara swiped at the tears on her cheeks again. "I can't help how I feel. I'm still in love with you."

Liv stared into the darkness. No words came to mind, and she felt completely lost. Did she still love Sara? Yes, but as her best friend. Not as a lover or partner. She was pretty sure she'd never loved Sara in that regard and felt guilty for it. It was partly why they broke up, right? Liv once thought she was in love. And lived with that mistake for years.

No matter what, she was going to hurt Sara and that increased her guilt a thousand fold. She understood that kind of pain and didn't want to inflict it on anyone else.

"I didn't say it to get a reaction or declaration of undying love from you," Sara said with a weak laugh. "Not that I'd be upset if you did. I only needed to say it out loud. To tell you how I feel, so you understand why I'm a little jealous of Grace."

"Uh, there's really not much to be jealous of, Sara. We're dating, but that's it."

"No. There's a lot more to it than that. I'm jealous of the possibilities that Grace represents. I know you won't believe me, but you're one helluva catch, Olivia Templeton. You're beautiful, kind, amazing and haven't stopped talking about Grace since you first took her to the pub for dinner. She's the first person since Jane that you've done that with."

Liv kept being shocked into silence. She didn't believe she

was any kind of "catch," though she was sure Sara had one thing right. There was something special about Grace. Her brain said no, but her heart was screaming yes. She very much wanted more with Grace.

Sara said, "Look, I probably—"

"No. Sara, it's fine." Liv took hold of Sara's hand and gave it a quick squeeze. "You'll always be my best friend. Always. I'm sorry I can't give you more than that."

"Me, too." Sara gripped Liv's hand and rested her head on Liv's shoulder. "Do me a favor and let me fight my own battles from now on. Much as I love it, it's not good for either of us."

"Probably not," Liv replied in a noncommittal manner.

"No more sex either."

Liv grinned. "I was going to say the same thing. I'd feel like I was cheating on Grace because you're right. There's something there. At least for me. I don't know that I'm in love with her, but I think I might be falling."

Sara snuggled closer to her. "Please be careful. I couldn't take it if you got hurt." A sob escaped Sara when Liv put her arms around her.

"Don't cry, sweetheart. We're still okay, and I promise to be careful. I'll even let you fight for me if she breaks my heart."

"That's not even funny," Sara said and playfully punched Liv's arm.

"At least you and I are still okay."

"We are. So how's Grace?"

Liv sighed. "She's okay. Bruised ribs and minor concussion."

"Wow. What happened exactly?"

Liv repeated all the details of Grace's accident. "It could have been much worse and I'm glad she's going to be okay. She's bummed about the hiking since we were planning on doing that tomorrow."

"You can always visit with her instead."

"I plan to. It's weird, but I think with any other woman I'd have already slept with her. Before the accident, that is."

"It's not weird. You've been talking to her constantly for a couple of weeks now. It's not like you don't know anything about her. You even know some of her family."

"Yeah, but the weird part is that I have the feeling that we need to go slow in the sex department. And trust me, my libido doesn't want to go slow. I wish I could ask her some stuff about her history, I don't want to pry. I think her ex did some serious damage to her. Seems to me like she's pretty messed up. I mean, what if we're in the mood, and she misreads something I do and kicks my ass?"

Sara kissed her on the cheek. "Honey, she already did."

"I know, right? So what the hell do I do?"

"What comes natural. You think you should go slow, then go slow, but make sure you tell her why."

"You're not helping."

"I mean it. Talk to her. She's already opened up to you, and I'd be willing to bet she'll open up even more. If you're serious about her, and I'm very sure you are, then you two have to talk. Let her know you aren't just looking for a tumble in the sack."

"I don't know. The idea of a relationship with Gracie is enticing and scary at the same time."

"Which is why I really want to beat the crap out of Jane. If she ever dares show her face here again, I just might."

"I seriously doubt she'll come back. Her girl toy has money, remember? They're living it up in   Vancouver somewhere."

"I still want to kick her ass. But enough about that bitch. Grace seems like a good person to me. Communicate with the woman. And trust your instincts."

"Heh. That didn't help much with Jane."

Sara faced Liv. "You didn't trust your instincts with Jane. So I'm telling you to do that now. I'm not the best person to give relationship advice, but I do know you better than anyone else. Talk to her. The sooner the better."

"You know me too well, I think." Liv embraced her. "Thanks, Sara. You're the best. Why don't we go inside for a while? It's a bit chilly tonight."

"I can't." She started down the porch steps toward her car. "Call me tomorrow and let me know how it goes." Sara was in her car and gone before Liv could reply.

Of course it was a bad idea for her to come into the house. Every other time they'd done that, they ended up having sex. Liv slapped herself in the forehead and went inside. It was going to be a long, lonely night.

****

The phone rang, jolting Liv out of a fitful slumber. She didn't bother to see who it was before swiping her finger across the screen to answer it. "Hello?"

"Have you heard from David?"

Her father's words were hurried, and it took a second for them to sink into Liv's brain. "No. Why?" She squinted at the time on her phone. It was ten past three.

"He called to tell me he was on his way to the shop because Hank was there causing problems. That was two hours ago."

Liv swung her legs over the edge of the bed. There was a lot of background noise as her father spoke. "Are you on the way there?"

"I am."

Now Liv was up and getting dressed. "Slow down, Dad. Get there in one piece."

"Says the woman who broke the sound barrier to get to a certain mine earlier today—well, yesterday."

"Says the child of the man driving like a maniac. I know you as well as I know myself, Jonas Templeton. Slow down. I'm closer and I'll call as soon as I get there and find out what the hell is going on. No arguing."

There was a brief silence. "Have I told you how much you remind me of your mother?"

"I'll accept the compliment. See you soon." Liv disconnected, shoved the phone into the back pocket of her jeans, and rushed out of the house.

She pulled onto the lot of their maintenance building half an hour later. The entrance to the workshop was closed, and the security lights at the corners of the two-story structure shone like daylight. She parked her vehicle after spotting David's pickup close to a mechanic bay. The roll door was open, but the only illumination came from the security lights.

She stepped out of her truck and heard David's raised voice. She sprinted to the bay just as David tumbled out. Liv was in time to help him to his feet. "What's going on? You hurt?"

David swiped his hand across his face, but it wasn't light enough for Liv to see if he was injured. "I can't get that stupid son-of-a-bitch to leave."

"Did you call the police?"

"No. I can't find my fucking cell phone. I must have lost it when I pulled his ass off the Black   Monster. And I didn't want to leave him to go and use the office phone."

"He was on top of the wash plant we just finished building? The one that's already sold for almost a million dollars? *That* Black Monster?" Liv felt the anger building, but judging from the expression on David's face, he was already furious.

"Yep. I don't know if he did any damage, but he was climbing out of the trommel when I got here. He's pissed drunk and ranting on and on about being fired and who knows what else. I can't understand half what he says with that stupid accent of his."

"When did you fire him?"

"At the end of his shift yesterday. He ran a loader into one of the new trailers and bent the hell out of it. I was standing there, and if I hadn't seen him coming, I'd have gotten hurt. I fired him on the spot." David pointed toward the bay. "I forgot to get some paperwork earlier today and came back here. I called Dad when I found Hank on the trommel. I managed to get him down, but he ran into the bay and won't leave. He says it's a sit-in."

"Whatever. Let me call the police and then Dad. He's on his way, freaked out that you aren't answering your cell phone."

"I'm sorry, Liv."

"There's nothing to be sorry for. It's not your fault. Except that you left the bay door open and he ran inside. That's your fault." She cuffed him on the shoulder to take any sting out of her comment and called the police.

She'd just finished giving them details when Jonas pulled in, his headlights blinding Liv. He left them on and jogged toward them.

"David? Are you okay? What the hell is going on? Where's Hank?"

Liv said to David, "Told you."

David quickly brought Jonas up to speed. "He's still in there."

"Not for long." Jonas strode into the bay, Liv and David close on his heels.

"Dad, this isn't a good idea. The police will—"

"Be here in time to take him to jail," Jonas said.

"Well I'll be damned," Hank said from the back of the bay. He was seated on a stool near one of the tool-storage areas. "Big Daddy Templeton comin' here ta save the boy's ass."

"I'm here to get you off my property, Hank. You've been fired, and David gave you your last check. If you leave now, I won't add trespassing to the charges I'm going to file against you."

"Charges? What for? You don't got no rights to be filing nothing agin' me." Hank staggered to his feet and shook a wobbly fist at Jonas. "Kiss my ass. I gotta right to be here. I'm a squatter."

Liv resisted the urge to roll her eyes. Though she now understood David's issue with Hank's drunken Tennessee slang. "You're not a squatter, Hank. You're drunk."

"Don't mean I ain't a squatter, girly. Now you jus' run along home."

Liv stepped between Hank and Jonas when she noticed Jonas clench his fist. "Hank, you've been fired. This is private property and you're trespassing. I don't want to have you arrested, but that's what's going to happen. You're drunk, and I'm trying to make this easier on you—"

"Fuck you!" Hank's meaty fist came out of nowhere, aimed for Liv's face. His slowed reflexes helped her duck the blow.

David tackled Hank and pinned him to the ground. "Don't you ever take a swing at my sister!" He pulled his arm back, but Liv rushed forward to stop him.

"No! David stop. He's not worth it." She kept hold of David. "Don't. Please."

There was hesitation, but David relented. Hank didn't move again. Jonas said, "Why don't you two go outside? I'll stay in here.

I think I hear the police out there."

Jonas was right. Liv heard at least two vehicles' tires crunch along the gravel parking lot. She took David by the hand and guided him outside. Once there, they were met by the police and Liv directed them into the bay.

David squeezed Liv's hand. "I wanted to kill him for trying to hit you, Livvy. You and I might have our issues, but no one comes at you without me getting in between. If he'd hit you—they'd have to take him out of here in an ambulance."

Liv loved her brother dearly, but sometimes he was too reactionary. She pulled him into a tight hug. "He didn't and you didn't need to do anything. I promise I can take care of myself, but I love you for looking out for me." She kissed him on the cheek, knowing it would make him blush. It was too bad she couldn't fully appreciate it in the dim light. "How about we go try to find your cell phone? I'll call it and you can get on your hands and knees to look for it."

"Thanks. I think. Why do I have to get on my hands and knees?"

"Because it's your phone, shithead. You're the one that lost it."

"I didn't lose it. It's just misplaced."

"Uh-huh." Liv dialed his number. The muted music of whatever ringtone he'd chosen to use this week filtered toward them. "It sounds a little tinny. Maybe it's in the trommel."

David hung his head and trudged to the Black Monster, which, as the name indicated, was painted black. He grumbled about not being able to see anything and climbed onto the giant wash plant. Liv giggled when she heard him inside the cylindrical part of the plant, calling for her to dial his number again.

It may have been the middle of the night, but Liv decided she'd get a little pleasure out of it. She dialed again, now knowing that the phone was actually under the wheel of the trailer the plant sat upon. She could see the light when she called it. David couldn't.

The only thing she now wondered was how long she could keep him busy.

"Where's your brother? The police need to talk to him." Jonas now stood beside Liv.

"He's in the trommel looking for his cell phone. He lost it when he pulled Hank off the wash plant."

Jonas retrieved the phone and tilted his head when he asked, "This one? He thinks it's in there?"

"He does because I told him to go look in there." Liv smiled. "Consider it payback for getting us up in the middle of the night."

"David!" Jonas stood beside the trommel. "I found your

phone. Now get out here so the police can talk to you. You need to fill out some paperwork."

"You're no fun," Liv said as Jonas rejoined her.

"And you're hiding how scared you are. You always do stupid crap like this when you're nervous or worried. Or scared."

Liv tucked her phone away and met her father's gaze. He was right, of course. She'd managed to calm David down, but her insides were in turmoil. "I didn't expect him to try to hit me. If he'd hit me my jaw would be broken. Or I'd end up with a concussion. I'm not helpless, Dad, but I felt like I was for that split second."

Jonas put his arm around her and pulled Liv against him. "You're not helpless. That's absolutely right. And if he had hit you, you probably would've slugged him back. But that doesn't mean it wasn't scary."

She nodded toward David as he scrambled down the ladder of the Black Monster. "Give dummy his phone back. I'm going home to get some sleep. I'll call you later, okay?"

Jonas kissed her temple and let her go. "I love you, Liv."

"Love you, too, Dad. Get David to bed safely, okay?"

"Yes, dear."

As Liv drove home, she thought about the punch Hank had thrown at her and how it scared her. She wondered if that was how Grace felt every time Carly raised her hand against her—a second of panic   followed by the sick feeling that she was about to be hurt. That Grace had experienced such helplessness saddened her.

Chapter Nine

The trip from the front room to the bathroom was more arduous than Grace expected. She'd nursed broken ribs before, so she shouldn't be surprised. Pain, combined with the inability to take a deep breath, sapped any energy she had. Once she reached the chair again, she was exhausted.

"This sucks."

"I know," Harry said, "but it won't last forever. Two weeks and you should be moving around better. By the end of the month, you won't notice the pain as much."

Grace eyed Harry as he wandered around the room. "Thank you, Doctor Kato. I appreciate the   prognosis."

"Don't be grumpy with me."

"I can't help it. It's how I feel." Grace watched him make his second path around the room. "What are you looking for?"

"I don't remember."

"You don't remember? Then why are you still looking for it?"

Harry shrugged. "If I keep looking, I might find it."

"And that makes sense to you?"

"It would make sense to you, too, if you were nearly a century old."

Grace couldn't resist the urge to roll her eyes. "Is that your way of telling me you're old?"

Harry stopped what he was doing and faced her, hands on his hips. The expression on his face was meant to be stern, but it made Grace giggle. "I may end up telling you I'm too old to fix your lunch."

"I can fix my own lunch."

There was a knock on the door, and Harry moved to answer it. Over his shoulder he said, "Perhaps we'll see if you can manage to do that."

Grace was about to reply when Harry allowed Liv in. It didn't look as though Liv had slept much, and her smile didn't reach her eyes. She quietly greeted Harry then came to Grace.

"How's the patient doing today?"

Grace and Harry answered at the same time.

"Fine."

"Grumpy."

Grace shot Harry what she hoped was a reproachful glare. He was still grinning when he left the room.

Liv knelt beside Grace's chair and gently took hold of her hand. "It's got to suck to be stuck inside all day."

"It does. But I don't think it's as bad as whatever's bothering you."

Liv smiled weakly. "That obvious?"

"Totally. What's wrong?"

"It's a long story, but I'll sum it up to say that David fired a guy named Hank from our repair shop yesterday."

"You told me you were going to do that. So what's the real issue?"

Liv kept her gaze on their linked hands. "I feel guilty because I should have fired him when David told me he was drunk on the job. I shouldn't have given him a second chance."

"But?"

"But I did and he almost got David hurt and managed to mess up some of our equipment. David fired him on the spot, but I'm responsible for all our employees and their actions on the job."

"So why did you give him a second chance?"

Liv shrugged. "He's got a family, and David asked me to let him handle it. But Hank came to the shop in the middle of the night, pissed that David fired him. He was drunk. David caught him climbing on our million dollar wash plant—that we just sold— and managed to pull him down. Then Hank got into one of the mechanic bays and wouldn't leave."

"What happened then? Didn't you call the police?"

Liv nodded. "We did, but Dad and I got there first."

"And? There's something you're not telling me."

"Hank took a swing at me."

Grace opened her mouth, but Liv placed a finger to her lips to quiet her. "He never touched me. He was too drunk, and David was a lot faster. He shoved Hank to the ground, and that was the end of it."

"Bullshit." Grace spoke around the finger on her lips.

"You're right. There is more." Liv lowered her voice as she said, "When he swung at me—I guess—it must be how you felt when Carly hit you. I felt this horrible sense of helplessness. The only reason I could avoid the hit was because he was drunk. Is that how it was for you? Every time she did that?"

"Yes." Grace cupped Liv's face in her hands. "And I'm sorry you felt that way, even for a second. It's horrible and I lived like that for years. I didn't get that feeling every time she hit me. I got it every day when I woke up, and it stayed there until I fell asleep. It was there in my nightmares, and sometimes it creeps up on me now. I have to fight against it all the time."

"I'm sorry. If that bitch ever comes near you again I won't be responsible for my actions."

"I don't want you to—"

"If you're going to say you don't want me to protect you, too bad. I will always protect you, even if you don't think you need it." Liv's gaze met hers, and it felt like a caress as her blue eyes held Grace's for a long time.

Grace's pulse quickened. She gripped Liv's hand. Had any woman ever cared for her that much? It excited and frightened her at the same time. "Tell me what happened next."

"I took David outside to calm him down because he wanted to beat Hank to death. The police came and arrested Hank. I have to meet with them later today to file charges for attempted assault and get his work visa revoked. I've never done that before, but one of the guys at the station knows how to get it taken care of. So it's all over now."

It didn't feel like it was over to Grace. The idea of Liv being near someone that could hurt her worried Grace. It bothered her that she hadn't been there with Liv. Not that she could do much in her current state, but Grace felt a wave of protectiveness come over her. Was this what Liv felt about her?

"How soon before he leaves the country?"

"No idea. It can take a few days or a few weeks. You know the government. Never fast when you want it to be. I just feel bad for his family. At least his girlfriend is a citizen. Probably a good thing they aren't married." Liv kissed the back of Grace's hand then placed her palm against Grace's cheek. "If he causes any more problems, I'm sure they'll speed the process up."

"You think he'll come after you? To retaliate?"

"Don't know. He'll be in jail awhile, I'd guess. I'm not going to worry about that right now." She placed a sweet kiss on Grace's lips. "I'd much rather spend the afternoon with you."

"You'd rather be inside on a beautiful day? Cooped up with me?"

"Hell, yes."

Grace laughed. "You're weird."

"Nah. My mother would say I'm 'smitten.'"

"Smitten? Seriously?" Grace laughed so hard it hurt.

"Hey, easy there." Liv kissed her again, this one longer, more involved. They parted, breathless.

"Okay," Grace said. "No laughing."

"Kissing is okay?"

"Yes. Very okay."

Liv gave her a crooked grin. "Well, aside from kissing, I was hoping to hang out and relax with you. If you're up to it. I can't stay all day, but I can certainly stay a few hours."

"You're very sweet. I think *Ojiichan* would appreciate the break. He's been running himself ragged, and I'm worried about him."

"Worry no more. I'll be your nurse for a while. What's your first order?"

"Um, another kiss?"

Liv complied. "Next?"

"Some water and maybe a sandwich."

"I thought you could make your own lunch," Harry said as he entered the room.

"She offered to help, and how long have you been listening?"

Harry didn't answer. He spoke to Liv. "If you don't mind babysitting my grumpy grandchild, I could use the time to go into town. Whenever she gets hurt, she feels the need to eat. A lot. I need more food."

"Of course," Liv said. "I'll take over babysitting duties for a while. I'm sure you need a break."

"You have no idea," Harry said on his way out.

Once the door was closed, Grace narrowed her eyes at Liv. "Babysitting?"

"Baby, I love sitting with you, so yeah. I'm babysitting."

"Nice save."

"I do what I can. Now I'm going to make you the best damn sandwich you've ever had."

"As long as it's big. I'm starved."

"So I heard."

****

Grace released a contented sigh. Liv could open her own sandwich shop and make a fortune. Grace's belly was full and happy. She eyed Liv who was finishing her own lunch. "If you cook as good as you make a sandwich, I'm going to have to marry you."

Liv nearly choked on her food. "What?"

"If you can cook, I'll rent a U-Haul and move in."

Liv made a nervous laugh. "It's just a sandwich."

"Clearly, you've never had Harry's cooking."

"You haven't had mine either."

"You haven't invited me for dinner." Grace kept the grin on her face, letting Liv know she was teasing.

"Hmm. It was most certainly an oversight. And since you already believe I'm a fabulous cook, I extend the invitation."

"Most gracious of you." Grace giggled and winced from the pain. "It sucks when laughing hurts."

"I know. I shouldn't make you do it so much." Liv reached for Grace's plate, but Grace took hold of her hand. "What?"

"Don't ever stop making me laugh," Grace said, her voice softened. "I've never really had that."

"Seriously? None of your girlfriends ever made you laugh?"

"Not as easily as you do."

Liv kissed the fingers now intertwined with hers. "That's a shame. I promise to do my best to keep that beautiful smile on your face."

"Thanks."

Liv gathered the plates and put them into the sink. She returned and sat cross-legged on the floor, so she was facing Grace. "Can I ask you a personal question?"

Grace watched the serious expression on Liv's face and tried to quell her sudden nervousness. "You sit with me at the hospital for hours, come out here and make me lunch, call me 'Baby,' and give the best kisses of anyone I've ever known. I think you've earned a personal question."

Liv's features relaxed a little. "It's just—I've never known anyone that was, um, in an abusive relationship."

"You probably do or did. It's not always obvious."

"Was it that way for you? Not obvious?"

"You mean did I manage to hide it from my family?" At Liv's nod, she said, "Yes. For the first few years at least. After she started hitting me."

"She didn't always hit you?"

"No," Grace said. She'd never discussed the details with anyone other than Abby. She was too ashamed to tell her family. But now, looking into the kind eyes of the woman seated in front of her, Grace found that she wanted to share. "We started out pretty normal, I guess. Carly was always a control freak. It's almost funny now, but she wasn't my type. I've talked it over with Abby, my counselor, many times, but I still don't know what attracted me to her."

"Is she pretty?"

"Beautiful. And I mean in the class of women you see on magazine covers. She did a bit of modeling in college but said it bored her, so she went on to get a business degree. She worked for the county government. At first, she was kind and considerate. Very sweet. But after a few months she became possessive.

"I never liked possessive women, but she was so amazingly cool about it. She'd make a joke, or make sure any woman near me knew who I was with. I thought it was great. I mean, how cool is it that this beautiful woman is making sure you're with her? I'd never had anyone remotely like that, and I found it pretty damn sexy."

"Sounds like you two got together fast."

"We did. Probably part of the overall problem. I was joking with you about a U-Haul, but that's exactly what I did with Carly. I was so damn sure it was the right thing. She made room for me and my stuff, and we were set. For the first year or so."

"What changed?"

Grace shrugged. "Good question. After I got out of the army, the possessiveness ramped up. If I so much as had a conversation with a waitress, she'd get pissed off. She only wanted me to go to work and come straight home. Anywhere else, she had to go with me. Eventually that came to include visiting my family, who never liked her."

"I can certainly understand why they wouldn't."

"That's just the first few years. I was fed up with her and threatened to leave after she slapped me during an argument. She apologized profusely, and we made up. It was the start of an ugly cycle. She'd get angry, hit me, then apologize. She was always sweet and loving afterward. After a while, the sweet and loving no longer existed."

Liv clenched her jaw. "Your family didn't notice bruises?"

"Yes, but I explained them away as part of my job. By the time she was hitting me with objects other than her fist—like a ball bat—I was working as a climbing instructor. Bruises and broken bones are part of the job. I only saw my family on the days I was stuck at home, unable to work. My mom would come over to make sure I was okay, or I'd see my brother, Matt, or his wife, Sherry. I didn't see my dad a lot, but looking back, I think he stayed away so he didn't beat the shit out of Carly. They only came over while she was at work. Otherwise, I didn't see them much. I can't tell you a specific time when I got scared of Carly, but I did."

Liv was chewing her lower lip, and Grace could see the questions in her eyes. She spoke before Liv could. "Why did I stay with her? I spent eight years in the army. Why didn't I just kick her ass?"

"Um, yeah. You kicked mine. Why not hers?"

"She convinced me no one else loved me like she did. I bought it at first. She made me believe I was worthless, and for six years I bought into it. There were times I wanted to leave her, but I was afraid. Terrified she'd find me and maybe kill me. Terrified she'd make trouble for my family somehow. I once got the courage to pack a bag and only made it to the bedroom door before she beat me unconscious."

Liv's tan face paled. "Is that when she broke your arm?"

"No. I woke up two days later. I have no idea what I did or didn't do. At some point I got into bed, but that whole time is a blank to me. The last time she beat me is also a blank. That's when she broke my arm and crushed my hand." Grace pointed to the jagged scar on her arm. "I only remember Carly hitting me with a baseball bat and then waking up in the hospital with Matt at my side. My mom told me I called her and that she and Dad showed up at the house. I had what they call a traumatic brain injury. *Ojiichan* flew to Seattle on the first plane he could get because the doctors weren't sure I'd wake up. That's part of why I didn't want him at the hospital with me and why he was worried about whether or not I told the doctors about my history. Carly hit me in the head numerous times over the years."

Liv's face paled.

Grace gave her a weary smile. "The last neurologist I saw told me everything was fine. The biggest remnant of the TBI is that I have amnesia at the time of the injury. He said that's not abnormal. I'm glad for it. I'm sure it's not something I want to remember, even if there's always a chance I will. Someday. But this is also why I've been in therapy with Abby for so long. She's helped me get back to something close to normal."

Liv scooted forward and knelt in front of Grace, her hands holding Grace's face. "I'm so sorry that happened to you. Baby, I won't ever do that to you." She gently wiped her thumbs across Grace's cheeks, removing her tears.

"You can't say that, Liv. You don't know what you will or won't do."

"You're wrong there, love. I do know. Even after Hank tried to hit me today, I didn't react with violence. I know I talk a big game, but it's not part of me. Clearly, it was part of Carly. But not me. I've never hit anyone in my life." She kissed Grace tenderly then said, "I will never intentionally hurt you. Physically or emotionally. Better?"

"Yes. Better. Don't make too many promises, Liv. You don't always know you can keep them, okay?"

"I'll do my best. It's just that I want to protect you. I don't understand why anyone would physically hurt the person they claim to love, but you're the strongest woman I've ever met."

"Strong?" Grace wanted to laugh at the irony. "I'm not strong, Olivia. If I was strong I'd have left her years ago."

"You survived everything she threw at you, Gracie Lee. You got away and didn't look back. You came all the way out here to get your life in order, and that's exactly what you're doing. If that doesn't describe a strong woman, then I don't know what does."

"I'm not sure I agree, but I don't want to argue with you either."

"Good girl." Liv pressed her lips to Grace's forehead, her cheeks, then her lips. "I won't always get to be right, but I do enjoy a 'yes, dear' moment anytime I can get one."

"Yes, dear." Grace gazed into those blue depths and knew she was falling hard and fast. Her brain told her to slow down, but her heart didn't want to listen. "Thanks."

"I didn't do anything."

"You did plenty." Grace leaned forward to share another kiss.

"I didn't leave you two alone so you could make out," Harry announced as he came in. His sly grin and cheerful tone made it clear he was teasing them. He also looked quite pleased with himself.

"You left us alone without any rules," Liv said as she stood. "If you don't want any hanky panky, then you have to be specific."

"Of course." Grace could hear him putting the groceries away as he spoke. "I saw your father in town, Olivia. He seemed to think you had a meeting today."

"Shit. We were supposed to go over the paperwork on Hank."

"Then you should get moving," Grace said. "That's more important."

Liv held both of Grace's hands in hers. "Nothing is more important than you, Gracie. Don't ever think there is. But this one thing is something I have to take care of." She kissed Grace's fingers, then her mouth.

Grace was aware that Harry was giving them some space, and she loved him for it. Liv's kisses energized her and made her feel special. "Call me later?"

"Of course." Liv headed for the door and called out, "You can come back now, Harry. I'm leaving."

"Bye, Olivia," Harry said, closing the door behind her. He made himself comfortable in his recliner. "Tell me everything."

Chapter Ten

Harry, always a little overprotective, eventually gave in and let Grace leave the house after two weeks of sequestration. She and Liv chose Monday evening for a home-cooked dinner at Liv's house. Grace was more than ready to get out of Harry's tiny cabin. She intentionally didn't tell him her ribs still ached. Otherwise the mother hen would have insisted upon driving her to Liv's.

The forty-five-minute trip caused more pain than she anticipated, and she almost wished she'd given in and allowed Harry to drive her. Once Grace pulled into Liv's driveway, she needed a moment to rest. That's when she saw Liv at the front door. Her arms were wrapped around a slender, blonde-haired woman. Their lips met in a brief kiss before the woman bounded down the steps.

The woman's gaze met Grace's, and she smiled broadly, as if seeing an old friend. Liv waved to Grace, but Grace felt frozen to the spot. She'd just seen Liv kissing another woman. What the hell was she supposed to do? Pretend it didn't happen? Even though that's exactly what she'd done with Carly?

Liv's voice startled Grace. She'd come to her car door and was speaking to her, though with the window up Grace couldn't make out her words. Liv opened the door and gently touched Grace's hand, which held the steering wheel in a death grip.

"Hey? What's wrong?"

"You...I...I have to go." Grace heard herself speak, but she still couldn't move. How could Liv do this to her?

"You just got here." Liv touched Grace's cheek and turned her head so they were looking at one another. "Baby, why are you crying? Are you hurting? Maybe it's too soon for you to be driving."

"Who is she?" Grace asked when she could speak around the lump in her throat. "I should have...I thought we—"

"You thought...oh shit." Liv wiped the fresh tears from Grace's cheeks. "That's Sara. My best friend."

"You kissed her."

"I always kiss her. But it's not a romantic kiss. I promise."

Grace shook her head as if that would help this all make sense. "I've never seen anyone kiss her best friend on the lips."

"We've done that forever." Liv pried Grace's hands from the steering wheel. "Come inside. Let's talk. Okay?"

Once again Grace found herself conflicted. Her brain said leave, but her heart told her to stay. The sincerity in Liv's eyes gave movement to her legs, and she climbed out of the car. They quietly walked onto the porch.

Grace stopped, whirled around to face Liv, and said, "Are you sleeping with her?"

Liv paused and Grace's heart clenched. She recognized the guilt in Liv's eyes and backed away from her. It must have been clear that she was going to leave, because Liv moved closer, but not close enough to touch Grace.

"Please don't go," Liv said.

"I can't go through this. Not again." Regardless of how affected she was by the magnetism of Liv's eyes, Grace would not—could not—repeat the worst mistake she'd made in her life. She'd allowed Carly to manipulate her for years. If she did it again, it would break her.

"I was sleeping with her when I met you," Liv said, her voice soft and soothing. "But when I realized I have feelings for you, we stopped. There wasn't anything between me and Sara. It was friends with benefits. That's all."

"Friends with benefits? Are you serious?" Grace shoved Liv away and started down the steps.

"Stop!" Liv blocked her, and Grace was tempted to send her tumbling onto the sidewalk. "Don't leave. Please."

"I don't want to hear it, Olivia. I've heard it enough."

"I'm not her, Grace." Liv stood her ground and didn't move when Grace tried to get past her. "I didn't lie. Sara and I were sleeping together. We broke up more than two years ago because we're just not compatible as a couple, but—"

"But you're compatible enough for sex?"

"Yes. Look, neither of us has had much luck in the dating arena, so when we really needed each other it sometimes ended in sex. We had a long talk after I met you and realized we can't keep doing this. We're not getting back together. I promise."

"You kissed her," Grace said, unable to get the sight out of her mind.

"I did. I've done that for years, even when I was with Jane. Sara's been my best friend since high school."

"Jane?"

Liv hesitated, as if contemplating whether she should answer or not. "My ex-wife."

"You were married?" Grace knew she sounded like a simpleton, but her brain didn't want to form complex sentences. She was trying to absorb so much that her head hurt.

"For three years. I'll tell you about her in a bit. Sara first. I love her. I'm not in love with her. She knows this and accepts that our arrangement had to stop." Liv caressed Grace's cheek with the tips of her fingers. "I really care about you, Gracie Lee. You're the only woman I want to be with. I don't know where our relationship is going, only that I want to continue to explore it."

Grace exhaled the breath she'd been holding. If she'd had a best girl friend, would she kiss her goodbye? Maybe. But she'd never had a best girl friend. She was closest to Matt and Harry. All her female friends had to be abandoned after she married Carly. It was all about Carly and only Carly. Grace's entire life revolved around one person for so long, she couldn't remember what it was like to have friends surrounding her.

Yet the woman in front of her, with the kind eyes, warm smile, and quick wit who always made her laugh, was unlike anyone she'd ever met. No one made Grace feel so safe and wanted. No one had ever caused her stomach to do flip-flops. Certainly no one ever turned her on with a simple look. Like Liv was doing right now. And it all terrified her.

Grace wrapped her arm around her ribs when pain flared up. She didn't want to think anymore. She just wanted to sit down.

"You need to rest. Please, let's go inside so you can sit for a while." Liv gently touched her arm, and Grace allowed her to lead the way inside and to the couch. Liv put a pillow behind Grace's back to help her be more comfortable. "Do you want something to drink? I can get you some Tylenol, but I don't have anything stronger for the pain."

"Water and Tylenol would be great, thanks."

Liv headed for the kitchen and returned with a bottle of water and two tablets. She removed the cap and handed it to Grace and waited while she swallowed the pills. "You rest and I'll talk. Okay?"

Grace remained silent. She wasn't ready to speak, afraid of what she might say.

Liv knelt in front of her and rested her hands on Grace's knees. "I'm shitty at relationships, and I have the past to prove it. I never stayed with anyone more than a few weeks before I met Jane Grady. It took all of three weeks to get the U-Haul and move her into my house. We were married two-and-a-half months later." Liv glanced down for a few seconds, then she raised her eyes to Grace's. They clouded over, and Grace could almost feel her pain as she continued.

"I was in love. Head over heels. Our first year together was amazing. Not a single disagreement between us. Only love and laughter. Like some kind of romance novel. All perfect. It was like I was living a dream, and I guess I was. But there were problems underneath it all. I just denied they existed.

"We both worked in Whitehorse, and I always made sure I was

home on time to have dinner ready for her. Hell, I used to surprise her with lunch at her office. At the time, she worked half a mile from my office. I mean, how much better could it get?

"But a year and a half or so in, she started getting distant. Nothing I did seemed to work. We started fighting until it got to the point where we just didn't talk anymore. I thought we had this perfect marriage. Except that it was falling apart, and I was too blind to see that. I figured I was doing something wrong. It had to be me, right? Maybe that's why she wasn't talking to me."

Grace finally found her voice. "Was she having an affair?"

"No. At least not a sexual affair. We had this friend named Nicolette. Jane spent a lot of time with her and her various girlfriends, including a few weekend trips that she'd take during the mining season. I figured it was because I was so busy and she needed the company.

"But one day Jane came home and said she was leaving me. I was stunned. Devastated. I knew we were having problems, but the one problem I never saw coming was that we'd fallen out of love. There wasn't anything left. I still had feelings for her, but Jane moved on."

"With Nicolette?"

Liv nodded. "I'm not sure whether they slept together or not, and I don't care. It doesn't matter anymore. The only thing that mattered at that time was Jane left me. We never discussed it. She literally came home, announced she was leaving, handed me the divorce papers, and that was it. Two weeks later she was gone, and I haven't seen her since. She even moved her office to Toronto."

"What did you do?"

"Nothing. For almost two months I stayed home. My mom came over every day to make sure I ate, and Sara practically moved in with me. Dad took over the business, and most of my friends gave me space, checking on me through Sara. I couldn't function. I didn't want to go out in public. I was humiliated."

"Why? You didn't do anything wrong."

"I know that now, but it felt like Jane was telling me in a very direct way that I wasn't good enough for her or anyone else. Far as I was concerned, Jane was the top of the food chain. If I couldn't make it work with her, what good was I to any other woman? And why would another woman even want me?"

Grace wiped the sudden tears from her eyes as she let Liv's words sink in. "Jane is a cruel-hearted bitch."

Liv barked a laugh. "She certainly is. Thanks to Sara and my family, I see that now. But it took a long time. Sara got me out of the house, and we spent nearly every waking moment together. Shouldn't come as a surprise that she was my rebound girlfriend."

"Is that why it didn't work out between you?"

"Probably. We're better off as friends anyway. Besides, I wasn't looking for love. Not with Sara and not with any of the other women over the last year or so."

Grace reached out and held Liv's face in her hand. She looked deeply into those pools of blue. Her heart skipped at the visceral touch of Liv's gaze. "And now? Are you looking for love now?"

Liv rose up enough that they were eyelevel. She never lost that connection with Grace. "I'm not so sure I need to look anymore. I'm beginning to think I've found it."

Their lips met in a kiss so tender and meaningful that it brought fresh tears to Grace's eyes. As they parted, she saw that Liv was crying as well. "Me, too," Grace said around the lump in her throat. She leaned in for another kiss but grimaced at the pain it caused.

"Easy does it," Liv said. She moved closer and softly pressed her lips to Grace's. "Take it slow, okay? And I don't just mean because of your ribs. I can see you're scared. So am I."

"If we're so scared, how can we do this?"

"We do it together. We do it by talking, just like we're talking right now. That's the deal we'll make. No assumptions. We talk things out. Okay?"

Grace saw the loving gaze on Liv's face and felt her heartbeat speed up a little. Could she do this? Was she ready? Her heart certainly was. She wanted to love Olivia Templeton for all she was worth. Part of her knew she already did.

She reached for Liv's hand and squeezed, feeling strength in the fingers wrapped around hers. "Okay. On one condition."

"Sure."

Grace almost laughed at the serious look on Liv's face. "We have dinner first. I'm starving."

Liv's smile nearly swallowed her face. "Drink your water like a good girl, and I'll finish dinner. I just need to heat it up."

"Hey, I thought I was getting a freshly cooked, homemade meal."

"You are." Liv kissed her again and got to her feet. "I homemade it last night. It's my famous lasagna. Just need to heat it up, and we're good to go."

"Mmm. I love lasagna."

"I know." Liv flashed a crooked grin before going into the kitchen.

"How did you know?"

Grace heard Liv opening cabinets and clanging something metal before she answered, "A little white-haired man told me."

"He did?" Grace should have known. "What else did this old man tell you?"

"Did I say he was old?"

"You didn't have to."

"Huh." Liv continued working, clearly ignoring Grace's question.

"Do I need to have a chat with this old man? Or has he already given up all my secrets?"

She heard some more clanging, a muttered curse, then Liv was in the living room again. "You have secrets? Oh, I have my own ways of getting those out of you. No, the sneaky old man didn't give up more than your favorite meal of lasagna, which is second only to the meatloaf from Marge's, but I chose not to compete with her."

"He's got a big mouth."

"Because he loves you." Liv's eyes twinkled with mischief as she said, "So, want to know how I plan to get more secrets directly from you?"

"Is this something I want to hear?"

Liv smiled and walked away. "When your ribs are healed. I think I'll wait until then."

"That could be weeks!"

Liv's hearty laugh gave Grace a smile. "You must be patient."

"Patient?"

"It'll be worth the wait." Liv appeared at her side again and kissed her deeply, eliciting emotions Grace never felt before. It was as if Liv could lift her up with a touch of her lips. When they parted, Grace was breathing heavily. Liv winked and left Grace to contemplate the meaning behind her words.

****

Three weeks felt like a lifetime to Grace. It took two different doctor visits for Harry to accept it was okay for Grace to be active again. He'd banned her from the mine until Monday, but today she would to break free. She and Liv were going for a hike in a place Liv guaranteed would be without tourists. Butterflies made circles in her stomach as she kept watch for Liv's truck to pull in the drive.

Harry said, "A watched pot never boils."

"Ha-ha." Grace didn't turn away from the window. "I can't help it. I'm excited to be getting out for a while."

"We've had dinner at Marge's almost every day this week."

"It's not the same."

Harry made a "harrumph" sound. "You mean I'm not Olivia."

"Well, she is better looking." Grace yelped when Harry pinched her arm. "Be nice you old fart. Remember who's going to take care of you in your old age."

He laughed. "I'm already in my old age. You're too late."

"You're going to outlive all of us, *Ojiichan*." Grace heard Harry grumble something but was too fixated on the truck pulling up to the cabin. She was out the door in a flash, not caring how silly she might look. She met Liv halfway to the porch and threw her arms around her, nearly knocking her to the ground.

"Whoa!" Liv grabbed hold of her to steady them both.

Breathless, Grace planted a kiss on her mouth and grinned. "I've been waiting forever for that."

"For a kiss?"

"Yes. I'm lonely all the way out here in the wilderness." Grace spread her arms wide as if to encompass the area around them. It was hardly the wilderness, but they both knew that. "All I have for company is a grumpy old man."

"I can hear you," Harry said from the porch.

"I know you can, you voyeur." Grace enjoyed another, slower kiss with Liv before taking her hand and heading to the cabin to get her knapsack. "See what I mean?"

"Oh yes. Must have been torture," Liv said. She mock saluted Harry as they walked by him.

"Kids."

****

Liv kept a steady pace along the well-worn mountain path. Grace managed to keep up, but suspected Liv was going slower than normal. Her ribs still ached, but it was nothing she couldn't handle. She'd dealt with a lot worse. She shook off the memories and focused on the woman in front of her. While the view from the path was amazing, it was nothing compared to the stunning view in front of her.

Tight shorts, long slender legs, well-muscled calves were a pleasant feast for Grace's eyes. Strong back muscles worked hard and stood out well beneath the white, sleeveless T-shirt. Grace felt a powerful, physical pull toward the woman in front of her. She'd been attracted to other women, but not like she was with Liv. It wasn't so much a pull as a need. Grace recalled the gentle strength in Liv's embrace and how, for the first time in years, she felt safe.

Was it just a physical thing? Or did this mean more? Each night she went to sleep with thoughts of Liv, and when she awoke she found her mind on Liv again. They sent text messages to each other during the days of Grace's recovery. When Liv had time, she'd call and it would be nearly impossible to disconnect. She enjoyed listening to Liv's silky smooth voice for hours. After they hung up, Grace felt a sense of loss.

Was she truly falling in love with Liv? Even though they barely knew each other? It was a scary thought. Grace didn't think she was ready for love again. Ready for a steady woman in her life, sure. Abby recently convinced her to take that step. It could be a lot of fun. But love? Commitment? She didn't think she'd ever be ready for that again. And yet, since being around Liv, her nightmares were silenced and Grace never believed that would happen.

"So, you were in the army?" Liv's voice broke into her thoughts.

"I was. Four years of ROTC and eight active duty."

"Wow. Did you have to go to the Middle East?"

"No. They didn't need my particular skill-set. I ended up staying in the states and traveling wherever they needed a translator. I really wanted to go to Afghanistan."

"You wanted to go? Why?"

"I wanted to serve my country. Even if I'm a homebody at heart."

"I was never much into travel either. I mean, look where I live." She stopped and indicated the mountain vista around them, sweeping her arms out like Julie Andrews in *The Sound of Music.* "Why would I leave?"

Below them, needle pine trees dotted the landscape like giant, green arrows pointing to the sky. Grace let her gaze wander along the rocky outcropping upon which they stood as it rolled downward,   ending amidst the trees where it met the green-blue lake below. She sighed and inhaled a deep breath of air filled with the scents of pine, dirt, and a hint of a flower she couldn't identify.

Grace said, "I think I'd be happy to stay here. It's what I loved about Washington. Lots of mountains."

"A woman after my own heart." Liv pretended to swoon before starting along the trail again. "What did you do in the army that they didn't need you in the Middle East?"

"Translation services. I speak Japanese, Chinese, and Korean. I've always had a love of languages and being raised bilingual helped me there. I can write in all three as well, so that gave me a specialized job. And since I'm not fluent in any Arabic languages, I wasn't needed."

"Wow. I'm impressed. I mean, like most Canadians, I can speak some French—though not all that great—but four languages is a lot."

"Six actually. I was learning Farsi and Arabic when I left."

"Seriously?"

"Yeah." Grace sighed. She hadn't been in the army for several years now and missed it a lot. "It was my best shot at being deployed to Afghanistan, but when my time was up, I mustered out."

They reached a bend in the trail, and Liv stopped. When she

turned to her, Grace saw something different in her expression.

"You were planning to go to a war zone and then just left the army? What happened?"

Grace looked away from her. She wasn't proud of that time in her life and ashamed of what she'd done. "Carly happened. She told me that if I didn't muster out when I had the chance, she'd report me as being gay. It would have devastated my dad to have me discharged dishonorably, so I got out. I loved what I did, and I didn't want to leave like that. But I knew how serious she was. She'd have done it. I wasn't willing to take that chance.

"I had no idea what I was going to do once I was out. We went back to Seattle and stayed with Matt and Sherry for a little while—that was rough." Grace adjusted her stance so she was looking across the valley below them. It no longer held its calming essence. "It took awhile to find another job. Not much need for a language specialist in Seattle. At least not a specialist in Asian languages."

Grace felt Liv move closer and resisted the urge to flinch when Liv's gentle hand settled on her shoulder. "That must have been horrible for you. I don't understand how she could do that to you."

"I was completely under her control, Olivia. And she knew it. It was easier for her to get a job, and in a month she was working at the county government offices. We moved into an apartment, and once we were settled, I got bored. We had one car, and she needed it to get to work. I had my bike and that's good enough since we were in the city, but what the hell was I going to do? I considered looking for a translation job I could do remotely, but there just wasn't anything around."

"How'd you end up as a rock-climbing instructor?"

"It's always been my hobby. I went on a climb one afternoon while Carly was working, got to talking to the guide, and sort of fell into the job." Grace looked down at her feet. Getting that job without Carly's permission ended up with Grace receiving a black eye. It was a miracle Carly hadn't made her quit.

"But I get the feeling you loved the military." Liv now stood in front of her and placed a finger under her chin until Grace looked at her. "She couldn't have loved you to threaten such a thing. Not even for a second. I don't know Carly, but I know I hate her for what she did to you."

Grace tried to shrug it off, but it was so hard to do under Liv's intense gaze. "Once I finished my study of Farsi and Arabic, I was set to be shipped out immediately. Carly liked having a wife in the military, but only as long as she was stateside, or in a cool country like Italy or France. Deployment to the Middle East would mean we'd have to live apart and she'd lose control over me. I didn't have the strength to fight her. We'd been married a few years then, and DADT wasn't yet completely gone from the military. I mean, it got repealed, but that stuff can take years to go into effect. I didn't want to take that chance."

Liv put her hands around Grace's cheeks and placed a gentle kiss on her lips. "I'd never do that to my wife. That's more than just selfishness. I don't think I have the words to describe it other than to say it makes me angry."

Grace smiled and caressed Liv's fingers. "Don't be. It's old news. I still miss the work, but I moved on."

"You're a better woman than me, Gracie Lee." Her next kiss was long and thorough and made Grace's body tingle. "I can't seem to get enough of kissing you."

"Is that a bad thing?"

Liv gave her that adorable, crooked smile. "I don't think so. It's something I look forward to every time we get together."

"Then we should get together more often."

"Hmm. I think I agree with that." Liv cocked her head to one side, as if she was contemplating something interesting. "Has anyone ever told you how beautiful you are?"

"Me?" Grace couldn't keep the astonishment out of her voice. Her fingers ran along the jagged scar on her face. "Uh, no. Pretty maybe. But not beautiful."

"Then you've been around some seriously blind people." Liv reached up and tucked a stray bit of hair behind Grace's ear. She'd decided to put her hair in a ponytail today, but now wished it was down so Liv would run her fingers through it.

"Maybe you're the one that's blind."

"No. You've got such soft hair, smooth skin, rich, mahogany eyes...I can't get enough of you."

Grace sucked in air and wondered if she was living in a dream. She released a slow breath as Liv moved closer again, taking her into her arms and kissing her. Their tongues danced together, and Grace felt the passion building. She slid her hands under Liv's shirt and along her strong back. The muscles beneath her fingers flexed as their bodies melded together. A perfect fit.

Breathless, Liv pulled away again. "I think we should stop before I throw you down and have my way with you right here on this trail."

"Who says I wouldn't like that?" Grace ran her fingernails along Liv's heated skin and felt her shiver.

Liv leaned her forehead against Grace's and sighed. "I don't think there's a single doubt we're attracted to each other."

"Nope. No doubt."

"I don't want to rush this." Liv's blue eyes darkened with desire. "Let's take our time, okay?"

Grace gave Liv a tender kiss and stepped away from her. "You're an amazing woman, Olivia. Now, why don't you show me how to get down from this mountain. I'm hungry and really want to dig into those sandwiches *Ojiichan* made for us."

Liv took Grace's hand and entwined their fingers. "Let's go."

Chapter Eleven

The July sun beat down on Grace's back as she shoveled tailings away from the wash plant. She'd only been at it half an hour, but it felt like all day. The ball cap she wore was soaked with sweat. She tipped it back to wipe her forehead with the sleeve of her T-shirt. She so wanted to be done for the day. Her stomach told her it was close to dinnertime. And Josie was already at the cabin cooking.

"Hey, Gracie! Catch!"

Grace turned in time to grab the water bottle that tumbled through the air at her. It was blessedly cold, and she held it against the back of her neck. Mike, the bottle thrower, grinned as he joined her.

"It's too hot for hard work. What do you say we head back to camp?"

"I'd say I need to finish this up first." She used the shovel to point out the work left. "If you were to help me, I'd be done sooner and my very empty stomach would be happy." She gave him her best smile.

Mike found another shovel and dug in beside her. "Two hands make faster work than one, right?"

"Something like that. You manage to get the D9 running? It'd be great if we could use both dozers tomorrow. Charlie hit pay dirt, so we could start filling the wash plant up first thing."

"The D9 is dead. I think it's electrical, but I need someone from TNT's shop to come look at it. I put a call in before I came up here. Problem is they can't get out here until Friday."

"We're not going to get much done with one dozer the rest of the week. It's only Monday."

"I know." Mike stopped working and put a hand on Grace's arm. "Think you could call your girlfriend? Get someone out here sooner?"

Grace almost laughed. "Seriously? You want me to get Olivia to pull strings? Are you using me for my connections now?" She lifted one eyebrow and watched the brief conflict flash across his ruddy features.

"Um. Yes." Mike grinned, realizing she was teasing him. "You got connections and strings. I'm pulling all of them and then some."

"I'll call her tonight and see what I can arrange."

"Cool. While you're on the phone with her, why don't you see if she wants to go on an overnight climb. A group of us are heading out Saturday morning to a nice local spot away from all the tourists. This crag is nice, has a good route and amazing views from the top. And there's a cave at the bottom that's perfect for camping. I've got some fireworks so us Americans can celebrate the Fourth. Whatcha think?"

Grace considered that a moment. Two things gave her pause. First was the climb. She'd not done one outside since Carly broke her arm. While she was okay inside, an outside climb would be higher and could prove more difficult. Second was the overnight part. She and Liv shared some amazing moments together, but they had never crossed that line to lovemaking. It was never quite the right time. Even though Grace's hormones begged for it to be the right time with every kiss or touch from Liv.

She mentally shook herself and said, "I'll ask her. Okay?"

****

Grace sat back in her lawn chair and stared up at the clear, night sky. The Aurora Borealis stretched across the horizon in all its wispy splendor. She never tired of watching the greens and blues float above her like some alien mist.

The ringing of her phone broke the moment, but a smile spread across her face when she saw Liv's number on the display.

"Hi there."

"Hey, baby." Liv's husky voice made her heart skip a beat. "Tell me you're lying in bed, naked, and waiting for me."

Grace's smile widened. "I'm outside, under a beautiful sky, fully clothed, and wishing you were here. Sorry to ruin the fantasy."

"Aw. That sucks."

"I know. But if it's any consolation, I liked where you were going with that."

"I knew I liked you." Liv chuckled. "How was your day?"

"Tiring and it's just going to get worse tomorrow. We're down a dozer and can't get the mechanic here until Friday, and we just got to the pay dirt on our newest cut. We'll be through the pay dirt we have by Wednesday."

"And a quiet wash plant means no money coming in." Liv was silent for a few moments, and Grace could hear her shuffling papers. "I can be there tomorrow at ten. Any idea what's wrong with the dozer? I'm assuming it's your D9."

"Yes, but what are you going to do? Fix it?"

"That was the plan."

"Seriously?" Grace asked. "Don't you have people for that?"

"I do, but according to the work order, my people can't get there until Friday. Lucky for you, I have the afternoon free. Unless you'd rather wait—"

"Hell, no." Grace laughed. "Besides, I get the added bonus of seeing you."

"There is that."

"And before I forget, we've been invited on a climb this weekend by Mike. It's an overnight one." Grace crossed her fingers, hoping Liv would say yes.

"Yes."

"That was fast."

"It's a weekend with you. Why would I say no?"

Grace opened her mouth to respond but stopped. Her brain gave her lots of reasons why Liv would say no. Insecurities cropped up again, but she tried to ignore them. "I wasn't sure you'd like the idea of camping in a cave."

"The cave camping sounds fun. So does the climbing—unless you don't think I'm ready to start going outside? I mean, we've been going to Rock World for a few weeks now, and my arms have finally stopped hurting."

Grace laughed softly. "I'm sure you'll do fine with the climb. You bring the sleeping bags, and I'll bring the climbing gear. Deal?"

"Deal." Liv hesitated, and Grace had the impression she was struggling with her words. After a few seconds she said, "Is it weird if I say I just want to stay on the phone with you until I go to sleep? That I want to listen to you breathe?"

"Um." Grace closed her eyes and tried to imagine Liv lying beside her. It wasn't weird at all. She'd often thought of the same thing. "No. I think I like that idea. Are you heading to bed soon?"

Grace heard a door open and close. "I'm walking home now. Stay on the phone with me for a while longer?"

"Try to get rid of me." Grace spoke quietly as a feeling of calm spread over her. Why the hell she'd been insecure moments before was lost on her. Liv was amazing, and she wanted a lot of the same things Grace did. Chief among them was any kind of contact they could get. Whitehorse was a solid two-hour drive from the mine, but at times it felt like they were worlds apart. How could anyone survive a real long-distance relationship?

That brought back thoughts of the few times she'd had to live apart from Carly and the consequences those brought when she returned. The separations incited Carly's decision to force Grace out of the military.

"Gracie?"

Liv's voice startled her. Had she been talking to her? "I'm sorry. I guess my mind wandered for a minute there. What did you say?"

"Are you okay?" The concern was clear in Liv's voice.

Grace tried to brush it away. "Fine. You home now?"

"I am." Liv didn't sound convinced by Grace's words. "You sure you don't want to talk about it?"

"How is it you can read me so well over the phone?"

"Because I called your name four times before you answered." Liv sighed heavily. "Don't hold back from me, Gracie. Let me in. Please."

"I'm sorry. I didn't mean to shut you out. It's just that...I really wish you were here. Right now. I mean, it's not like you're all that far away, but at the same time you are."

"I can be there in two hours. Less if I don't go the speed limit."

"No, Liv. You need your sleep as much as I do."

Grace was pretty sure she'd heard a door close and the jingling of keys.

"I just tossed some clothes in my backpack. I'll stop by the shop, get a few things, and be at your camp before you're ready to fall asleep. We can stay on the phone if you'd like."

"Liv...you're really coming out here?" Grace could hardly believe it.

"Of course. There's something wrong, and I can tell that you need me. I won't be able to sleep for worrying about you. So, yes, I'm coming over." The sound of a car door opening and closing and an engine coming to life told Grace that Liv was on her way.

"You're...you're the best damn girlfriend ever."

Liv gave a gentle laugh. "I want to hold you, Gracie Lee, while you tell me your troubles."

"I get that. And I'm beyond grateful for it."

"No worries. Now, tell me what's wrong with the D9 so I know what to bring."

****

Liv awoke as sunlight first peeked through the blinds of the cabin window. The bed was meant for one person, but she and Grace managed to curl up together in a comfortable position. Were it not for her screaming bladder, Liv wouldn't move. She could stay like this forever.

She snuggled against Grace's back, breathing in the flowery scent of her shampoo. She felt muscles flinch under her arms and wondered if Grace was waking up. An elbow slammed into her neck seconds before Grace jumped out of bed in a blind panic. She struggled with the handle to the door and managed to get it open. She was out of the cabin before Liv had a chance to get her bearings.

She found Grace pacing a few steps away from the porch, wild eyes searching the area, but not really seeing anything. Liv watched her for a moment, not sure whether she should approach her. Did she awaken from a nightmare? Was Liv holding her too tightly? Her gut clenched at the thought she might have caused this panic in Grace.

"Gracie...are you okay?"

"What?" Her response was terse as she stopped pacing to stare at Liv. "What'd you say?"

"I asked if you're okay."

"I—I don't know."

Grace's voice shook. Liv took the few steps to her and gently gathered the trembling woman in her arms. "Talk to me."

"I haven't had one in over a year."

"One what?"

"Panic attack." Grace tightened her hold on Liv. "I couldn't move, couldn't breathe...I just had to get out of there."

"Did I do something wrong?" Liv was surprised by the tremor in her voice. "I don't want to hurt you, Gracie."

"It's not you." Grace sniffled and pulled back enough to face Liv. "I get them sometimes. I'm not always sure what the trigger is. I'm sorry."

"Hey, what'd we say about apologizing?" Liv brushed strands of hair from Grace's face and gave her a soft kiss on the forehead. "Want to go back inside? Or would you rather the rest of the camp wake up and see you in your T-shirt and undies?"

Grace nodded. She led the way into the cabin and to the small room in the back. She sank onto the bed and held her head in her hands. "I really wish I could be rid of these damn attacks. It's like no matter what I do, Carly still has control over me."

Liv knelt in front of her and pulled her hands from her face. "No, she doesn't. She's not here, baby. I am."

"I know, but she's still in here." Grace tapped a forefinger on her temple. "Every insecurity I have is from her. It doesn't take long to think you're worthless when the one person you love most in the world tells you that every day. Sometimes in those exact words. Abby's told me plenty of times that nothing Carly told me was true. I'm a good person. I'm worth being loved, and I've got a lot of love to give. That's the line of thought I've worked so hard to hear and believe."

"But?"

"But it's not that easy. I spent years feeling as though I didn't have a life to live. I thought about   suicide more than once, and I'm ashamed of that."

"Don't," Liv said, ignoring the hitch in her voice. "Don't be ashamed of that time. Be proud of the strength you had and have.

You should think about how you didn't kill yourself. It takes a stronger person to stay alive, in my opinion. And I'm so thankful you did." She kissed her thoroughly, hoping that her love was obvious. And it was love. Liv was never more certain of it in her life. She loved Grace with all her heart and soul.

"It wasn't strength, Olivia. It was fear. Fear that I wouldn't succeed, and what Carly might do to me if I failed. I never thought she'd outright kill me, but I knew I couldn't bear going through the pain she'd inflict."

"She's an evil, sick, twisted bitch."

"I loved her. No matter how many times she yelled at me, scorned me, beat me, I loved her. I only ever wanted to make her smile. I wanted to do whatever it took for her to love me back." Grace closed her eyes as tears streamed down her cheeks. "The worst of it is that there's a part of me that still loves her. Or, as Abby says, loves the idea of the relationship I wanted with her."

Liv swiped at the tears with her thumbs as she cradled Grace's head in her hands. "You're worthy of that kind of love, Gracie. I promise you are."

"I'm broken, Liv. I just didn't see how bad it was until now. I mean, I've got this amazing, caring, attentive girlfriend, and my ex-wife is still haunting me. How can I move forward if I can't let go of the past?"

"What does Abby say? You must have talked to her about this."

Grace let loose a long sigh. "We have. She wants me to go to group therapy. Says that talking to other people who survived abusive partners will help me out."

"Sounds sensible. Did she find one out here that you can go to?"

"She did."

"I'm sensing another 'but' coming."

Grace's lips twitched into a tiny smile. "I have the info, but I'm not ready to go there just yet."

"You'll at least consider it, right?"

"I have and I will."

"Good." Liv kissed her softly, tasting the saltiness of her tears. "When you're ready, I'd like to take you. I'll even go inside with you if that's what you want."

New tears pooled in mahogany eyes, accompanying a smile. "What did I do to deserve you?"

"Came to the Yukon?" Liv teased with a crooked grin. "Your granddad and my dad are like two old ladies playing matchmaker. Only this time I think they actually got it right."

"You do?"

Liv sensed the question was genuine, and by way of an

answer, kissed Grace again. "I do. I'm here for the duration, Gracie Lee. If you'll have me."

The hesitation gave Liv pause. Did Grace really have to think about this? If she did, did that mean Liv was moving too fast? Maybe she shouldn't have worded it quite the way she did. Maybe—

"I always did have trouble saying no to a beautiful woman." Grace ruffled Liv's curly hair, which was probably standing on end. "We've got a couple more hours before breakfast. Want to cuddle some more?"

Relief washed over Liv, and she grinned. "You have to ask?"

Chapter Twelve

July fourth dawned with a warm, shining sun and the prospect of perfect weather through the weekend. Grace double-checked her climbing gear as she waited anxiously for Liv to arrive. For the tenth time, she heard Harry clear his throat. He'd already told her to stop fussing with her stuff, but she couldn't. She was nervous as hell for a multitude of reasons.

"Gracie..."

"I can't help it." She twirled around to see his smug face. She narrowed her eyes at him. "What?"

"I was going to say that I haven't seen you this nervous over a woman since your first date. Remember that?"

Grace sank into the empty recliner and resisted the urge to roll her eyes. "How can I forget? I was fourteen and lucky you and *Obaachan* were there to visit. If not for you, I'd never have been allowed to go."

"Well, your father has always been too conservative for his own good. Though I must say I did make a nice chauffeur for you two."

"In a candy-apple-red family sedan. But you were so sweet to us. I'll never forget the look on Cammy's face when you opened the door for her. It wasn't like we were going to a five-star restaurant. It was just McDonald's."

"It was my grandchild's first date," Harry said with all seriousness. "It was a very big deal. You changed your clothes twelve times before *Obaachan* stopped you. Then you paced and paced until it was time to get Cammy." He rested his arms on his knees. His eyes sparkled as he recalled the memory. "Your cheeks were rosy-red after she kissed you goodnight. It was the most beautiful moment, and I was honored to share it with you."

"I was glad you were there, *Ojiichan*. But I've always wondered how you, raised with such traditional Japanese values, can be so liberal about certain things, and my dad, who was raised by you, is such a stick in the mud."

Harry barked a laugh. "Your father has always been more traditional than me. *Obaachan* insisted he be raised with all the traditions of our heritage, even if we didn't strictly follow them ourselves. She wanted him to be able to choose. As for your love of women...it was never a question for me. You are who you are, Gracie Lee. Who am I to judge you? I love you unconditionally, and so does your father. He just took longer to accept it. Even if your *obaachan* slapped the back of his head a few times over it."

Now Grace laughed. "*Obaachan* slapped Dad? I would have loved to be witness to that!"

"She was his mother. In her opinion, it was her duty to set him straight. And it usually worked."

A horn sounded from outside, accompanied by the crunch of gravel beneath tires. Harry stood up with Grace. "Gracie, I want you to enjoy the weekend. Don't feel you have to come home in any rush. Okay? You deserve to have fun."

His unspoken permission nearly made Grace cry. She hugged him, gathered up her backpacks, one for her and one for Liv, and waved at him before heading out the door. Harry Kato was the most amazing man she'd ever known, and Grace was blessed to have him in her life.

His words gave her an extra spring to her step as she met Liv in the driveway. She kissed Liv the moment they were close enough.

"Wow," Liv said. "Awesome greeting. Can I get that more often?"

"As often as you want, but first you have to take your backpack. I left you room for at least two changes of clothes. Rock climbing is dirty, ya know? You did remember to bring the right clothes?"

"I did as instructed." Liv gave her a quick kiss before they climbed into her truck. "You ready to have a good time?"

"More than ready. Let's hit the road, woman!"

****

Grace stared at the crag, letting her gaze move along the rocky surface until she spotted the top, about fifty meters above the group of climbers. Mike and four of his friends were already setting up the belay lines and other safety measures, while Grace checked over her equipment. Like all the climbers there, she had her helmet, climbing shoes, harness, and chalk bag, among other essential pieces of equipment, stuffed into her backpack. Under all that, she managed to fit two changes of clothes.

She put down a set of carabiners and rubbed the scar on her left arm as she tried to settle her nerves and focus on the route she'd take. Five routes were laid out with hooks secured in the rock, and she was having trouble choosing which one to take. She didn't want to use the easiest one, but this was her first outdoor climb in almost four years.

Indoor climbing wasn't all that different, with the obvious exceptions. Outdoors, the rocks could rain down on you from above, be more slippery, or you could uncover various creepy crawlies where you chose to hold on. Those didn't usually bother her, but she wondered if she was up for those kinds of surprises. She tried a few breathing techniques to ease the tension and erase the doubt clouding her brain. Was her arm strong enough? Had the indoor practice conditioned her enough to make such a high climb? She'd climbed twice as high more times than she could count. But not since the damage to her arm. She wanted to rub the damn scar off and pretend nothing ever happened. But, of course, she couldn't do that.

Strong arms curled around her waist from behind and pulled her against a warm, familiar chest. She breathed in the lavender scent of Liv's shower gel and sighed. Liv leaned down, rested her chin on Grace's shoulder, and whispered, "What's wrong?"

"Are you psychic?"

"Nope. But I can read your body language, and right now it's telling me something's wrong." She placed a kiss at the nape of Grace's neck. "Talk to me."

"It's been years since I've done a climb this high. I'm a little scared." She pivoted in Liv's arms so she could face her. "I've never been nervous before a climb. Not even my first one, and I was fifteen then. I've always gotten this huge adrenaline rush."

"Then Carly came along and broke you." Liv's words were harsh, but her tone was loving and caring. "I'm going to make it my mission to fix you, Gracie Lee."

"Really?" Grace searched Liv's eyes, comforted in the love there. Their connection was growing, but still...

"Yes. Really. You know how every gold miner is searching for a glory hole—that ancient deposit of gold that could be worth millions?"

"Of course."

"I want to help you find that glory, Gracie. For me, your glory is worth more than all the gold in the world."

Grace smiled through her tears, and despite the doubts and insecurities that swirled around inside her, she spoke the words from her heart. "I love you, Olivia."

"I love you, too, Gracie Lee." Liv pressed her lips to Grace's, and in that moment, Grace felt a love she never dreamed she could know. They parted breathless. Liv said, "Now go climb that damn mountain."

"It's hardly a mountain. Just a crag."

"Whatever." Liv reached into Grace's pack and handed her the helmet. "Go."

"Bossy ass."

"Kiss my ass."

"Later. If you're a good girl."

"Oh, I'm a very good girl."

****

Liv thought she hid her nervousness pretty damn well. Except for the pacing. And the covering of her eyes now and then. Grace was almost halfway up the crag. She made it look easy, swinging from hold to hold like she was born to climb. Liv was thankful for the rope that hung to Grace's harness. But the thought of her falling...

Liv shivered.

She stayed close enough to keep an eye on Grace, but far enough back to be out of the way. The route Grace used was well marked with the safety hooks shining in the late morning sun. If not for the glint of metal now and again, they'd be invisible from where Liv stood. But clearly Grace could see them as she made her way in a zigzag pattern to each one.

Liv estimated ten meters separated each hook. The route Mike wanted Liv to take was straighter with the hooks closer together. An easier climb he'd told her. The route Grace was on took a lot more skill to complete. Grace's strong fingers clung to crevices Liv couldn't see as Grace propelled herself from one spot to the next.

Until she didn't. The fall was so fast it caused Liv's heart to skip a beat. One moment, Grace was hanging by her left arm and the next she was swinging in a downward arc. Her feet kicked out to bounce off the crag-face and control her movement. Liv let out a shaky breath once Grace was again settled and climbing the same direction as before.

Determination must have fueled her because Grace was at the next hook at an amazingly fast pace. Liv wanted to look away, but she couldn't tear her gaze from the woman she loved. The woman she'd only made that announcement to less than half an hour ago. Were they incredibly crazy to be doing this?

It was then Liv realized Grace wasn't moving. She'd hooked in and was leaning back, her legs braced against the rock. "That can't be good," Liv muttered.

"She's resting," Mike said as he joined her. "She'll be fine."

"She just fell. How can you say she'll be fine?"

"Because I know how good she is. We climbed together when we were kids, and even then she was amazingly good at it."

"She hasn't done much climbing the last few years."

"I know that, too." Mike stepped in front of her so Liv had to look at him and not Grace. "Don't be worried. She's a pro."

Liv released a deep sigh. "I'll feel better when she's back on the ground."

"Maybe you'd feel better if you were up there with her."

"It's not my turn."

Mike shrugged. "I doubt anyone will mind. You ready for this?"

"As I'll ever be."

"Grab your gear."

****

Her arm hurt like hell. Painful spikes drove into her muscles as Grace pulled herself closer to the top of the crag. Twice she lost her footing. The last one almost caused another fall. She hoped Liv wasn't watching.

Fortunately, no one could see her force back the panic attack just after her fall. Everything closed in on her, despite being out in the open. Clear skies surrounded her. So why now? What triggered it? Her nerves? Maybe it was the weakness of her arm. She hadn't expected to tire so fast. The arm felt like it was made of rubber.

She used her breathing techniques and managed to calm down enough to continue climbing. Now she reached the zenith and forced herself upward. Tiny rocks rained down the crag after her foot slid on a hold. She adjusted her position, reached up with her left arm, and curled the tips of her fingers into a crevice. She kept her hold and swung right to grab the next one. Two more and she was hauling herself over the precipice and standing atop the crag.

Adrenaline won out over exhaustion, and she fist-pumped in the air. She looked over the edge and saw Liv getting ready to start her climb. She gave her a thumbs up and stepped back to keep from knocking any rocks down on her.

Grace lifted her face toward the afternoon sun, enjoying the warmth on her skin. She was sweating, but the sun energized her. She gazed out at a stunning vista. Pine trees lined the mountainside, deep and green. Water from the lake below shimmered as if sprinkled with diamonds. She closed her eyes to listen to the birds sing, breathed deeply of the fresh, mountain air, and smiled broadly. Maybe Liv was right. Maybe Grace could now find her glory.

She stood atop the crag for a time enjoying the solitude. She had no clear idea how long she'd been up there until she heard the very distinct sound of someone grunting. And cussing. She nearly laughed out loud when she realized it was Liv.

Grace stood to the side of where Liv was climbing. She was a few meters from the top and was hanging off the last safety hook. Grace squatted and said, "Not much farther now, baby. You can do this."

"I...am...never...again...tired...painful..."

Grace felt sympathy for Liv. It was a tough climb for your first time out. But once she got to the top, Grace knew Liv would feel so much better. Besides, they planned to rappel back down. Who wouldn't enjoy that?

"I was, too. But just a couple of meters and you're done. There are lots of holds for you to pick from. Just take a deep breath and push yourself up. You can do this."

Liv moved back enough to look up at Grace. Sweat beads rolled down her reddened face. Damp hair clung to her forehead. "Promise?"

"Of course. Come up here so I can give you a kiss."

"That...is a good...incentive." Liv managed a tired grin. She tucked her hand into the chalk bag at her hip, dusted off the excess, and reached up for a hold. In no time, she was at the top and Grace was helping her over the edge.

Once there, Liv rolled onto her back and splayed her arms out spread-eagle. "Fuck."

"Fuck?" Grace asked with a laugh. "Is that a good 'fuck' or a bad 'fuck'?"

"Both." Liv sucked in a breath. "I had no idea...it'd be that...damn tiring. It's...it's so different than indoors."

"Well, duh." Grace reached for Liv's hand and helped her to her feet. She unhooked the safety line and pulled her farther from the edge. "But the view is worth it."

"It damn sure is," Liv said. Except she wasn't looking out at the mountain valley. She was staring at Grace. "I'm pumped and exhausted at the same time. I sort of see the rush in this outdoor stuff."

"Me, too," Grace said, unable to tear her gaze away from eyes as blue as the water of the lakes below them. "You've earned some TLC once we get back down there. We'll eat lunch and maybe go for a swim. There's a smaller lake not far from here. Mike showed me the trail earlier. What do you say?"

"Will there be nakedness?" Liv teased.

"Maybe." Grace added a light kiss to Liv's lips. "You'll just have to wait and see."

****

Grace took off at a run, closely pursued by Liv. Reenergized after lunch, Grace turned a jog to the lake into a full-out race. She followed the worn path around a copse of pine trees and ended at the edge of the water. She slid to a stop and heard Liv breathing before she saw her round the bend.

Grace couldn't help laughing when Liv dramatically collapsed at her feet. "You can't be that tired. It was a short run."

"Can't. Breathe. Just. Died."

"Wuss," Grace said and started stripping to her underwear. "You're not going to cool off lying there in the grass."

"I'm dead. I don't care. Where the hell does your energy come from?"

"I'm an adrenaline junkie. And I really want to jump in the water and cool off. C'mon." Grace extended her hand to Liv and yelped when she was pulled down, nearly landing on the supine woman. "Hey!"

Liv rolled over so she was on top of Grace. "I need resuscitation."

"You're on top of me. How can I do CPR like this?"

"I only need mouth-to-mouth."

"That so?"

Liv's lips hovered above Grace's. "Yeah. Mouth-to-mouth. You'd be saving my life."

Blue eyes locked with Grace's, and her heartbeat quickened as their mouths touched. Gently at first; exploring; needing. Tongues met, and suddenly Grace wanted nothing more than the feel of Liv's skin against hers. She lifted Liv's moist shirt up and slid her hands along sweaty skin until she met the fabric of Liv's sports bra. She hated that her prize was covered up and slid a finger along the edges, dipping in to feel the soft skin hidden beneath.

Liv's breath caught, and she pulled back enough to meet Grace's gaze. "Not here," she whispered.

"Why not?" Grace missed her warmth when Liv sat up and settled beside her. "Did I do something wrong?"

"It's not—not how I want our first time to be."

"What? You've been thinking about this?"

"Haven't you?" Liv ran her fingers along Grace's cheek. "It's all I've been able to think about for a long time. Gracie, there's so much I need to tell you."

"About what?" Grace sat up when Liv moved away from her. Grace crossed her legs and sat facing Liv. "Is there something wrong?"

"No, nothing's wrong. I'm not good at this, that's all." Liv took hold of Grace's hands. "I don't want to just have sex with you. I want to make love to...I want to love every centimeter of your body so you know how special and cared for you are. I want it to be a time we'll never forget." She placed soft kisses along Grace's fingers. "I want to worship your body."

Grace swallowed the lump in her throat. Words failed her. The tender look in Liv's eyes was her undoing. Tears trickled along her cheeks. Her hands shook, and in an instant she was wrapped in Liv's loving embrace.

Liv whispered reassurances in Grace's ear, her breath tickling the sensitive skin. Grace rested her head against Liv's chest and listened to her rapid heartbeat. Liv's confession stunned her, but in a way that made her heart soar. Never had anyone said something so amazing to her. She hardly felt worthy of Liv. In fact, she was certain she wasn't good enough for a woman like Olivia Templeton.

After a few moments, Grace pulled back and swiped at the wetness on her face. Her chest ached at the knowledge that there was no way her love would ever be what Liv deserved. She fought back the urge to cry again.

"You okay?" Liv asked softly, her hands resting on Grace's waist.

"No one has ever...I don't think I can do this, Olivia."

"Do what?"

"This." Grace's hand fluttered between them. "Us."

"I—I'm confused. You said you love me."

"And I do. With all my heart."

Liv's gaze met hers, and Grace could clearly see her determination.

"I love you," Liv said. "Whatever's wrong we'll figure it out."

"I'm not good enough for you, Olivia. I could never give you what you need."

"Nonsense." Liv kissed her softly. "You have a lot of love in your heart. You've just never been given the chance to let it out."

"But what if I'm not—"

"Shh." Liv quieted her with another kiss. She let her hands slide along Grace's bare neck, across her shoulders to her back. "You are exactly what I want and what I need."

"I can't think if you keep kissing me."

"Exactly my point." Liv's voice was soft in her ear. "Let me love you, Gracie. Let me promise to do everything I can to make you happy and never hurt you." Liv pressed her lips to Grace's mouth for a long, sweet, tender kiss. "I think we've got a good thing going. Let's take it slow."

"Okay."

"Yeah?" Liv gazed at her with smiling eyes.

"Yeah. We could start by taking a swim. It'd be nice to feel clean and refreshed."

"Deal." Liv removed her T-shirt, tossed it aside and said, "I'd go butt naked, but I don't want a surprise visit from anyone in the group. What I got to show off is for your eyes only."

Grace smiled. "My eyes thank you. It'll be my honor to see what you have to show off."

Liv waggled her eyes brows. "It'll be worth the wait." She ran into the water calling over her shoulder, "Race you to the other side!"

Chapter Thirteen

Liv spent the better part of Monday morning going over spreadsheets to reconcile the latest gold   royalties with the leased properties, as well as the gold from last week's cleanouts of the two properties they still mined. There was nothing from Clear Creek. She dialed David's cell phone and jumped when Adele's "Skyfall" filtered in from the hallway. David answered the phone as he entered her office.

"I'm here," he said and tucked the phone into his pocket.

"Good timing. So how'd it go at Clear Creek?"

David plopped onto the couch and rested his head on the back. "I'm fine, thanks. Had a great weekend. Saw Timothy when I had dinner with the parents. Oh, we tried to invite you, but apparently your phone only works on weekdays. Care to share?"

"No. And my phone was on all weekend. If you did call, you didn't leave a voicemail."

"You never check your voicemail," he said.

"I do, too." Liv narrowed her gaze at him, trying to gauge what he was getting at. "For the record, I spent most of the weekend with Grace. When I wasn't with her, I was with Timothy. In fact, I'm the one who took him to the airport." David opened his mouth to speak, but Liv talked instead. "How did I know he was home? He called me last week. Now, what's up?"

"You suck. Why didn't you tell me about Grace? You told Timothy but not me?"

Liv wasn't sure if he was hurt by that or not. It wasn't usual that she'd tell anything to Timothy before David, but it sort of slipped when she took him to the airport. "How do you know?"

"Timothy texted me asking how well I know Grace." David sat forward and rested his arms on his knees. "Livvy, I thought we were good."

"We are. I just haven't seen you and—I guess I got a little excited when I was talking to Timothy. David, I don't know how to explain it, but this time's different. I can hardly wait to see her, and when I can't, we're on the phone or on Skype. I want to be with her all the time."

"You were pretty damn sure about Jane, too."

The comment stung, but Liv knew he didn't mean to be unkind. He was making a valid point. "I was, but it never felt like this with Jane. I think I was in love with the idea of finding someone to spend my life with when I met Jane. We moved way too fast. But with Grace...” She shrugged. “I’m in love with her. I can’t put it any plainer than that.”

“What does Sara say?”

“Sara says she needs to slow down.” The voice came from the doorway, where Sara’s slim figure stood. She walked to the couch and settled beside David. “And yes, this is an intervention. We wanted your dad here, but he thought it was better with just the two of us.”

“Ah, so not a full-on coup. Just a partial one.”

“Something like that,” Sara said. “Look, I don’t know anything about Grace, and that scares me a lot. No one’s met her yet. We only know what you tell us, and I’m going to be blunt here. Your track record with women is horrid. You only ever see the good. Never the bad.”

“Was it so horrid with you?” Liv asked.

Sara gave her a wry grin. “Not for the first week. But yes. It did get bad and you know it. At least we came to an agreement to split up before we hurt each other. Liv, I love you and you know that. So does David. We’re here because we don’t want to see you repeat what happened with Jane.”

Liv considered Sara’s words for a moment. “I’m not sure how this will work out. I don’t know if Grace is even interested in living in Canada. I only know that in a couple of months I’ve fallen in love with her. We’ll figure the other stuff out. I promise we’re going slow.”

“Have you slept with her?” Sara asked.

David covered his ears. “I do not want to know this information.”

Liv laughed at him. “No. I have not.” Liv held up her hand to stop Sara when she opened her mouth again. “Enough. I’ll make you all a deal. Let’s plan to have dinner at my house tomorrow night. I’ll cook, we’ll eat, chat, and have a nice time getting to know Grace. Deal?”

****

“You make the best lasagna,” Grace said. She wiped her mouth with a napkin. The evening with David and Sara had gone well so far. She enjoyed their easy banter and immediately felt like she was part of the group.

“It’s the only meal she can cook,” David said with a smirk.

Liv punched him in the arm. “I’m trying to impress my girlfriend here, you shit. Don’t tell her crap like that.”

David wore the same crooked grin as Liv, and it made Grace smile. He replied, “Crap. Good word to describe your cooking.”

Liv shot him a look that Grace expected was meant to shut him up. She'd done that with Matt on many occasions. It didn't work any better on David than it did on her twin brother.

Sara piped up just as David opened his mouth to retort. "Liv makes the very best S'mores Pop Tarts in the world." Her voice filled with playful pride. "I wanted to marry her, but she dumped me."

Liv snorted. "You two are so full of shit I need to get my boots on."

They all shared a laugh as Liv and Sara cleared the table. Grace listened to their continued playful chatter in the kitchen. "They really are a pair, huh?" she said to David.

"Best friends for years. I told Livvy it was a bad idea to date Sara, but as usual she didn't listen." David leaned across the table and whispered, "I'd date Sara if I could get her to switch teams."

Grace smiled. "Good luck with that. She seems pretty firmly set on our side."

"Yeah. All the good women are gay."

"And I thought that was what straight women say about men."

David shrugged, his crooked grin firmly in place. "Same difference. So, how are things for you over at Gracie's Glory? I heard you had some trouble with your D9."

"We did, but Liv is one damn good mechanic. She had it up and running in a few hours. Saved us a potential downtime of three days or more. We ended the week with a decent clean out. Eighty-seven ounces."

David whistled. "That's great. Charlie told me you were averaging around ninety or so. You must have found some good ground."

"Yep. Ironically, in that area you guys argued over."

David's jovial manner turned serious. "Hey, I'm so sorry about that. I was under a lot of pressure and listening to the wrong person. I never should have gone after Charlie like that. He's a good guy."

"He is, and it's water under the bridge. How was your week? Liv told me you've been doing pretty well up at Clear Creek."

"Amazing. Managed 250 ounces on the first clean out for our new cut."

"Wow. That's, what? Around a quarter million dollars?"

"Just over 305 thousand." David's grin was back, and there was a certain sparkle in his eyes. "Best clean out yet. I'm just over 800 ounces for the season, and I'm hoping to get 2000 before we're done."

"Lofty goals, brother. You don't know if that new cut is gonna pan out or not." Liv joined them and rested her hand on David's shoulder. "Don't set yourself up for failure. Get what you can get.

It's all profit from now on anyway."

"Exactly." David pushed back from the table and stood. "I want to push for more gold so we can pay off the expense of breaking two trucks. Next week we're going to run the wash plant twenty-four hours a day. If I'm right, we'll double that clean out."

Liv started to reply, but Sara moved between them. "Work talk on Monday. Not the weekends." She gave Grace a sad smile. "And this is why we broke up. Don't let her do this too much, okay? All work and no play makes for a wiped out Liv."

"I'll do what I can," Grace said. She moved to Liv's side and slipped her arm around her waist.

"And that's our cue to leave," David said. He took Sara's hand and headed for the door. "Thanks for dinner, Livvy."

"Yes, thanks," Sara said. "You still make the best S'mores though."

"Yeah, yeah, yeah." Liv playfully shoved them toward the door. "Out. You've done enough damage to my rep."

David turned to Grace and gave her a quick hug. He whispered to her, "Please don't hurt her."

"I'll do my best," she replied and watched him and Sara leave.

Liv closed the door and took Grace into her arms. "I thought I'd never get rid of them. Pay no attention to anything those two said."

"Oh, I plan to commit every word to memory. No way are you getting out of this one. I think I've found two new friends. Great pair to dig up dirt on you when I need it."

"Ugh." Liv rested her head against Grace's. "I'm doomed."

"You're being dramatic. Though I do find it kinda cute."

"You do?" Liv brightened instantly. "I could keep it up."

"Don't." Grace rolled her eyes. "It's not that cute."

"It's okay. I have something better planned anyway."

"You do?"

"Mmhmm." Liv ushered her into the living room. "Have a seat on the couch. I've got a surprise for you, but I need a few minutes to set it up." She kissed Grace and bounded out of the room like a kid on Christmas day.

Grace was excited as well. Not so much about the surprise, but that Liv wanted to do something special for her. When was the last time someone surprised her? Tonie. Of course. Her high school sweetheart.

Grace warmed with memories of Tonie, the best being the afternoon she stood outside Grace's window to serenade her. Their fathers were stationed in Charleston, South Carolina. In a list of favorite bases, Grace still considered it at the top. Even if the weather sucked during the summer. She'd never been a fan of hot, sweaty summers.

She laughed, recalling Tonie dressed in a short tank top, Daisy Duke cut-off jeans, and flip-flops. Her wild, orange-red hair plastered to her face in the sweltering heat. Despite the July weather, she smiled brightly and let loose a melodic tune that Grace couldn't recall. It was something Tonie wrote just for her. But the sweet sound of Tonie's voice filled her room, even before she opened the window. The gesture was so amazing that it made her cry.

Now it made her smile.

Would she and Tonie still be together if her dad hadn't been sent to Spain?

"You have a beautiful smile, Gracie." Liv knelt in front of her and rested her hands on Grace's knees.

"I do?"

"Yes. I hope I'm the reason it's there."

Grace cupped Liv's face in her hands and gazed into her eyes. She saw love shining back at her. "All because of you. I was remembering a surprise I got many years ago. I hadn't thought about it in forever." Grace pressed her lips to Liv's. "I'd almost forgotten how happy I used to be."

"Before Carly."

"Yes. There have been some amazing women in my life, but none of them compare to you, Olivia. I love you."

"I love you, too. Now come and see your surprise." Liv pulled Grace to her feet and led her up the carpeted stairs to the second floor. She stopped at the first door they came to. "Close your eyes."

Grace did and allowed Liv to guide her in. The door shut softly behind her.

She breathed in the scent of fresh roses mixed with a hint of chocolate and vanilla.

Liv, still behind her, said, "Now take off your shoes and socks."

"Are you going to massage my feet?"

Liv chuckled and placed her hands on Grace's waist to help steady her. "I might."

The shoes and socks tossed aside, Liv urged Grace forward. A few steps and her feet sank into luxurious softness. Grace wiggled her toes. "Nice."

"It gets better. Two more steps and you can sit."

Grace followed Liv's instructions and settled onto the floor. She heard Liv move about for a moment before she said, "Open your eyes."

Grace did. The flickering glow of candlelight highlighted her Liv's features. The desire in her eyes sent a pleasant tingle through Grace. Butterflies fluttered in her stomach. It was nearly impossible to look away from her, but Liv broke their contact and glanced to her left.

In front of the fireplace sat a breakfast tray. Three bowls, filled with strawberries, melted chocolate, and cream, sat beside two champagne flutes. Next to the tray stood a silver ice bucket, in the center of which rested a bottle of champagne. Pillows of varying sizes and shapes surrounded them, creating a soft environment.

"I—I don't know what to say," Grace said.

"Do you like it?" Liv asked.

"Of course I do. It's perfectly romantic."

"And all for you." Liv's voice was deep, husky. Every word sent chills down Grace's spine. Liv opened the bottle like a pro, not spilling a drop of the bubbly liquid. She half-filled both flutes and handed one to Grace. "To us. And many more romantic nights to come."

"To us." Grace gently clinked her glass to Liv's and took a sip. A smile broadened her face when she heard the low, sultry voice of Nora Jones fill the air. That Liv thought to play her favorite singer, in addition to all the other things, caused a lump in Grace's throat. She fought against the urge to cry.

Liv must have sensed this as she took the flute from Grace, placed it on the tray alongside her own, and kissed Grace's lips. "Baby, I told you I wanted our first time to be special."

"I had no idea you were a closet romantic." Grace leaned forward and crushed her mouth to Liv's, one hand behind Liv's neck. Their tongues danced as the kiss became more heated. Grace felt the wetness between her legs and longed to strip the clothes off Liv and ravish her. Liv broke the spell when she pulled back to speak.

"You bring out the romance in me." Liv placed feathery kisses on Grace's cheeks, neck, lips. "What can I say?"

"You don't need to say anything. It's perfect."

"Almost." Liv gave her that sexy, crooked grin. "You haven't tried a strawberry yet. Chocolate or cream?"

"Surprise me." Grace closed her eyes and parted her lips. Dark chocolate, her favorite, assaulted her taste buds in the most pleasurable way. She bit down and savored the sweet strawberry/chocolate combination.

"You missed a bit." Liv licked the corner of Grace's mouth and Grace turned her head so their lips were in contact again. She placed her hands on either side of Liv's face and luxuriated in the feel of her amazing lips; so soft and supple. How could one kiss send such incredible feelings through her entire body? One sexy, amazing kiss.

Liv's tongue traced the edges of Grace's mouth. Her lips

pressed softly along Grace's neck, trailing to the edge of her shirt. "This needs to go," Liv whispered as she unbuttoned it. She kissed, nipped and sucked her way down Grace's body until the shirt was gone and tossed aside.

Then she moved to Grace's nipple, biting gently on it through the fabric of her bra. Liv ran her fingers along the edges of the soft cotton until she reached the back and unhooked it in one, swift motion. It joined the shirt somewhere on the floor.

Grace inched closer to Liv, wanting to feel their bodies touching each other.

Liv had a different idea and nudged Grace to lie down. Liv continued kissing Grace's body, moving along every inch of it as she undid Grace's jeans. The kissing never stopped and soon the jeans were gone. The fire warmed Grace, but not nearly as much as when Liv took a nipple in her mouth and sucked on it. There was fire in Grace's belly and she badly wanted Liv naked as well.

Her hand reached for Liv's shirt, but Liv pulled back a bit. "Not yet. This about you, Gracie. Not me."

Grace started to reply, but all thought went out the window when Liv's hand pressed against her center. She traced her fingers along the edges of her undies and Grace raised her hips in invitation.

"You're so wet."

"All for you, baby," Grace touched the side of Liv's face. "You're amazing."

"I love you," Liv said as she gently tugged Grace's undies down her legs, never losing eye contact. She tossed them over her shoulder and replaced the covering with her hand. "I'm going to love every bit of you, Gracie Lee. I want you to know how special you are."

Grace sucked in a breath when Liv's fingers touched her. She easily found the spot Grace needed her most, slowly stroking her. Grace's need was intense now, and the more Liv touched her the higher she flew. She'd never experienced this intense passion with anyone in her life. Never felt the mind numbing pleasure as she did the moment Liv's fingers were inside her.

"Liv, please. I need you."

"I'm right here," Liv scooted down and settled between Grace's thighs. While her fingers did wonderful things to Grace, Liv used her mouth on Grace's lips, sucking them in and sending a shockwave through Grace's entire body.

Her breath caught and her hands fisted the bedsheets. Grace threw her head back as her hips moved in concert with Liv's motions. Liv continued to love Grace with her mouth, never letting up on the rhythm of her fingers. Their movements got faster and Grace place a hand on the back of Liv's head, tangling her fingers in Liv's curls.

Liv pumped harder, faster and when she pushed just a little harder she found the spot that made Grace scream. The orgasm shot through her body and Grace threw her head back and let out a scream that surprised herself. Never done that before. Never had such an earthshattering orgasm as the one she was riding right then. Fireworks exploded behind her eyelids as her body twitched in pleasure.

Arms held her close as the last bits of the orgasm rippled through Grace. Her body shook slightly when she finally began her descent, her eyes rolled back and she soaked in the last shutters of orgasm. She didn't realize she was crying until Liv was wiping the tears from her face.

"Baby, I'm so sorry. Did I hurt you?"

"No. You didn't hurt me. It was all—so perfect. I've never felt anything like it. I don't have the words..."

Liv gently kissed her lips and pulled her into a warm embrace. "You don't need them. Your tears scared me a little. That's all."

"They're tears of joy. I promise."

"Good."

"I love you so much, Olivia." Grace rested her head against Liv's shoulder. "Thank you."

"I love you, too. Now save your energy. I'm not done yet."

Grace leaned on an elbow so she could see the expression on Liv's face. Her eyes gleamed with passion and it sent another tingle through Grace's body. "You're not?"

"Nope. This is your night, baby. I plan to love you well into the morning."

"Wow." Grace settled down again. "You really are the best girlfriend ever."

Liv laughed and snuggled into her. "You have no idea."

"Show me."

****

Liv trailed her fingers along the thin scar on Grace's cheek. How could anyone willingly hurt the amazing woman in her arms? Thinking of the violence that caused the mark made her physically ill. Liv wanted five minutes alone with Carly. Just five minutes...

Grace leaned on her elbow and wiped tears from Liv's face. Liv hadn't realized she was crying. "Did I do something wrong?" Grace asked, her voice trembling. "I'm so sorry."

"What? No. Baby you're amazing." Liv kissed her tenderly, slowly. "Never think you're anything less. Okay?"

"Why are you crying?"

"Because...because you've been hurt." She touched the scar

again. This time Grace flinched. "I'd love to get my hands on that bitch."

"Liv—"

"What she did to you makes me so damn angry."

Grace's voice was soft as she said, "I'm sorry, Olivia."

"Stop apologizing. Remember our deal? I'm going to have to try a new technique to break you of this habit." Liv trailed tender kisses along the scar then pressed her lips to Grace's. The kiss was slow, sensual, and, Liv hoped, full of promise.

"I like your technique," Grace teased. "If this is how you break habits—well, I might need attention for more habits."

"That could get interesting. Maybe I need a special technique for each habit?"

"Maybe."

Liv kissed her again then reached toward the food tray and retrieved a gift box. She placed it on Grace's bare chest. "I got you a present."

"It's not my birthday."

"No, but we're lesbians and required to celebrate certain days. This is the first time we made love, so it's now an anniversary."

Grace sputtered and laughed. "Anyone ever tell you you're weird?"

"Many. Often. Now open it."

"Okay, okay." Grace took her time removing the silver wrapping paper. Liv was tortured by how long it took just to open the damn box. Once she did, Grace gasped. "It's—are you serious?"

"As a heart attack." Liv removed the multicolored key chain and dangled the bronze key above Grace. "I'd love for you to move in, but if you aren't ready, it's okay. No matter what, I want you to have a key to my house. Come and go as much as you want. Every day if you really want to." She waggled her eyebrows and grinned.

Gracie laughed again. "You're so very sweet." She took it from Liv and examined the keychain. A gold nugget painted in rainbow colors swung from the end of it. "Seriously? Who comes up with these tacky things?"

"Gay souvenir shops?" Liv kissed her.

"Of course. Who else." She placed the key on the floor beside her. "Thanks. But I don't really have to think about it much. We might be moving too fast, but Liv, I love you. I don't want to be with anyone else. Soon as the mining season is over, I want to move in with you. I want us to be together."

"You've just made me the happiest woman on the planet." Liv kissed her with great enthusiasm. "I wish the season was over already."

"You can't wait six weeks?"

"Can you?"

Grace pretended to think that over. "Uh, not really. But it makes sense. I'm closer to the camp at *Ojiichan's*, and most of the things I have are split between the two places." She traced her fingers along Liv's cheek. "I promise to make it worth the wait."

"That's awesome, but it does nothing for my patience. How about we spend the rest of the weekend playing house?"

"Now that sounds like fun. What should we do first?"

When Liv kissed her again, she left no doubt what she wanted to do, though she said, "Stop talking."

Chapter Fourteen

"Asking her to move in is not exactly taking it slow." Sara pushed her salad plate away and sat back in her chair, arms akimbo. She glared at Liv.

Liv sighed. She'd expected this reaction, which is exactly why she'd waited almost a week to have lunch with Sara. Friday night at Pot O'Gold wasn't her first choice to have this discussion, but it gave her the least chance of Sara yelling at her. Except Sara hadn't gotten the memo.

"We've been going out for a few of months, Sara. How long am I supposed to wait?"

"I don't know. A year? Two years?"

"Be serious."

"I am serious. I don't want you to make a mistake."

"It's not a mistake. Besides, she won't be moving in until the end of the season. That's still another five weeks away." Liv took a sip of her beer. From the look on Sara's face, she reckoned she'd need something much stronger to get through this.

"You know what I mean. I don't want to see you broken again. It's amazing you even decided to date Grace after the way things ended with Jane and then me. I honestly never thought you'd be in another serious relationship. Don't get me wrong. You know I'm glad you are."

"Let me stop you right there." Liv placed her elbows on the table and leaned forward. "Don't compare Gracie to Jane. They are worlds apart. I know you're only looking out for me, but this is my decision. I didn't come by it lightly, either. I've been thinking about it for a couple of weeks now."

"Why didn't you tell me?"

"Because I knew how you'd react. And that intervention with you and David proved I was right."

Sara was uncharacteristically quiet for so long that Liv thought she might get up and leave. At last, she said, "I—you're right. I'm probably overreacting. Is it so bad not to want to see my best friend hurt?"

"Nope. Your opinion matters. But it's a done deal, so there's no sense arguing over it. Just wish us the best. Okay?"

Sara lifted her beer and clinked it against Liv's. "To you and Grace."

"Thanks."

"Sara Hyatt? Wow. I think my day just got better."

Liv glanced up to see a familiar woman standing by their table. She wracked her brain for her name. Her smile was brilliant, and her deep-brown eyes twinkled as she stared at Sara. She adjusted the bright blue frames of her glasses and tucked a strand of coal-black hair behind her left ear.

"Terry Alexander?" Sara asked.

Terry's smile widened and created crinkles along the edges of her eyes. The light-brown skin of her face tinged slightly with a blush. "You remembered."

"Of course," Sara said. They continued to stare at each other, neither offering anything in the way of an introduction.

Liv cleared her throat. "I'm Liv Templeton."

"I know." Terry slowly moved her gaze to Liv. She held out her hand to shake Liv's. "Your dad owns TNT, right?"

"Yep. Have we met?"

"I don't think so, unless you saw me at the bank. I was there last week about a loan. I'm buying Frank Trane's business. He's retiring this year."

"So I heard," Liv said. "Frank's the best geologist in the territory. If he's letting you buy his business then you must be damn good."

"Thanks. I hope I can live up to the reputation he's building for me."

"I'm sure you will." Liv nudged Sara with her foot. "You can ignore my rude friend and have a seat if you'd like. Sara, move your ass over."

"Huh?" Sara looked like she only just realized Liv was there.

"Move over so Terry can sit."

"Oh, it's okay. I need to head out. I'm on my way to the bank to finalized the paperwork for the loan. I believe I have an appointment with Sara." Terry's eyes twinkled with mischief and Liv smiled.

"Oh, that's me!" Sara practically jumped out of her chair. "I'm heading that way. Why don't I walk with you?"

"I'd like that." Terry indicated for Sara to lead.

The two women said goodbye to Liv and headed for the door. Liv tossed a twenty on the table and left, relieved that Sara had someone other than Liv to occupy her time.

****

Pile after pile of pay dirt slid out of the scoop and into the wash plant through the feeder. Usually, the monotony of it helped Grace think. Yet today, she was restless. A dream woke her around two in the morning, but she had no recollection of it other than the haunting emotions it brought about.

As the day progressed, bits and pieces flashed through her brain. None of it made sense. The pounding headache certainly didn't help any. Grace tried hard to concentrate solely on her job, but that just wasn't happening.

The teeth of the dozer's scoop scraped against the steel bars of the feeder. The sound was like fingernails on a chalkboard, and Grace shivered. Her fingers slipped off the joystick that operated the arms of the dozer. The scoop jolted and the cab of the dozer rocked.

Something caught Grace's attention beyond the trees that marked the edge of their claim. A woman dressed in black jeans, white peacoat, and sunglasses stared in her direction. She didn't move. She didn't speak, though Grace would never hear her anyway above the noise of the dozer and wash plant.

The woman ran her fingers through light-blonde hair. It was that motion—a motion Grace had seen thousands of times before— that brought a scream to Grace's lips.

No sound came out. She kept trying to call for help, but her voice no longer worked.

Her hands scraped against solid glass.

The frame of the dozer closed in on her.

She couldn't breathe.

Couldn't get out.

Darkness formed along the edges of her vision.

Rough hands grabbed her. Grace kicked out with her left foot and reached for a weapon with her right hand.

She slipped from the seat in the cab, and before she could react, found herself lying on the hard, cold ground. A figure hovered over her, trying to control her flailing arms.

Grace couldn't think. She was out there and she was going to get Grace. She had to run. Grace needed to get away before the woman caught up to her.

The scream finally made it past her lips.

The person standing over her jumped back, and Grace scrambled to her feet.

She had to get out of there, but she couldn't figure out where she was. Her eyes searched the area, the woman no longer in view. Was she closer now?

"Gracie!"

The voice was strong and familiar.

"Gracie Lee, it's okay. Calm down."

Grace's heart was beating so hard it felt like it would come out of her chest. She swiped at sweat that dripped down her face as she tried to focus. The woman...who was she? Where was she?

"Mike, get me a bottle of water," the person in front of her said.

Grace took a tentative step forward. Her eyes focused on Josie, who watched her closely. Josie's face was pale, her eyes wide with concern. Grace tried three times before words made it past her lips. "I'm okay."

"You don't look okay," Josie said. She came closer and handed the water to Grace. "Sweetie, you were freaking out. I thought you were going to kick Mike's ass."

"He grabbed me," Grace said between long drinks of water. "He shouldn't have grabbed me." She took a few wobbly steps to lean against the tracks of the dozer. "I had a panic attack."

"I gathered." Josie leaned beside her. "What brought it on?"

"I'm not sure." Grace looked toward the tree line but saw no one there. She'd only half-expected to see the woman again. The woman she now realized was Carly. "It's hard to know exactly what causes them."

"You'd tell me, right?"

Grace nodded, though she kept her eyes averted from Josie's. "It's not easy to explain."

Josie placed a gentle hand on Grace's shoulder. "You don't have to. But I think it's time you stopped for the day. Mike and I can get the mats and take them back to camp for the clean out. Charlie said that Harry's coming over this evening with food for a barbeque. Why don't you get cleaned up and lay down for a bit? Get some more sleep. You look like you could use it."

Grace understood Josie was being nice, but sleeping was the last thing she wanted to do. "I'll head to the cabin. Thanks, Josie. And tell Mike it's safe now. I won't hurt him."

"I'm not about to tell him that," Josie said with a laugh. "It's good for him to be scared of girls. Keeps him honest."

****

Liv pounded a steady beat against the steering wheel of her truck, not quite matching the song on her CD player. She didn't care. No one could hear her off-key singing either, but she kept it up as loudly as she could. She was in the best mood ever and wanted everyone to know it. Liv was going to enjoy an evening bonfire and barbeque and take home the most amazing woman ever to walk into her life.

She teased Grace by saying she wanted to play house, but the reality of it was that she wanted to test the waters. The previous two weekends had gone very well. She and Grace fit into an easy rhythm that was almost scary. But only almost. It was like they were meant to be together. And with each moment they were, Liv got closer and closer to popping the one question she was terrified to ask.

Liv wanted to be with Grace every moment of every day for the rest of her life. If they were to get married, Grace would be able to stay in Canada and not worry about her work visa. More important, they would be together.

The only thing that stopped Liv was Grace. While there was no doubt that Grace loved her, Liv sensed the time wasn't right. Grace was still settling into their relationship. She'd wait a while to ask. But she'd already spotted the ring earlier in the week in a window display in Whitehorse. Was it a mistake to put a deposit on it?

Liv pulled into the parking area at Gracie's Glory and parked beside Harry's old pickup. It was already dark, but the glow of the bonfire lit a path for her. As she headed toward the steady murmur of voices, Liv realized the ring was a good idea. She was going to ask Grace to marry her. She only needed to pick the right time.

The moment she approached the fire, Liv saw this was far from the right time.

Grace stood staring into the flames. Her posture was slumped. Conflicting emotions rolled off her in waves that nearly knocked Liv off her feet. She moved forward, gently slipped her arms around Grace, and pulled her close.

"Hey. What's wrong?"

Grace leaned into her and rested her head against Liv's. "I had a panic attack today."

"I'm sorry, babe. Want to talk about it?"

Liv felt Grace's deep sigh and held her a little tighter. Grace said, "I had a nightmare last night that I don't remember. Then today, while I was loading pay dirt into the wash plant, I started freaking out."

"Did you hurt yourself?"

Grace adjusted herself so she was facing Liv but remained tucked into Liv's arms. "No. I don't remember much of that, either, but Mike will. He grabbed me and I guess I scared him."

Liv placed a soft kiss on her forehead. "I'm sure he's fine. What happened then?"

"Josie got me to calm down." Grace looked away, and in the light of the fire, Liv could see the fright in her eyes. "I thought I saw Carly. I was so sure of it that I kept looking for her even after I got to the cabin, took a shower, and helped Harry set up the food."

Liv cupped her palm around Grace's cheek and urged her to meet her gaze. "Honey, that bitch is seared into your brain, and I wish like hell I could make you forget her. But I'm more concerned about the panic attack. I think it's time you followed Abby's advice."

"About the group therapy?"

"Yes. She said it would help you progress in your healing. She told you there's only so much she can do. You don't want to have to take any medication, so you have to do something. If she thinks group therapy will help you, then that's what you need to do."

"I don't know, Liv. I don't know that I can face a bunch of strangers..."

"I'll go with you."

"I know you've said that before, but are you sure?"

Liv felt a pang of hurt at the surprise in Grace's voice. "Of course. I'll take you there, and I'll sit with you and hold your hand if you want me to. Whatever you need to get better, I'm there."

"Are you real?" Grace half-laughed as she trailed her fingers along Liv's jaw. "I mean, you're amazing."

"I'm in love with you, Gracie Lee. Why wouldn't I do this for you?"

Grace shrugged, but Liv understood the answer she wouldn't voice. Grace still found it hard to believe in and trust Liv. How could she help Grace get past that? How could Liv get her cleansed of all the poison Carly poured into her?

"Hey...I don't mean to doubt you," Grace said, as if sensing Liv's thoughts. "I love you, and I love that you are so gung ho about helping me. I'm not sure I'm ready for the group therapy. Let me talk to Abby again. Okay?"

"Sure," Liv said reluctantly. "You have a call with her on Monday, right?"

"I do."

"Is there any chance I can come over? I don't want to intrude on your call, but I'd like to talk to her for a few minutes. Would that be okay?"

Grace stared up at Liv with questioning eyes. "Of course it's okay. But what do you want to ask her?"

"How best to help you," Liv said and pulled Grace into a tight embrace. "I want to ask for her advice. You're my partner, Gracie. I want to be there for you, and I want to understand what you need from me. I figure Abby's a good start."

"I'm your partner?" Grace asked. Liv thought she heard a hitch in her voice, like she was crying. "Not just your girlfriend?"

"I think we passed the girlfriend stage awhile back," Liv whispered against Grace's ear. "We might not live together yet, but you're my partner. There's no one else in the world I'd rather be with."

"I—I don't know what to say."

"You don't need to say anything." Liv kissed her ear and gave the lobe a playful tug with her teeth. "Let's get something to eat so we'll have energy later. Okay?"

Grace pushed her away with a smile on her face. "You're worse than a guy. Is sex all you think about?"

"Not all, but it's in there a lot. Why? Don't you?"

Grace narrowed her eyes at Liv and wagged a finger at her. "I asked you first."

"Which is a positive response. So you're thinking about it as much as I am."

"Am not."

"Are, too."

"If you two children are done squabbling, the food's done cooking," Charlie announced from behind them. "Best come eat before Mike takes a swipe at the table and clears all the good stuff."

Grace took Liv's hand and dragged her toward the area set up with food. "Am not."

"Are, too."

Grace started to speak, but Liv cut her off with a kiss. "Let's settle this later tonight."

The blatant look of passion on Grace's features was nearly Liv's undoing. If she could, she'd have dragged the woman into the cabin and stayed there the rest of the weekend. Grace ran her fingers along Liv's face, circled her sensitive earlobe, and trailed along her neck. The movement sent tingles along Liv's body.

Grace said, "Am not," and walked away.

Liv exhaled loudly. "Damn woman."

****

The following Monday, Liv drove Grace back to Harry's cabin. Once there, Grace settled in to her scheduled Skype appointment with Abby. For the first time, she invited Liv to join in. After nearly half an hour, Liv walked out of Grace's room, and closed the door, leaving Grace to have some private time with Abby. She stepped into the living room and plopped into the chair opposite Harry's. He muted the TV and waited for her to talk.

"Abby's pretty damn awesome."

"She's been good for Gracie."

"She has."

"Did she answer your questions?"

Liv sighed. "She did. But I'm not sure I can get Grace on board. Abby is adamant that Grace start going to group therapy."

"And Grace continues to put it off," Harry said. "I tried to give her time to make the decision on her own, but I think the idea of sharing her experience with people she doesn't know scares her too much."

"I agree. But Abby gave me the information for the group in Whitehorse, and I happen to be friends with the woman who runs it." Liv grinned. "I'll take Grace to introduce them before the meeting and maybe slowly work our way in. I promised I'd go with her and hold her hand."

Harry smiled, but to Liv he looked like he might cry. "I never expected you'd be this good for her, Olivia. I only hoped she'd find a friend."

"She did, Harry."

"Stop talking about me," Grace said as she joined them. She sat on Liv's lap and wrapped her arms around Liv's shoulders.

"Who says we were talking about you?" Liv teased, giving her a light kiss on the lips.

"You're sitting next to my *ojiichan*. Of course he's talking about me. And anything he says is either a great exaggeration or something you just don't need to believe."

"I don't lie," Harry said. "Nor do I exaggerate."

"I didn't say you lie. But you totally exaggerate and get pretty damn far from the truth. I think it's old age. Maybe it's time to put you in a nice home."

Harry stuck his tongue out at Grace. "You will need an army to drag me from my cabin. I'm going to die here."

"Eww. I don't want to think about that."

"Me either." Liv eased Grace off her lap and stood up. "And I'm using this weird turn in the conversation to leave. Harry, I'll see you Friday when I come to steal Grace from you."

"Steal? You can have her. No need to steal."

Grace literally shoved Liv out the door. They walked hand in hand to her truck. Grace said, "Are you and Abby really going to gang up on me over this group therapy thing?"

Liv stopped at the truck and pulled Grace toward her so she could hold her in her arms. "Yes. But it won't be painful. I know the person who runs the group. She's very sweet, and I think she'll make you comfortable. I'll introduce you guys next weekend. We can talk, and you can decide when we start going."

"We? You're seriously going with me?" Grace's open expression made Liv smile.

"Of course. Besides, Abby thinks it's a good idea for me to be there with you. I want to be there for you, Gracie Lee. Please don't forget that."

"I won't." Grace returned her kiss with enthusiasm. She'd become more daring in the last few weeks, and Liv thoroughly enjoyed it. Her passion was ignited with each step Grace took.

"I better leave before I have my way with you in front of the voyeur. You know he's watching us."

"I do, and while I'm tempted to give him a show, it's kind of a creepy idea."

"Totally creepy." Liv hugged her close and kissed Grace again. "I'll call when I get home. I love you."

Grace's smile spoke volumes, and it was that smile that

remained in Liv's brain the two hours back to Whitehorse.

Chapter Fifteen

Grace steered into the parking lot of Marge's and turned off the ignition. Yesterday, Sara called her and asked to meet for lunch. It was Friday, and she had to be in Whitehorse anyway, so she agreed. Sara specifically wanted it to be the two of them, and that made Grace a little nervous. She recognized that Sara wanted to get to know her. Probably needed to be sure Grace was good enough for her best friend.

Grace liked Sara but got the impression that Sara was protective of Liv.

A tap on the window beside her startled Grace. Sara was staring at her with a bemused expression on her face. She said, "I thought we'd actually eat inside."

Grace laughed and got out of the vehicle. "Sorry."

"No big deal." Sara hooked arms with her and led Grace inside. "I think we were both waiting for each other to show up. I just happened to spot your Jeep. I remembered it from that day we first met at Liv's."

She and Grace entered and found a booth to settle into. "That wasn't my best moment," Grace said.

"It's okay. Liv explained things to me."

"She did?"

"Of course. I should tell you now, there's no such thing as TMI between us. We've known each other since high school."

The waitress came at that moment to take their order. Grace chose her usual meatloaf, even if it was lunchtime, but held back on the pie. Her stomach was on the verge of upset, and she wasn't certain how much it could handle. Just what had Liv told Sara about her? Did she know about Carly? When they laughed and enjoyed the evening at Liv's, Sara didn't seem like a judgmental type of person.

Some people were hard to read, and if Sara didn't like her, Grace wondered how much that would influence Liv.

"Whatever you're thinking about, you probably should just ask me." Sara spoke quietly and with the hint of a smile on her face. "I honestly thought you and I should take the time to get to know each other. Liv is important to both of us. We both love her, and we're going to be around each other a lot. I don't want anything to be awkward or weird."

"Sorry. I just...I don't know what to say."

"Say what's on your mind. Please."

Grace held Sara's gentle gaze. "I want you to like me, Sara. I don't know what all Liv told you about me. She never mentioned anything specific, but I don't want you to think badly of me."

"Why would I do that? You haven't done anything." Sara reached across the table and covered Grace's hand with hers. "Liv told me about your ex. No details, but enough so I'd understand why certain things have happened. I don't know what judgment you think I'm going to make, but I can tell you that I think your ex is a horrible person. It makes me sick to think of someone as sweet as you going through that."

"You think I'm sweet?" Grace said, hoping to deflect the conversation away from her past.

Sara picked up on the cue and patted her hand. "I do. I wouldn't let just anyone date my best friend."

"Is that so? That's why we're here, right? So you can determine if I'm worthy?"

"Something like that." Sara sat back as the waitress delivered their food.

Grace hadn't paid much attention to Sara's order and was shocked at the number of dishes arranged in front of her. Sara was skinny, but if Grace ate a hamburger packed with everything imaginable, along with a double order of steak fries, coleslaw, and a milkshake, she'd be sick for a week.

"Your food's getting cold," Sara said.

"Can I ask you a question?"

"Of course."

"How can you eat all that? You've got enough food for two people."

Sara laughed outright. "You sound like Liv. She's always on me about what I eat." Sara had a fry in her hand and used it like a pointer, aimed at the burger. "I've got a high metabolism. I've tried to gain weight, because my doctor says I'm too skinny. But that ain't happening." She popped the fry into her mouth. "I stay skinny. Most of the girls at work hate me for that, but it's in my genes. My mom's skinny, too."

Grace dug into her meal, her stomach calmer with the change of topic. "I don't have any problems with my metabolism. I'm the same size I was when I was eighteen, though I did weigh more when I was at my height of fitness."

"You're not at your height now?" Sara lifted an eyebrow, and the gesture gave Grace a laugh. "Have you looked in a mirror lately? You're not exactly out of shape."

"Well, I'm not like I was. Three years ago, I was a climbing instructor and worked out every day. My muscles were solid, and I could boulder a V14."

"V14? What's that?"

"Climbs are rated by how tough they are. V14 is near the top of the difficulty level. I've done a couple of V16s, but that was before..."

"Before Carly?" Sara's voice was soft and compassionate. "I've seen the scar on your arm."

Grace rubbed the reminder of Carly's worst damage to her body. It seemed no matter what, the topic was going to be Carly. "Yes. It took two years of surgeries and therapy to get my arm conditioned enough to climb again. I'm not anywhere close to doing the climbs I used to do, and I miss it. Climbing has always been my escape."

"Do you still have to escape now?"

Grace pondered that question for a moment. Did she? Her thoughts turned to Liv, and she realized she no longer felt the need to run or hide. The biggest need she had was to simply be with the woman she loved. The woman she could spend the rest of her life with.

Grace said, "No. For the first time in years I very much feel at peace. Olivia is the love of my life. She's there even when I don't realize I need her. I don't know what I'd do without her."

"I have a feeling you're not going to find out, either. I've never seen Liv look at a woman, or talk about a woman, the ways she does with you. And trust me, I've helped Liv through a lot of relationships, including our brief time together. She falls fast. I was so worried because I could tell it was different with you. I don't want to see her hurt like she was with Jane."

"Me either. I've never felt this way before, and sometimes it's scary. But scary in a good way. It's exhilarating, exciting, and amazing."

"Liv says the same thing, actually. It's so weird to see a woman as butch as Liv gush over her girlfriend."

"She gushes? Seriously?"

"Oh yeah. Like a teenager with her first crush. It's hilarious, really. She'll start talking about you, and she rattles on and on to a point where I can't really follow her anymore. And she tends to tell me the same thing more than once." Sara gave a dramatic sigh and rolled her eyes. "She's insufferable."

"Oh, you poor dear. How can I help?"

"Marry the woman. Give her someone else to talk to every day. Hell, give her something else to do everyday."

"Marry her? Isn't it a bit soon? I mean, we're only just planning to move in together."

Sara made a hand gesture like she was shooing away a fly. "You're getting the U-Haul. Might as well make it official."

"Does that mean I pass the test?"

"There's a test?" Sara feigned surprise. "I mean, I know there's a rule book, but I had no idea there's a test."

"Could be different here, but in the U.S. there's a test and I'm hoping like hell I passed it."

"I'll have to think very hard about this. Here in the Yukon we take this stuff very seriously."

"So seriously that you didn't even know there was a test?"

"Um..." Sara pretended to look around as if someone were eavesdropping. "I was hoping you didn't notice that. I mean, what kind of best friend would I be if I didn't know to give the new girlfriend the test?"

"I think we can keep this a secret. Just between us."

"Oh good. In that case," Sara lifted her glass of cola in a toast, "I hereby pronounce you have passed the test and may proceed as girlfriend to one Olivia Templeton."

Grace good-naturedly tapped her glass against Sara's. "Well said."

"So, how much dirt do you want on Liv?"

"Dirt? Like what kind of hell she raised at university?"

"For instance."

"Hmm." Grace rubbed her hands together. "I think I'm going to like being friends with you, Sara."

"Of course you will." She waved the waitress over. "Could you get me a piece of apple pie?"

"Me, too," Grace added. "That's my fave, but I need two scoops of ice cream with it. Cinnamon if you have it."

"Seriously?" Sara giggled. "Are you reading my mind?"

"Apparently." The waitress cleared the table and after she was gone, Grace said, "Every time *Ojiichan* and I come here, I have my dessert first. It's like a weird tradition I started when I was a kid."

"It's not weird. As a matter of fact, if you want to meet me here sometime next week for lunch, I'll join you in that tradition."

"Sara, I think this is the beginning of a beautiful friendship."

Sara joined her in a fit of giggles that only stopped long enough for them to enjoy dessert.

****

Saturday nights were always a crazy time at the Pot O'Gold. Liv sat at the bar and watched Izzy and two other women pass drinks to people so fast she was amazed they could keep up. She checked her watch to see that Grace was now ten minutes late. Liv considered heading back to the house to see what was keeping Grace, but it would be her luck they'd pass each other. She'd rather show some patience. Easier said than done, considering the gift she carried in her pocket.

"Is this seat taken?" The sultry voice in her ear caused a tremor, and not in a nice way. She would recognize her anywhere. Liv had to put her drink down before she dropped it. The woman spoke again, "It's been awhile, Livvy."

Liv closed her eyes and willed her to go away. She was hallucinating. Or having a bad dream. A nightmare. But when she opened her eyes, she found herself gazing into a pair of gray eyes she knew almost as well as her own.

"Jane." It was all she could say. Her throat felt like it had seized shut.

"You look like you've seen a ghost, Livvy." Jane brushed her fingers along the bare skin of the arm Liv rested against the bar. It was the only thing keeping her from falling over. Jane's touch was sensual, and goose bumps trailed behind her fingers.

"Wh-what are you doing here?"

"Just came in to get a drink."

"I meant what are you doing here, in Whitehorse. I thought you went to live in Toronto."

Jane lifted one shoulder in a half shrug. Her eyes searched Liv's, and Liv was unable to look away. "Got bored. I'm not cut out for life in the big city. I much prefer to live here."

"And Nicolette?"

"Even more boring. She made me realize the mistakes I've made." Jane slid closer and soon there was barely air between their bodies. "I never should have left you, Livvy."

It was hard to breathe. Liv felt the familiar warmth rush through her body and knew her face was flushed. Jane's lilac perfume filled her nostrils and brought back vivid memories. Wild nights of passion and discovery. She never realized she wasn't truly in love with Jane until Grace Kato entered her life and stole her heart.

Jane pressed her body against Liv's, her knee slipping in between Liv's legs to press against her crotch. Jane's breath tickled her ear as she nipped the edge of it. Her tongue followed the curve of Liv's ear, down the side of her neck until she reached her pulse point. Jane's lips caressed the sensitive spot, and Liv had to grab her by the arms to pull back enough to see Jane's face. The smoky gray eyes stared back at her with an important question in them.

"I'm with someone," Liv said shakily, cursing her own body for its reactions to Jane.

"So what? I don't see her here." Jane's lips met Liv's in a searing kiss.

Liv shoved her back with enough force that Jane nearly fell on her ass. Liv wished she had. "You bitch. How dare you."

"How dare I what? Kiss you? Ha! As if you didn't enjoy it as much as I did." Jane's eyes narrowed for a second when she glanced at something over Liv's shoulder.

"Get the fuck away from me."

"But, baby," Jane said as she touched Liv's cheek with her fingertips, "I came back for you."

"Because Nicolette kicked your sorry ass out. I don't care, Jane. I don't want anything to do with you."

Jane whispered in her ear, "You'll think differently when you end up alone."

"Go fuck yourself, Jane." Liv shoved Jane away again and headed for the door, figuring she'd wait for Grace outside. But Grace stood near the entrance, her face pale as tears streamed down her cheeks. "Gracie—"

Grace spun on her heels and ran out the door. It took Liv a stunned second to follow her. Grace hadn't gone far and leaned against a car in the parking lot. Her body shook with her sobbing.

Liv was afraid to touch her. Instead she stayed within arm's reach and spoke softly. "Gracie, please. Talk to me."

"You—I trusted you. I...I...go away. I can't do this."

"Do what? Gracie, what you saw—it's not what you think. Jane surprised me and—"

"Jane? That was Jane?" Grace made a sound like a cross between a hiccup and a laugh. She still wouldn't look at Liv. "Guess I can't blame you. She's gorgeous. Who wouldn't rather be with her than me?"

"That's not true. I'm not interested in Jane."

"Don't lie to me." Grace spoke so quietly that Liv wasn't sure she'd heard her correctly. "Don't lie to me. It's the only thing I ever asked of you. It's my fault. I knew better than to trust again."

"I'm not lying."

"I saw you kissing her. Her hands were all over you, and you weren't in a hurry to push her away." Grace began sobbing again, and Liv's heart ached to hold her. "How long? How long has she been back—with you?"

"She's not with me." Liv grabbed her arm and turned Grace around so they were facing each other.

Grace yanked her arm free. "Don't touch me. Don't you ever touch me again."

"You have to let me explain."

"I don't have to do anything. Not anymore. I've learned my lesson. I should thank you for that."

"What are you talking about?"

"I don't ever want to see you again, Olivia." Grace started past her, but Liv took hold of her arm again. In a flash, Grace shoved Liv against a car and pinned her there with her forearm under Liv's chin. "I told you not to touch me."

The expression on Grace's face was somewhere between anger

and hurt. The pressure she put against Liv's neck made it hard to respond, so Liv tapped her elbow. "I—can't..."

Grace released her and backed away. "I loved you, Olivia. More than I ever thought possible."

"Loved?" she squeaked out, rubbing her sore throat. "Gracie, you're not giving me a chance to explain."

"What's to explain? I saw you with her. She was smiling, laughing, and when she—when she kissed you...just stay the hell away from me."

Grace turned again to leave but didn't move. Liv wanted to go to her, but she was afraid to activate that fight reaction again. "I love you, Gracie Lee."

"That's what Carly always said." Grace's voice broke. "It was a mistake. She didn't mean it. She loved me. After every affair, after every beating...she loved me."

"I would never hurt you, Grace."

"Too late." Grace quickly walked away.

Liv felt frozen to the spot. She couldn't move. Couldn't breathe as her entire world fell apart. She watched until Grace was beyond her sight, lost in the crowds of people milling along the sidewalk.

A hand touched her arm and she flinched. When she looked it was directly into Sara's worried eyes.

"Liv? What happened? I saw you run out of the pub." She reached forward to move Liv's hand from her neck. "Are you hurt? Terry!"

"I'm fine," Liv said, though she was anything but.

"Bullshit. Your neck's blood red. What the fuck happened? Who did this?"

Liv avoided Sara's gaze. "Grace."

"Grace?"

"What's wrong?" Terry asked as she joined them.

"Her neck," Sara said, but her voice held less anger.

"I'm fine." Liv tried to protest, but she lacked any strength behind the words. "Grace left me. She thinks I was cheating on her with Jane."

"Jane?" Sara's voice went up a decibel. "What the fuck? Jane's been gone for—"

"She was at the bar just now. Probably still is. She came up to me and acted like nothing ever happened between us. She...kissed me and Grace saw it."

"Liv..."

"She ruined my life again, Sara. And it took her less than five minutes."

Liv hadn't realized she was crying until Sara wiped a thumb across her cheek. "What exactly did Grace see?"

"Jane with her hands all over me. But Grace didn't see me shove Jane away. She didn't hear me tell her to fuck off. I turned around and saw Grace standing there, staring at me and crying. I saw in her eyes how hurt she was. I tried to talk to her, but she never wants to see me again."

"She knows about Jane, right? About what that bitch did to you?"

Liv nodded, not trusting herself to speak.

"Then you have to go after her. If she won't talk to you, then you do all the talking."

"I tried that."

"Then try again. Try harder." Sara held Liv's face in her hands so their gazes met. "I mean it. She's the one, Liv. You and I both know it. You have to go after her and do whatever it takes to get her to listen to you."

"When I did that just now, she almost killed me."

"That's an exaggeration," Sara said.

Liv pointed to her neck. "Is it?"

"Grace did that?" Terry asked, reminding Liv she was also there.

"Yes. I made the mistake of grabbing Grace's arm. She pinned me to the car before she ran off."

"You still have to talk to her." Sara glared at Liv. "If you don't, I will."

"Oh no. You're not going to—"

"You think I won't?" Sara took a step in the direction Grace left.

Terry kept looking between Sara and Liv as if at some very weird tennis match. When neither woman spoke, Terry finally did. "I'm going to stick my nose right in this one. Sara, you're not going anywhere. Liv, you're going after your girlfriend. I've heard about this woman endlessly from Sara, and if half of what she says is true, Grace is an idiot if she doesn't at least let you try to explain. The only way to know if she is or not, is to go after her." Liv still didn't move, so Terry said, "Now. Right now, Liv. Before she gets too far away."

Liv fingered the gift box in her pocket again. "I was going to ask her to marry me."

Tears pooled in Sara's eyes as she smiled at Liv. "And she'd be stupid to say no. Go. Find her. Talk to her. Keep telling her how you feel."

"K." Liv pulled Sara into a warm embrace and leaned down to whisper, "I don't know why you stick around. You're too good for me."

Sara kissed her on the cheek. "I am too good for you," she teased. "That's why we broke up. But Grace—she's perfect for you."

"I hope she feels the same way," Liv said. She thanked Terry and took off at a jog through the maze of people on the sidewalk.

****

Grace's chest tightened with each step. Breaths came in sharp, shallow gasps. She was forced to stop and lean against a wall to prevent falling over.

The world collapsed around her.

It was happening all over again.

No. Liv would never hit her. But she'd done the one thing she promised never to do. She'd hurt Grace. Hurt her in a way Carly never could.

Grace didn't love Carly with all her heart and soul. She never loved Carly so much that a touch from her could steal her breath away. Liv—she loved Liv that much. Maybe more.

Her heart hammered in her chest as though it wanted out.

Tears blurred her vision as Grace sank to the ground.

The pain only worsened as sobs wracked her body.

"Hey? You okay?"

The voice startled her. It was soft and kind, and through her tears Grace saw the young man kneeling in front of her. Other people, maybe three or four, milled behind him.

The young man used a tissue to gently dab at her cheeks. His smile was kind and reflected in his eyes. He had short, spikey hair and smelled of cheap beer and aftershave.

"Are you hurt, honey? Can I call someone for you?"

Grace shook her head, unable to speak around the constriction of her throat. She accepted a fresh   tissue from him.

He leaned closer and whispered, "Look, I've been there. We all have. But you got to pick yourself up and move on. Especially from this mangy spot." His expression nearly brought a smile to her face. He took her hand and helped her to her feet.

They stood eye to eye. He gripped her upper arm and said, "Butch it up, buttercup. And if she's really worth the tears, fight for her."

He kissed her cheek and joined his friends as they continued into the night.

Was Liv worth fighting for?

Or had Grace already lost the fight?

****

Twenty minutes later, Liv came to Burke Park and found Grace on a swing, gently swaying, her gaze on the ground. She hugged herself, and even at a distance, Liv could tell she was crying.

Liv took a moment to catch her breath before carefully moving toward the most important person in her life. Her heart broke again at the agonizing sight before her. How could Liv fix this much damage?

She felt the need to run away, but unsteady legs carried her forward.

"Gracie—"

"Go away," Grace said. Her voice was quiet and broken by the hiccups of her sobs. "I don't want to see you."

"No. I can't just leave you like this." Liv knelt in front of her, purposely not touching her. "You're angry and hurt, but I'm not about to walk away. At the very least, let me take you home. We can talk tomorrow."

"No, we can't. I called *Ojiichan* and he's on his way. You can leave."

"Grace, would you at least look at me?"

Grace did and Liv nearly fell over at the hurt in those soft eyes. Grace said, "Please. Just leave me alone."

Liv spoke around the lump in her throat. "I'm not giving up on you, Gracie. I love you." Liv said those last words softly. Grace looked away and Liv stood. She waited near the merry-go-round until Harry pulled up and Grace was safely inside his truck.

Harry glanced at her as he drove away, and Liv saw the sadness in his eyes as well. She'd made one helluva mess. No. Jane made the mess and once again left Liv to clean it all up. She stuck her hands in her pockets, kept a strong hold on the velvet box in her right hand, and headed back to the bar.

She walked by Sara and Terry and zeroed in on Jane. She was leaning on the edge of the bar talking to some unsuspecting young woman. Once Liv actually saw Jane, she couldn't hold it back any longer. She shoved the young woman aside, grabbed Jane by her upper arms, and slammed her against the nearest wall.

Jane was obviously dazed, and for an instant, Liv felt bad for hurting her. But that only lasted an instant. "You fucking bitch! I can't even begin to tell you how much I hate you right now. Two years ago you screwed me over, and I didn't think I'd ever be able to function, let alone fall in love. But I did. I was so happy with you gone. I got my shit together, and I built a good life for myself. Then you fucking walk back in like you own me. You knew about Grace. I don't know how and I don't care. You kissed me in front of her to make sure you caused trouble between us. It wasn't enough that you shattered my heart when you left me. You had to come back here and do it again. What the fuck did I ever do to you, Jane? Why do you feel the need to hurt me?"

A crowd had gathered around them, and Liv let Jane go. Jane slumped against the wall but didn't speak. Live didn't actually care if she did or not. It wasn't a rhetorical question. It was something she'd never understand.

"I don't fucking care where you go, Jane, but you damn sure best stay away from me, from Grace, from anyone that I care about. You got that?"

Jane stared at her, but Liv was pretty sure her head nodded slightly.

Liv shoved her way out of the bar and into the fresh, night air. She felt Sara's arm go around her just as she crumpled to the ground and sobbed.

Chapter Sixteen

Liv hung up the phone and resettled herself in her desk chair. She stared out the window at a beautifully sunny afternoon. Over the past week, she'd called Grace's phone so many times that it now said the voicemail was full. Which meant Grace wasn't even listening to the pleading messages she left her.

Today Liv had called three times. Voicemail was still full, and Liv was tempted to try calling Harry. But she didn't want him to feel like he was in the middle of their problem. What Liv really wanted was to go over to Harry's and talk to Grace face-to-face. It wasn't a good idea, though. Grace clearly didn't want to talk to her. Still. She could be there in a couple of hours. Or maybe she could go to the mine.

"Fuck." Liv placed her head in her hands and put her elbows on the desk. "This sucks."

"Still not taking your calls?" Sara walked in and sat on the couch.

"No. Her voicemail is full. What am I supposed to do? I can't just leave it like this."

"Let me talk to her."

"No." Liv's tone was more forceful than she wanted, so she calmly said, "I'm sorry, but no. You don't know her all that well, and I don't think she'll be any more willing to talk to you than she is to me."

Sara sat forward. "Who says I'm going to let her do any talking?"

"Sara, remember how you told me not to get involved when Angel hit you? Well, this is me asking you to return the favor."

"Um, as I recall you interfered anyway and I was pissed as hell. Bad example there my friend. Look, you're right. I don't know Grace very well, but I do know you. I know you've barely slept, only eaten when someone else brought you food, and haven't left this office in three days."

"How do you know all that? You haven't even seen me."

Sara raised one eyebrow, her expression clearly saying, "Duh."

"Of course. My idiot brother called you."

"Close. Your mother." Sara held up her hand to stop any comments from Liv. "He called your mother when you refused to talk to him and he found you pacing the office at three in the morning. Your mother told me she's been bringing you food every day, and I've been going past your house all week. You're never there."

"Fine. So what? Maybe I don't want to go home." Liv sat back in her chair, feeling more deflated than before Sara came in. Hearing it all spelled out made it sound so much worse. If that was even possible.

"You won't go home because it reminds you of her," Sara said, "and because her key was in your mailbox." Sara tossed the rainbow nugget keychain onto Liv's desk. "I thought I'd check your mail. This is all I found inside."

Liv couldn't breathe. She gently fingered the nugget. It was such a ridiculous thing, but it seemed so appropriate at the time. Barely a month ago, Grace was going to move in with her. Start a new life with her. The black velvet box she'd carried all day Saturday sat next to where the nugget landed. If she'd waited for Grace at home, or maybe not gone into the bar ahead of her, maybe they'd be together celebrating. Grace would have said yes, right? She'd have wanted to marry Liv. Right?

"Hey." Sara's quiet voice startled her. "I'm sorry if I sounded harsh, but, honey, you can't keep   hiding."

"Why not?" Liv asked through her tears. "Why the hell not? I find someone I could love forever, and she didn't believe I'm not having an affair. Yes, Jane kissed me. She surprised me, and it took a few seconds to react. I was in shock, you know? And now Grace is gone. Sara, I wanted to marry her. I wanted to spend the rest of my life making her feel special. How am I supposed to come back from that? She won't talk to me. I managed to talk to Harry a couple of times, just for a few seconds, and he was sweet and sympathetic and still she wouldn't take the phone from him. I heard her say she's done with me."

"Bullshit."

"Excuse me?"

"Bullshit." Sara got to her feet and moved to Liv's side. "Get your ass up. We're going to lunch, and we're going to make a plan."

"There's no plan to make. You can't—"

"I can and I will." She pulled on Liv's arm until she was also standing. Sara wrapped her arms around Liv and held her as more tears sprang forth. Liv rested her head on Sara's shoulder.

"You always said I was broken after Jane." Liv sniffled and wiped tears from her cheeks. "I think I'm beyond repair this time."

"More bullshit." Sara moved back enough to look her in the eyes. "You're strong and you're going to make that woman talk to you. And if she says no again, I'm going to intervene. Like you said, I owe you one for Angel."

"You're never going to let me live down Angel, are you?"

"No way." Sara hooked arms with Liv and moved her to the door. "Besides, it was the best thing you could've done for me. I just didn't want to admit it at the time."

"Then I'm forgiven."

"That depends."

"On?"

Sara smirked. "On if I manage to get Grace to talk to you or not."

****

Grace avoided going into Whitehorse for days. Until Charlie convinced her to retrieve an order he'd made at the hardware store. The last thing she wanted was to be anywhere Liv could conceivably show up.

And since she was going, Harry added a few things to the list. It felt like a conspiracy to get her away from the mine. Maybe they were right to ban together against her. Most of the time she was either losing her temper over the smallest things or going off to any spot that had no one around. She hated taking her anger out on her family, but didn't seem to be able to stop it.

Liv was never far from her mind and that made things worse. Even now her temper rose and that was unacceptable. Grace needed to turn her back on Liv and move on. Except she couldn't. Liv was the first woman to ever show Grace what real love was like.

Images of Liv's face hovering above her as they made love; the feel of her soft lips against Grace's; the way a single touch would sent shivers through Grace's body...

Grace took a deep breath and tried to shove all thoughts of Liv out of her head. She needed to get on with her day. The sooner she was done the sooner she could get back to the mine and work until she was ready to collapse. It was the only way she could get any sleep.

Grace entered the hardware store and did her best to smile at Jim, the store manager. "I hear you have some stuff for Charlie."

"Not much," Jim said, the dark, leathery skin of his face crinkled into a grin. "But I'm glad he sent you to get them. It's nice to see a pretty face, instead of his ugly mug."

"Thanks, Jim," she said, feeling a tiny blush color her cheeks.

"You doing okay, Gracie?"

She shrugged, unable to bring to words the turmoil she was going through. "Life happens and we move on."

"It's a shame about you and Liv," he said as they headed to the rear of the store. "I thought you two made a nice couple."

"Me and Liv?"

"Yeah. I've known Liv her whole life." He slowly shook his head. "Harry was so happy for you."

"I didn't realize everyone—I mean that anyone knew we were together."

Jim stared at her like she had two heads. His eyebrows rose to his hairline. "Seriously? Honey, I don't think there's anyone in Whitehorse who didn't know about you two. You do realize that Harry Kato is the world's biggest gossip. Right? He plays poker with my wife and they talk about everyone."

Jim loaded some boxes onto a trolley. "Once Bernadette knows it, everyone knows it."

"Oh." Grace quietly followed him outside to the truck.

They loaded the boxes without speaking and when done, Jim said, "I'm sorry about what happen."

"Thanks Jim," she said, not meeting his eyes. She couldn't take the sympathy in them as she now wondered if she'd encounter others in town that would say the same things to her. She didn't need their sorrow. What she really needed was to be alone.

"See ya, Gracie." Jim rolled his trolley back into the store.

Grace felt her anger return and slammed the tailgate closed, spun around, and found Liv standing on the sidewalk staring at her.

"Hey, Grace."

Grace froze. She had a lot of errands to run and didn't need to deal with Liv just then. Or ever. Bad enough the whole city knew their business. She brushed past Liv and headed toward the bank.

"Can I walk with you?" Liv asked.

Grace felt a familiar tingle in her belly when Liv got closer and cursed her body for being such a traitor. She allowed herself a glance into those amazing blue eyes and her knees got weak. Those beautiful eyes searched her face and held her when she wanted to look away.

"I suppose. Free country." It was the first thing she'd said to Liv in more than two weeks.

Liv's face broke into a wide grin. "Cool."

Liv strode beside her in silence. Grace went directly to the assayer's office, took care of her business there, and started for the bank. Liv remained at her side.

"How have you been?" Liv asked. "You know I've been calling."

"I know. I got your messages."

"Why didn't you call me back?" They stopped next to the bank's door. Grace noticed that Liv was careful to keep some distance between them.

"We have nothing to discuss, Liv." Grace took hold of the door handle.

"We've got a lot to talk about. Please let me explain."

Grace shook her head and entered the bank. She was glad that Liv didn't follow and hoped she'd be gone when Grace finished her business. She was in line for the teller when she spotted Sara.

"Miss Kato, I'm so glad you're here. Could you step into my office?"

Grace sighed and followed Sara rather than argue in full view of the others in the bank. Once inside, Grace stayed close to the door. "I need to deposit my check so I can make a payment—"

"Please sit down." Sara was all business. "This is personal. Nothing to do with Harry's loan."

"If this is about Liv—"

"It is and you really need to sit down. Since you won't talk to her, the least you can do is talk to me. We are friends, right?"

"Did she put you up to this? Is that why she followed me here?"

"Wait, she's here?"

"Outside the door," Grace said, trying to keep the annoyance from her voice, but failing.

"Interesting, but no. She didn't put me up to this. In fact, she'll kick my ass when she finds out I'm talking to you, but it'll be worth it."

Grace plopped into one of the plush chairs in front of Sara's desk. "I don't know—I don't want to make you mad, Sara, but it's really none of your business."

"We can argue semantics another time. Right now I need to have my best friend's back. That bitch Jane is to blame here. She's a user. She came on to Liv to get a rise out of her. It worked. It always did. That's Jane's M.O. She'd break Liv's heart, walk away, then come back, turn on the charm, and Liv was hooked. Only the last time she never came back."

"She looked back to me."

"Yeah, after three years, but you didn't see everything."

"I saw enough. Liv wasn't being forced to kiss that woman."

"No. Jane's damn sexy, and I don't doubt that Liv reacted to her. But reacting to a woman's kiss and cheating on the one you love are two different things. Liv shoved the bitch away and ran after you. She stayed with you until Harry showed up. She went back into the bar and had it out with Jane. She shoved her against a wall but stopped herself from doing any real harm. I've never seen her that angry. When she came out, she was a mess."

"Sara, please don't..."

Sara leaned forward in her seat. "Jane has taken a lot away from Liv. Taking you was the last straw. We tried to get her to go homI let her cry on me until she fell asleep. It took two days to get her to leave the house and she's spent all her time at the office or one of the mines. She's sleeping on the couch in the office, if she sleeps at all. She only eats when her mom brings her food or I pull her over to the pub, which isn't often, I might add.

"She's a wreck. You need to hear her side of the story. She loves you, Gracie. And not like she loved me and sure as hell not like she loved Jane. She's in love with you. She wants to spend the rest of her life with you."

"Stop. I can't do this."

"You have to. You need to be an adult about this. She's been so good to you—and if you don't at least talk to her it might make me have to start calling you every day. And I will. I think Liv is close to giving up, and when that happens—I can't stand to think about that. It took me months after Jane left to get Liv back to life. If you leave her, I don't think there'll be anything I can do."

Grace stood so abruptly she startled Sara. "You act like she's going to kill herself over me. Don't try to lay that on me. That's not fair."

"She'd never hurt herself, Grace. That's not what I mean. But she will stop living. She'll work and work hard until that's all she has in her life. She'll push away her friends, her family—me. She's already started doing it, and there's nothing I can do to stop it. If you would at least talk to her, then she can tell herself she tried. At least give her closure. I think you can manage that."

Grace had no reply and walked out of the office, careful not to slam the door behind her. She made the deposit and hurried outside. Liv was still there and fell into step with her as Grace headed back to her truck.

They were silent until Grace reached the truck. "Look, I don't want to talk to you, but if it means you'll stop calling and following me, then I will." She faced Liv, careful not to be caught by those blue eyes. "Come by the cabin tonight at eight."

"Thanks."

Grace didn't reply. She got into the truck and drove off, hoping she'd hadn't just made a huge mistake.

****

At exactly eight o'clock, Liv stepped out of her truck and stared at the door to the cabin. The light was on, and she thought she saw someone seated near the window. Her brain tried to tell her legs to move forward, but they refused. Her chest tightened, and for a moment, she thought she might pass out. A feeling of dread kept her rooted to the spot.

She had no idea how long she stood there before the front door opened. A lone figure moved along the porch and onto the driveway. She stopped a few feet from where Liv stood.

"Are you coming in?" Grace asked.

"I—I planned on it." Liv ran fingers through her unruly hair, thankful for the darkened evening. She didn't think she could bear looking into Grace's eyes. "Gracie, I'm sorry. I'm sorry that you had to see that. I know you don't believe me, but I wasn't cheating on you. Jane did that to—to fuck with me. She found out I was seeing you and decided to do something about it. She's always gotten whatever she wants—including me. She was pissed to come back and find I wasn't available. Not to her. Not ever again."

Grace crossed her arms over her chest. "You're right. I don't believe you. How can I? I know what I saw."

"You don't know. Gracie, I wasn't cheating on you. She kissed me. Not the other way around. I love you. I asked you to meet me because I planned to ask you to marry me." Liv removed the velvet box from her pocket and held it up for Grace to see. "I bought the ring months ago. It took me that long to get up my nerve to ask you. I love you, and I want to be with you the rest of my life."

Grace shook her head, and Liv could tell she was crying. "No. Don't—"

"Gracie?" Harry was on the porch, leaning heavily on the rail, one hand clutching his chest. "Gracie—"

Grace ran to him and caught Harry as he collapsed. Liv was by her side instantly.

"*Ojiichan?*" Grace gently laid him on his back. "Call an ambulance," she said to Liv.

"Is he breathing?" Liv pulled out her phone.

"Yes. But his heartbeat's too slow. It happened once before and we—we almost lost him." Grace bent closer and spoke softly to him.

Liv made the call and prayed the ambulance would arrive in time.

Chapter Seventeen

Liv anxiously paced the length of the waiting room, sidestepping a toddler playing with Legos on one end and a passed-out drunk on the other. The helicopter carrying Harry had arrived at the hospital half an hour before she did. Grace rode with Harry, leaving Liv to race back to the city like the devil was on her ass.

During her long drive to Whitehorse Hospital, Liv managed to contact Grace's family, call Sara and ask her to make travel arrangements for the Katos, and leave a voicemail for her dad. She took her cell phone out of her back pocket and checked it for the hundredth time. When it rang, she nearly dropped it.

"Hello?"

"Olivia? This is Hariku Kato."

"Hi, Mr. Kato. I'm sorry, but I don't have any news on your father yet. Grace is with him, though."

"I understand. Matthew told me you called, but he was unclear exactly what happened."

His commanding tone left it clear to Liv he wanted answers. She did her best to control her hammering heart as she responded, "We aren't sure. Grace and I were in the driveway, and we heard him call out her name from the porch. When we got there, he—he wasn't —his heart wasn't beating very fast. We did what we could, but it took so long for the ambulance to get there, and they called in the helicopter, and I'm so sorry. It's all my fault..."

And it was. If she hadn't been there fighting with Grace, Harry wouldn't have had a heart attack.

Her legs collapsed, and if not for sudden, strong arms, Liv would have hit the floor. Tears she'd held back sprang forth. "I'm so sorry."

She heard him answer but didn't understand what he said. Someone took the phone from her. Cradled in a warm embrace, Liv sobbed. So many things whirled in her mind, none of them making much sense and all of them part of a chain reaction that caused this mess. Jane at the bar. Grace not speaking to her. Harry's collapse on the porch...it was too much.

"Hey, take it easy," a soothing and familiar voice said in her ear.

It took her a few moments to realize who was holding her so tightly. She'd expected her father, but when she leaned back, she stared into eyes so different from hers. David's concern was clear on his pale face. He wiped her wet cheek with his rough, calloused hand.

"You're okay," he said, taking a shaky breath. "When Dad said you were at the emergency room..."

"It's Harry," Liv said.

"I know. Dad told me. I pulled into the parking lot right behind him. Livvy, why didn't you call me?"

"I—I didn't think of it. I had to call the Katos first, and then I wanted to make travel arrangements for them so they wouldn't have to worry about it, but I couldn't. Thank God for Sara. She's getting that done. I could hardly think on my way here. I just had to get here."

"Where's Sara?"

"Probably still working out arrangements," Liv said.

A gentle hand landed on her shoulder. Liv glanced up into her father's worried face. "I gave Hariku all the travel details," Jonas said. At her questioning gaze, he responded, "Sara called me. The Katos get here tomorrow around eight at night. It's the soonest she could get them here. She'll be here later."

"Good."

"Let's go sit down." Jonas led them to a row of four empty seats. Once they were seated, he said, "Tell me why you think this is all your fault."

"Because it is." Liv explained to them what happened. "If Harry dies—I'll never forgive myself."

Jonas gave her a one-armed hug. "Harry's had a bad heart for as long as I've known him. This didn't happen because of you. Trust me on that."

"You can't be so sure, Dad. Our breakup put a lot of stress on him, and that could have caused the heart attack."

Her father seemed to consider her words for a moment, then he said, "He's been having problems for a while. Couple of months. I've taken him to the cardiologist twice. There's a block in a major artery, and not much can be done. Harry's old, sweetheart. And his heart isn't the strongest anymore."

"I get that, but—"

"But nothing. Instead of beating yourself up, maybe you should check on Grace. I'm sure she needs you right about now."

Liv shook her head. "No. I'm the last person she wants."

"Kato family?" A nurse at the emergency room entrance called out.

Liv was on her feet in seconds. "Yes?"

"Are you Olivia?" she asked.

Liv's heart beat triple time. She felt her dad standing behind her. "Yes."

"Follow me, please." Liv didn't hesitate to accompany the nurse. They walked a fast pace down a wide hallway. Liv kept her eyes on the woman in front of her, not daring to look at the people in hospital beds that lined one side of the hall. The antiseptic smell smacked her in the face and made her nauseous. She kept her mind on moving forward and nearly ran the woman over when she stopped at a door. "They're in here."

"Thanks," she said. Her hands felt sweaty as Liv turned the knob and entered the surprisingly large room. Her eyes were immediately drawn to the figure on the bed. Harry looked tiny, almost childlike, against the stark white sheets and huge bed he was in. Tubes and wires went everywhere. A machine beeped a slow, steady rhythm.

Grace stood beside the bed. She leaned on the metallic rail, Harry's hand clasped in hers.

Harry's eyes were closed. His skin pale.

"Hey," Liv said quietly.

Grace turned her head slightly and caught Liv's gaze. Liv almost started bawling again when she saw the strain on Grace's features. "Could you please stay with him for a bit? I need to call my dad."

"I already called him." Liv took a step forward but stood on the other side of the bed, keeping a distance from Grace. "Their flight details are all set. They should get here, to the hospital, by eight tonight."

"How—when did you call them?"

"On my way here. Sara took care of the flight stuff. It's the least I could do." Liv pulled her gaze from Grace and touched Harry's leg. Even with the blanket over him, it felt cold to touch. "I'm sorry, Gracie."

"For what?"

"For this. I should have left you alone when you told me to." Liv backed away so Grace wouldn't see her start crying again. "Let me know if you need anything."

"Wait." Grace was suddenly beside her. "You didn't cause this to happen. He's been sick for a while. But thanks for getting hold of my family. It means a lot to me."

"I'd do anything for you, Grace."

Grace touched her arm, urging her to turn around. "I meant what I said. Thank you."

"What can I do to help you?" Liv held Grace's gaze, hoping she'd want her there. She needed to be with Grace. She yearned to wrap her into a comforting embrace and never let go.

"I—I need you here. Please stay with me. I don't want to be alone."

Liv touched Grace's hand briefly. "I'm not going anywhere."

Grace's smile warmed her heart. "Thanks." She went back to her vigil next to Harry, and Liv sat in the chair on the opposite side of the bed. She took Harry's cool hand in hers and did the only thing she could. Wait.

****

Grace stepped outside the doors to the emergency room and took a deep breath of fresh air. At Liv's insistence, she left *Ojiichan*; there was nothing she could do while they waited on the results of some tests. The blockage in his heart was in a dangerous place, in an artery they called the widow maker. Appropriate, since lots of people died from blocks like this. The doctor said there was a remote chance they could clear the blockage, perhaps putting in a stent to support the artery, but *Ojiichan* had to be more stable first. There was no way to know how long that could take or if it would even happen.

On an adult level, she understood he was ninety-three and had lived a good, long life. He might even be ready to die, having been without his wife for so many years. Yet there was a little girl inside her that didn't want the most important person in her life to leave her. Especially not now. She'd lost Liv. Losing *Ojiichan* would kill her.

She paced along the sidewalk that paralleled the ambulance entrance. Selfish. Grace was being completely selfish. She was wrong to be worried about how it would affect her if he died. She should be more concerned about what was best for *Ojiichan*. Her life wasn't important. Especially not at that moment.

Grace walked for a few more minutes then went back into the emergency area. She glanced at her watch, surprised it was already well into the next evening. She couldn't remember much about the past twenty-four hours, only that Liv had yet to leave her side. As she continued into the hospital, she nearly walked into someone. She muttered an apology and started past him, but he called her name. She wheeled around and saw Jonas standing there.

"You okay?" he asked.

"No, sorry. I didn't see you."

"It's fine. David is on the way with your family. I was coming outside to let you know."

Grace felt a huge weight lift from her shoulders and needed to sink into a nearby chair when her legs gave out. "Thanks."

Jonas sat next to her. "Is there anything you need? I know neither of you girls has eaten, despite my wife's best efforts. Are you sure I can ask her to bring you something?"

"That's very sweet, but I'm not sure I can eat."

"You know what Harry would say right now?" Jonas asked.

"He'd say that your body needs the food, whether you want it or not."

"Yes, he would." She kissed Jonas on the cheek. "I'm going back to his room to let Liv know what's going on. Thanks."

"No problem."

She watched him go then leaned back and closed her eyes. Her body simply refused to move, even if the chair wasn't particularly comfy. The day's events came crashing down on her, and Grace felt an incredible need to give up.

"Gracie!"

Matt's voice spiked her adrenaline, and she was on her feet and in his arms in seconds. They didn't speak. Maybe it was a twin thing, or a close sibling thing, but they always knew each other's thoughts and feelings. She sank into his embrace and let his strength pick her up.

It wasn't long before their parents joined them, and Grace filled everyone in on the latest from the doctor.

"He's resting in the ICU. He's still not conscious, but we're allowed to go in to see him. Liv's with him now."

"Olivia?" Hariku asked, following Grace to the elevators.

"Yes. She's very close to him."

"I know," he said. "She's the one that paid for our flights out here, though it wasn't necessary. Her brother picked us up at the airport, too."

"She paid for the flights?" Grace asked, though she shouldn't be surprised. "Dad, the Templetons are a wonderful family. And they mean a lot to *Ojiichan*. I'm sorry you're meeting them like this."

"So am I," he said and shocked Grace when he put his arm around her. "I love you, Grace. You've taken care of your *ojiichan*, and I'm proud of you for that." He gave her a one-armed hug and kissed her cheek. "I'm here now. Let me take the burden from you."

Grace wanted to cry but kept her emotions in check as best she could. At least until they got to the ICU waiting room.

****

An hour later, Grace and Liv sat across a table from each other, finishing up the pot roast, mashed potatoes, and green beans brought for them by Liv's mom. It was probably the late hour, but Grace didn't think she'd ever had any meal that tasted better. Perhaps it was her father's presence and how he took charge of things, but her appetite managed to resurface and she was happy to oblige her empty stomach.

"Mom's the best cook in the world."

"Well, next to my mom," Grace said as she pushed the plastic lunch plate away. "Thanks for staying with me. I don't think I could have done this by myself."

Liv looked genuinely surprised. "I'm worried about Harry, too. And no matter what has or does happen between us, I'd like to think I could be your friend."

Grace forced herself to look away from the sad eyes that watched her.

Liv said, "I'm going to head out, but there's something I need to give you first." She reached in her pocket and carefully placed the rainbow nugget keychain and key on the table in front of Grace. "I haven't been staying there anyway, and your family needs somewhere to sleep. There's no sense sending them to a hotel when I have two nice beds and a couch you can use. Besides, my place is only ten minutes from here."

Grace stared at the key, unable to make her hand move to take it. "Olivia, I can't."

"You can." Liv stood and headed for the door. "Dad gave your brother the keys to his car so you guys can get around, since your Jeep and Harry's truck are still at the cabin. Use it as long as you want. He doesn't need it since Mom has a car, too." She hesitated at the door, leaving her back to Grace when she spoke. "I'm sorry for all this, Gracie. Please let me know how Harry's doing."

Still in shock, Grace stared at the door before it kicked in that Liv had walked away. She jumped up and ran after her.

"Olivia! Wait!" Grace nearly ran into her at the elevators. Liv half-turned to her, tears glistening in her eyes. Grace tried to speak, but nothing came out. Her heart pounded in her chest.

The elevator opened and Liv got in. She held Grace's gaze for a long moment.

"Don't leave," Grace said, her voice barely a whisper, though from the expression on Liv's face she knew she'd been heard.

The doors closed.

Grace punched the button to get the elevator back. Nothing happened. The opposite elevator opened, and she was about to step in when she heard her mother's voice.

"Gracie?" Marsha stopped her with a gentle hand on her shoulder. "Honey, where are you going?"

"Olivia—she left." Grace was torn. The impact of those words hit her like a physical slap to the face. Liv hadn't just left. She'd gone with no intention of returning. Grace's hesitation to accept friendship from her sent Liv away. For good.

Marsha said, "I came to find you because Harry's awake. He's asking for you."

"Mom..."

"I don't know what's going on between you and Liv, but she

can wait. Harry needs you."

Her mother's words finally sank in. "He's awake?"

"Yes." Marsha smiled. "And he's asking for you."

"Thanks, Mom." Grace hugged her and hurried to Harry's room. She stopped at the doorway. Hariku was at Harry's bedside, a smile on his face. He said something to Harry and motioned Grace to come in.

Hariku embraced her and whispered, "I love you, Gracie." He kissed her cheek and quietly left.

Harry held out his hand and beckoned her forward. "Where is Olivia?"

Grace cradled his frail hand in hers. "She left a few minutes ago."

"I will talk to her later, but first I need you to make a promise, Gracie Lee."

"Anything for you, *Ojiichan*."

"You listen to Olivia. Give her time to explain what happened." He took a deep, shaky breath and it pained Grace to see him struggle.

"Rest, please. I'll talk to her."

"No," he said, squeezing her hands. "You listen to her. She...you belong together. Like me and my Gracie. Forever."

"I love her, *Ojiichan*. I'm so angry and hurt, but I can't stop loving her."

"Don't stop."

"I'll try."

Harry gave her a weak grin. "There is no try. Only do or do not."

That made Grace laugh. "Okay, Yoda. Let her speak I will."

"Good. Your *obaachan* would be proud."

"You're going to be okay." Grace said it as much to convince herself as to convince him.

"I am. Even if my body fails, I will be okay. Promise you will be, too."

His eyes drooped, showing his fatigue.

"I promise." She kissed his forehead. "*Aishiteimas, Ojiichan.*"

His smile faded as his body succumbed to sleep. Grace sat in the chair beside the bed and watched him, wondering what she would do without him.

****

Liv stared out a window in the hospital lobby. Waning sunlight streaked across the glass, obscuring the landscape. But Liv wasn't actually looking at anything in particular. Which was a good thing since tears kept blurring her vision. Guilt constricted her chest.

Who the hell was she to be upset? Harry was in the ICU and might not come out again. His family was there, scared and worried. Especially Grace. Yet all Liv could think about was how she wanted to take Grace into her arms and hide her from the world until she realized just how much Liv loved her.

If she could take back what happened at the pub...but she couldn't. And it seemed nothing she did would get Grace to see the truth. Maybe it would be best if Liv left the hospital. She looked toward the door again. Her legs felt rooted to the spot. Just as they had for the last hour. She returned her gaze to the window, unsure exactly what the hell to do next.

"Olivia?"

Liv flinched at the sound of her name, recognizing the soft voice of Marsha Kato. She steeled herself and turned to face Marsha. "Yes?"

"I'm sorry to bother you, but could I speak to you for a few minutes?"

"Sure."

"I thought you might want to know that Harry is stable now. The doctor expects to be able to do the procedure on his heart as soon as he can get it scheduled this evening."

"Does he think it'll work? What if Harry's not strong enough?"

"It won't matter if they don't do the procedure."

Liv let that information sink in for a moment. Her heart was hammering in her chest at the thought of such a sweet man no longer being around.

"He wants to see you."

"I—is that a good idea? I mean, I don't want to cause him any stress."

"It'll be more stressful if you don't see him. Trust me." Marsha gently touched her arm. "But before you go in there, could you do me a favor?"

"Of course."

"Talk to Gracie. Whatever is happening between you two needs to be resolved." Marsha held her hand up to stop Liv when she started to speak. "I get that it's not easy, but if you don't talk it out, things are going to get worse. Your running out didn't help matters all that much."

"I didn't run. As you can see, I never left the hospital. Gracie needs her family."

"Doesn't that include you?"

Liv was surprised by Marsha's comment. "I wish it did. Look, maybe I shouldn't have walked away from her earlier, but I don't know what to do. I love her. So much that I want to spend the rest of my life with her."

"But?"

"But it's not what Gracie wants, Mrs. Kato. Not now. Maybe not ever—at least not from me."

"Are you sure?" Marsha's expression was expectant.

"No. I'm not sure of anything other than Harry's heart isn't working and mine's been shattered into a million pieces. Wait. It's not about me at all. It's about Harry."

"He's a convenient excuse. You and Gracie need to sit down and talk this out like adults. Period. If you love my daughter like you say you do, then get your ass back into that waiting room and fight for her. She's just as lost and broken as you are, and right now she's barely hanging on. I refuse to stand by and watch her be hurt again. And let me tell you, Olivia Templeton, you've got more power to hurt my child than Carly ever had."

Marsha's steely gaze held Liv's, and Liv felt herself shrink beneath it. "Mrs. Kato—"

"No more excuses. Get in the elevator and go talk to her. You'll never know the answers until you ask the questions."

Marsha walked away, leaving Liv to stare after her in amazement. In that moment, a strange thought occurred to her. Marsha Kato would get along well with Liv's mother.

****

Liv entered the family waiting room and found Grace seated on the gray vinyl couch. She sat with her elbows on her knees and her head resting in her hands. Her long hair fell forward, and Liv ached to brush it back from her face.

She took a deep breath, slowly released it, and sat on the opposite end of the couch, patiently waiting for Grace to notice her there. She didn't have to wait long.

"Why did you come back?" Grace sat straighter and tilted her head to see Liv. Her face and eyes were red from crying.

"Because you need me and I need you." Liv wanted to reach for her hand, but she held back. "And Harry needs us both."

"You left..." Grace didn't finish the sentence. Instead she got to her feet and turned her back to Liv. The gesture put a chasm between them the size of the Grand Canyon.

"Gracie, I'm sorry." Liv pushed into the corner of the couch as if she could make herself smaller by doing so. "No matter what happened, I never stopped loving you."

"You kissed her, Liv. I saw you."

"Yes, I did. She caught me off guard—I don't have any excuses. But it was a mistake, and I walked away from her and ran after you. I want—I need to spend the rest of my life with you. Jane doesn't mean anything to me. Not anymore. It was my libido that kissed her. Not me. You've got my heart, Gracie Lee. You always have and you always will."

Grace didn't move for the longest time, and Liv worried that she'd made up her mind. Maybe Grace really didn't want anything more to do with her.

"Whether or not I love you was never in question. It's not something I can just turn off, Olivia. I took a chance, and I let myself open up and love someone. For the first time in more years than I care to count, I trusted. And you broke that trust. How am I supposed to get past that?"

"But I didn't." Liv got up as well and stood behind Grace. "I never broke your trust. I didn't cheat on you. That kiss with Jane was just that. A kiss. It shouldn't have happened, and when my brain caught up, I stopped it. I shoved her away and went after you."

"Liv..."

"Let me finish. Please." Liv placed her hand on Grace's shoulder and gave it a squeeze. "When you finally said you'd talk to me. I was almost afraid to show up. But I did. When we started fighting...and Harry collapsed...I thought it was all my fault. That I'd caused Harry's heart attack. I know that sounds ridiculous, but timing is everything."

"You couldn't possibly have caused it," Grace said, her voice weak from her crying. "He's got a bad heart. It would have happened whether we were there or not." Grace turned so she was face-to-face with Liv. "But this isn't about Harry. It's about us."

"Is there an us?"

"I don't know. I'm miserable without you. The only nights I slept were after I'd cried myself to sleep or worked myself into exhaustion. I can't eat. I can't think. I never knew I could hurt as much as I have the last few weeks." Grace kept her gaze locked on Liv's. "The thought of you—that you didn't care enough..."

"I promised I wouldn't hurt you, and I did anyway. I won't blame you if you hate me. I won't blame you if you tell me to get out of here and never come back. I'll do whatever you ask of me. But please, please understand that I would give anything to fix this. There has to be something I can do, something I can say." She stepped forward, but Grace stiffened. "Do you think I'm going to hit you?"

"What? No."

"Then why are you acting like I'm going to? You stiffened when I got close, like I was going to hurt you."

"No. I stiffened because I was afraid you'd try to hold me."

"I don't get it. Why would that make you afraid? Gracie, I love you."

"I know. And if you take me in your arms right now, I'll fall apart. I can't stay mad at you if you touch me."

Liv curved her lips into a half-smile and opened her arms. "Then let me hold you."

Grace stared at her for a long time before she stepped into Liv's embrace. She rested her head on Liv's shoulder. "I don't want to be without you, Liv. Please stay here. Don't leave me again. I need you."

Liv held Grace as her body shook with tears. "I love you, Gracie Lee."

"I love you, too."

"Um, sorry to interrupt," Matt said as he joined them. "Mom wanted me to find you two. They're going to take *Ojiichan* to the cath lab."

"Cath lab?" Liv asked. "What's that?"

"It's where they'll do an angiogram to find the blockage in his heart." Grace accepted a tissue from Matt and dried the tears from her face.

"And if they find it?"

"They'll do the angioplasty to remove the blockage or put in a stent to reinforce the artery. If that doesn't work, the doctor said he'd have to go right to surgery for a bypass."

Liv still had her arm around Grace's shoulders, surprised by how steady Grace was now. Her face must have conveyed her thoughts, because Grace continued, "We've been through this four other times over the last twenty years. Plus Matt and I looked up a lot of information on these procedures."

"And?"

"And he's come through fine every time," Matt replied. "The last time he was home the next day, and after two weeks, he was up and going like nothing ever happened."

"I hope that's how it goes this time," Liv said.

"It will," Grace said. "It has to be."

Chapter Eighteen

"Hariku Kato, if you don't sit down I'm going to glue your ass to that chair." Marsha stood over him and glared at Harry.

Harry did his best to glare back as he sat down. The exchange gave Liv a chuckle. Harry'd been home for two weeks, and Marsha had yet to let him do anything. She wondered how long Harry would allow Marsha to have control. Was she like that at home? Maybe it was why Hariku and Matt returned to Seattle last week. A bit of vacation from Drill Sergeant Kato.

"And what are you laughing at?" Harry's question broke into Liv's thoughts.

She replied with a grin. "Nothing. Just wondering if you two are done. We do have to get Marsha to the airport before the plane leaves."

"Leave now."

"I'll leave when I'm good and ready to go," Marsha said, shaking her finger at him from the kitchen. "You're going to need something for lunch."

"I'm not a child, Marsha. I do know how to cook."

Marsha scoffed. "You know how to use the microwave. That does not count as cooking."

Harry shook his head and gave a dramatic sigh. "I've lived for ninety-three years and always   managed to feed myself. I don't believe I'll starve because you went home."

"The only way you won't starve is if my daughter comes over to cook for you." Marsha finished what she was doing and stalked to his chair. Liv leaned against the doorjamb, curious as to how this was going to conclude.

Marsha towered over him, but Harry clearly wasn't afraid. "I love you, you stubborn old man. You need to take better care of yourself."

"I'm fine, Marsha. I'll eat the vegetables you've packed away for me. I'll even re-heat the meals you put in my freezer. Does that make you feel better?"

Marsha bent down and gave him a kiss on the cheek. "It does. For now. But don't be surprised if I come back in a few weeks to check on you."

"A few weeks? That's all the reprieve I get?"

"Watch it," Marsha said. "You might convince me to stay."

"No. You go. I'll stay." Harry crossed his arms over his chest and narrowed his eyes at Marsha. "Please go. I promise to be good."

"I'll keep you to that."

"Mom, we need to get moving." Grace picked up Marsha's bag. "C'mon. I promise to keep a close eye on him."

Liv giggled when Grace winked at Harry behind Marsha's back. She pushed away from the doorjamb and took the bag from Grace. "You all get this sorted out. I'll be waiting outside."

"Chicken," Harry said.

Liv did a chicken walk as she went outside.

****

The hour long drive to the airport was pleasant, and Liv enjoyed the opportunity to spend more time with Marsha. They hit it off well, and Liv would miss her. She watched Grace say goodbye and worried that Grace might not be okay with Marsha's departure. Liv couldn't imagine being so far from her parents. Especially her dad.

Grace climbed into the truck, and Liv drove toward the city center. "You okay?" she asked.

"I didn't realize how much I missed my family. It's not like Seattle is on the other side of the world, but sometimes I just want to go see her."

"I was the same way when I was at university." Liv reached over and took Grace's hand. "I have something planned for today."

"Oh? Should I even ask?"

"Of course. I've set up a meeting with my friend Caroline. We're going to have lunch with her this afternoon."

"Caroline? Isn't she the one that runs the therapy group?"

Liv nodded and gave Grace's hand a gentle squeeze. "The very same."

"What brought this on? We haven't talked about the group therapy thing in a long time."

"Well, you and I haven't, but Harry and I have. He knows it's important for us that you go to this group to help you heal."

"I sometimes wonder if he talks to Abby, too."

"It wouldn't surprise me one bit." Liv brought Grace's hand to her lips and kissed it. "He loves you, baby. So do I. And you'll like Caroline. I promise."

****

Grace rested in the passenger seat of Liv's truck and closed her eyes. The meeting with Caroline was wonderful and left Grace with a lot of information to process. One thing was sure. The woman next to her was the best thing that ever happened in Grace's life.

She placed her hand on Liv's thigh. "I expected Caroline to be easy to talk to, but it was like she knew what I was going to say. And I felt so comfortable with her...like one of my sessions with Abby."

"Caroline is one of a kind. I don't think she's ever met a stranger. Counseling is the perfect job for her."

"I'll say. And she gave me a ton to think about."

"All good stuff, I hope."

"Yes. This group therapy thing has scared the hell out of me ever since Abby first mentioned it. It was hard to talk to you about Carly, still is sometimes. I couldn't imagine saying any of those things to people I don't know. But as soon as we sat down and started chatting, I wanted to tell my whole story to Caroline right then. It's like she gently pulls it out of you."

"So what do you think of group therapy now?" Liv took one hand off the wheel to cover Grace's.

"I still think it's terrifying."

"I'm happy to go with you to as many sessions as you need me to. I'll sit right there, hold your hand, and do anything else you want me to. If you want me to just sit in the car and wait for you to get done, I'll do that, too. It's so important that you have someone else to talk to about all this, Gracie. Just know I'll do anything you ask me to."

"And this is why I love you, Olivia." She kissed her on the cheek as they pulled into the driveway of Harry's cabin. "I wouldn't move in with just anyone, you know?"

"You better not." Liv brushed her lips across Grace's fingers. "But I'm serious."

"Me, too." Grace climbed out of the truck and met Liv at the steps to the porch. "I don't know what's going to happen with it, but I'm going to the group session tomorrow night. I would love for you to be there with me."

"Of course." Liv slipped her arms around Grace and kissed her sweetly. "I'm so proud of you right now."

"Proud?"

"Yes. This is a huge step. And I'm honored you want me to go with you."

Grace gazed into the face of the person she wanted to spend her life with. She felt their connection and, in that instant, knew exactly what she needed to do.

"At the risk of sounding corny, Olivia Templeton, you complete me. I never imagined anyone could love me so strongly, or that I could love someone as amazing as you. I never want to be a minute away from you."

"Good thing you're moving in with me then," Liv said. She was trying to lighten the mood, but Grace saw the glistening in her eyes.

"I don't want to just move in with you. Olivia, will you marry me?"

Liv's eyes were the size of saucers. Tears slid down her cheeks, and for a moment, Grace's heart dropped. "I—I don't know what to say."

"It's okay. You don't have to say anything. If you don't want to—"

"Shh." Liv cupped her hands around Grace's face and kissed her gently. "Yes. My answer is yes, I'll marry you."

Grace smiled against Liv's kiss. "I love you."

"I know." Liv swiped at her tears and took a deep breath. "It's a beautiful thing, you and me." She reached into her pocket and pulled out the black velvet box. "That night at the bar...I'd planned another romantic evening once we got home. But things took a different turn, and I didn't get to ask you the question." She opened the box and showed it to Grace. "I've kept this with me, hoping to find the right time to ask you. I think we've found the right time."

Grace couldn't see the ring through her tears. Liv slipped it on her finger, and Grace buried her face against Liv's chest. "Great minds think alike, right?"

She felt Liv's laughter. When they parted again, both of them had managed to stop crying. "I love you, Gracie Lee."

"And I love you, Olivia. Should we go inside and tell *Ojiichan*?"

"No need. I'm not deaf or blind," Harry said from the doorway. "Now get in here so I can see that ring."

"You dirty old man!" Liv shook her fist at him. "I oughta call the cops on you for spying on us."

"Ha! You're in front of my porch and the door was open."

Grace took Liv by the hand. "C'mon. Might as well go inside so the old man can have his way." They entered the cabin. Harry was already seated in his recliner.

"Your mom was right. He's like having a two-year-old that won't mind."

"I told you I'm not deaf," Harry said. "Do I get to see the ring or not?"

"Only if you're good," Grace said. "Are you going to be good?"

Harry gave her the same look he'd given Marsha that morning. It made Grace burst into giggles. She could never hold up against Harry. Instead, she knelt beside his chair and showed him the ring.

Harry examined it as if he were a jeweler making an appraisal. He eventually looked up and met Liv's gaze. Grace noted that something passed between them, and the feeling made her heart swell.

Harry gently gripped Grace's hand then reached for Liv's. "Welcome to the family, Olivia."

About the Author

Patty is the Goldie Award-winning co-editor of *Blue Collar Lesbian Erotica* with Verda Foster. She and Verda also coedited *Women in Uniform: Medics and Soldiers and Cops, Oh My!* and *Women In Sports*. Her first novel, *Souls' Rescue* was a finalist for the Ann Bannon Popular Choice Award. Patty is a retired paramedic and currently resides in The Netherlands with her wife, Sandra, and their kitties. Visit her website at www.pattyschramm.com

Books by Patty Schramm

From Flashpoint Publications

Reflections of Fate

Leoni Wolf lived and worked on the Qualla Boundry in Cherokee, North Carolina her entire life. It was her home and the place she belonged. Leoni once believed in fate and that everything happened for a reason. Until her wife, Tayanita, was killed in a tragic accident. What possible reason could there be for her death? The event shattered Leoni's world.

Each day Leoni awoke, gazed at her reflection in the old free-standing mirror and convinced herself she could get through one more day.

Nicola Daelis was tired of fate intervening in her life and wanted to throttle her. Before Nicola could act on the event that could change it all, fate landed a beautiful, dark-eyed woman in her lap and turned Nicola's world upside down.

Fighting for their lives, and often against each other, Nicola and Leoni must embark upon an adventure that could be the beginning of something new. Or the end of them both.

ISBN: 978-1-949096-12-5
eISBN: 978-1-949096-13-2

Available at:

Bella Books
Amazon
Nook
Kobo

Better Together

Mac Bradenton has never been south of the Mason Dixon Line or across a body of water wider than the Ohio River. But her best friend is sick and on a quest to complete her bucket list. First stop is Paris, France. Mac goes along expecting to enjoy the time with Kristy, never anticipating just how much her life will change.

They meet up with Kristy's friend, Lenie, who has promised to give them a guided tour of Paris and while there, romance blossoms between Mac and Lenie.

Once home, life takes some major turns for Mac. As she struggles to deal with the challenges thrown at her, will everything fall apart? Or will she be able to lean on Lenie knowing that, no matter what happens, they are better together?

ISBN: 978-1-949096-09-5
eISBN: 978-1-949096-10-1

Available at:

<u>Bella Books</u>
<u>Amazon</u>
<u>Nook</u>
<u>Kobo</u>

Souls' Rescue

Kelly McCoy is a firefighter and paramedic who's lived most of her adult life in New York. After 9-11, she relocates to Cincinnati, nursing a broken heart and looking for a new start. She takes one day at a time, trying not to let her losses overwhelm her.

Talia Stoddard is an insurance wiz who's always been smart on the job, but unlucky in love. After years of being told that she's too big, too tall, too black, too lesbian, and not a very snappy dresser, Talia has resigned herself to a life alone with only her dear gay friend Jacob for a diversion.

When Kelly and Talia's lives crash into one another, it's under the most stressful and threatening circumstances. Talia is in terrible danger, and it's up to Kelly to rescue her. In the horrendous situation they end up in, neither expects to find a friend, much less a soul mate.

Will they rescue one another and heal the wounds of their pasts? Or will they both continue to believe that they're not worthy of the kind of love the other might offer?

Souls' Rescue is the story of opening up to love, taking chances, and building a life that everyone dreams about, but few people ever find.

ISBN: 978-1-949096-06-4
eISBN: 978-1-949096-07-1

Available at:

Bella Books
Amazon
Nook
Kobo

From Regal Crest Enterprises

Because of Katie

Siobhan Landry's granddad had one wish before he died. That she would travel from their small town in Indiana to the place of his birth in southern Ireland and become the artist he knew her to be. She never expected how much her life would change when she got there.

Katie O'Briain nearly lost her life, but that couldn't stop her from doing what she's always loved—being a marathon runner. However, no matter how much she pushes herself, or convinces herself life is good, there's something very obviously missing.

But Katie has a lot of scars and even though her attraction to Siobhan is immediate, can she bare those scars to the lovely American?

Siobhan also feels that attraction. Will she be able to move beyond her broken past and let Katie heal her heart?
Or will the scars they both hide keep them apart forever?

ISBN: 978-1-61929-380-9
eISBN: 978-1-61929-381-6

Available at:

Bella Books
Amazon
Nook
Kobo

Love Is In the Air — w/Nann Dunne

Love Is in the Air is a collection of romantic short stories about love that comes to us in different ways, different forms, and in ways we   might never suspect. Whether we feel worthy or not, love is there. And   it will find us all.

ISBN: 978-1-61929-278-9
eISBN: 978-1-61929-362-5

Available at:

<u>Bella Books</u>
<u>Amazon</u>
<u>Nook</u>
<u>Kobo</u>

Women In Sports: Sweaty, Sexy and Hot, Oh My!
— w/Verda Foster

Women in Sports: A collection of romantic and erotic tales.

Hot. Sweaty. Tight shorts. Sports bras. Six-pack abs. What sparks your imagination? Muscular legs? Hands that are strong and sure? Baseball, soccer, hockey, track and field...does it really matter? She's sexy, she's incredible and she's all yours. Sit back, relax and enjoy some wonderful tales from this group of talented authors. Women in sports—does it get any better than that?

This amazing collection of romance and erotica includes stories from: Lee Lynch, Jessie Chandler, Mary Griggs, MB Panichi, Tonie Chacon, Kate McLachlan, A.L. Duncan, Jeanine Hoffman, Erica Lawson, Sharon G. Clark, Nann Dunne, Pat Cronin and Verda Foster.

ISBN: 978-1-61929-278-9
eISBN: 978-1-61929-279-6

Available at:

<u>Bella Books</u>
<u>Amazon</u>
<u>Nook</u>
<u>Kobo</u>

Women In Uniform: Medics and Soldiers and Cops, Oh My! — w/ Verda Foster

Cops, medics, soldiers, chefs, forest rangers...let's face it...who doesn't appreciate women in uniforms? Whether it's a nurse in Vietnam, a lesbian about to deploy to Iraq, a horny football player, a cop who likes bondage, a medic who needs pampering, or a security guard who finds out she's not past her shelf date, these stories of erotica and romance will rev you up, touch your heart, and make you feel.

You'll be delighted by great stories from some of today's top writers: Catherine Lundoff, J.M. Redmann, Lee Lynch, AnaIza Otis, Lori L. Lake, Chris Paynter, Sammo, M.J. Williamz, Ms. M, Diane S. Bauden, Karen D. Badger, V.W. Massie, Victoria Oldham, Bliss, R.G. Emanuelle, Andi Marquette, Jessie Chandler, Pat Cronin, and Lee Coats.

ISBN: 978-1-935053-31-6
eISBN: 978-1-61929-046-4

Available at:

<u>Bella Books</u>
<u>Amazon</u>
<u>Nook</u>
<u>Kobo</u>